WITHDRAWN

Dangerous
Alterations

**Center Point
Large Print**

Also by Elizabeth Lynn Casey
and available from Center Point Large Print:

Sew Deadly
Death Threads
Pinned for Murder
Deadly Notions

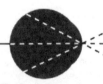

Dangerous Alterations

Elizabeth Lynn Casey

CENTER POINT PUBLISHING
THORNDIKE, MAINE

This Center Point Large Print edition
is published in the year 2012 by arrangement with
The Berkley Publishing Group,
a member of Penguin Group (USA) Inc.

The text of this Large Print edition is unabridged.
In other aspects, this book may vary
from the original edition.
Printed in the United States of America.
Set in 16-point Times New Roman type.

ISBN: 978-1-61173-269-6

Library of Congress Cataloging-in-Publication Data

Casey, Elizabeth Lynn.
Dangerous alterations / Elizabeth Lynn Casey. — Center Point large print edition
p. cm.
ISBN 978-1-61173-269-6 (library binding : alk. paper)
1. Sewing—Fiction. 2. South Carolina—Fiction. 3. Large type books. I. Title.
PS3603.A8633D36 2012
813'.6—dc23
                                                    2011038003

For my readers.

Thank you.

Acknowledgments

One of my favorite parts of writing this book was the chance it gave me to reach out and solicit the expertise of some dear friends. Fortunately for me, they didn't blink twice when I showed up in their inboxes asking about things like fire, murder, and sewing projects.

A huge thank-you goes to my Facebook friend Janet Armentani for answering my endless questions about various ways to poison a person.

An equally big thank-you goes to my fellow I-High grad and friend John Garizio. His experience as a firefighter proved priceless. Thanks also to his wife, Suzanne, who heard my cries for help and pointed me in John's direction.

And last but not least, a special thank-you to my friend Lynn Deardorff, who unknowingly started my mind plotting when she shared a pattern for a pillow with me!

Dangerous
Alterations

Chapter 1

One by one, Tori Sinclair ran through the order once again . . .

Rub eyes. *Check.*

Blink fast. *Check.*

Pinch hard. *Check.*

Yet it made no difference. Dixie Dunn was, in fact, *smiling.*

At *her.*

The first part was a rare occurrence in and of itself. But the second part? The part about Dixie Dunn smiling at Tori? Well, *monumental* didn't even come close to doing it justice. Especially since Dixie steadfastly believed her earlier-than-intended retirement was 150 percent Tori's fault.

Her. Tori. The one Dixie was smiling at like the proverbial cat who'd swallowed the—

Tori glanced down at the floor and took note of the carpet beneath her predecessor's feet, the absence of yellow feathers more surprising than she would have expected. She met the elderly woman's gaze. "You're twenty minutes early."

The woman's stout frame rose and fell, the smile never leaving her face. "I guess I'm just excited. It's been a long time." With a silent clap of her hands, Dixie stepped forward and motioned toward the shelves of books that stood like soldiers in formation. "I was up half the night thinking about the kind of changes we can make while I'm here."

"Changes?"

"All the libraries are going that way."

She swallowed. "All the libraries?"

"It's meant to breathe life into the place and liven things up a little."

Rub eyes. *Check.*

Blink fast. *Check*

Pinch hard. *Check.*

Once again, Dixie was still there. Only this time the smile was parting to allow foreign gibberish to flow between her pencil-thin lips. *Dixie*. Dixie *Dunn*. The same person who had waged a one-woman war against change at the library less than two years earlier.

It was a battle that had ultimately resulted in Dixie being forced to retire—and Tori being hired—as head librarian. Hence, the more-than-a-little-unsettling smile's effect on Tori.

"Things?" Tori repeated. "What kind of things?"

Dixie nodded, her voice a perfect accompaniment to the unmistakable sparkle in her eye. "First, there's the matter of chairs." With a beckoning gesture, Dixie turned on her sensible white pumps and led the way to one of the reading nooks Tori had created shortly after taking the library helm. The high-back armchairs had been found at a consignment shop for a ridiculously low sum, making it easier than expected to replace Dixie's wooden chairs.

"They've already been replaced."

"I see that," Dixie mused. "But I think we can make them even more inviting."

She stared at the woman, unable to think of a single thing to say.

"We want our patrons to feel comfortable here, don't we, Victoria?"

"Comfortable?"

Dixie nodded. "Of course. That's what all the up-and-coming libraries are doing these days, isn't it?"

"Up-and-coming?"

"The more homey the better, I say."

"H-homey?" She knew she sounded like a squawking parrot but she couldn't stop herself. Dixie Dunn wanted to enter the age of progress?

"In fact, I think we should talk to the board about opening a little coffee kiosk over there in the corner." Dixie gestured for Tori to follow, and, once again, she did. "It wouldn't have to be anything terribly elaborate just—"

"A *coffee* kiosk?"

Again, the woman nodded. "It's the wave of the future."

Tori stopped in her tracks, folding her arms in

the process. "Okay. Enough. Who put you up to this?" Periscoping her head from side to side, she strained to make out Margaret Louise Davis's graying hair and plump form in the mystery section. Or her always-stylish twin sister, Leona Elkin, smirking in periodicals. Or even Rose Winters, in her telltale cotton sweater and penny loafers, glaring at Leona from the local history aisle.

Rose.

A quick check of the wall clock put her morning in perspective. If there was a hidden camera lurking for the sole purpose of recording her reaction to the woman formerly known as Dixie Dunn, its location would have to wait.

"Look, can we pick this back up later? After Rose's appointment?" At Dixie's nod, Tori turned and made her way over to the information desk in the center of the library's main room. "There are no groups scheduled today, and no story time until tomorrow. So between that and the pool weather we're having right now, I imagine things should be fairly quiet while I'm gone."

Dixie's smile slipped momentarily only to return on the heels of a shrug. "That's okay. Quiet will give me time to make some adjustments."

"What kind of adjustments?"

The elderly woman pointed at the clock. "You better get going. You want to be there when Rose starts her treatment, don't you?"

Tori's eyes followed the path made by Dixie's finger, and she cringed. "Okay, you're right. I've got to go. But, Dixie"—she reached down, pulled her purse and tote bag from its spot on the bottom shelf, then straightened to meet the woman's eye—"why don't you hold off on any changes until I get back? It'll give us a chance to, um . . . brainstorm a little first."

Dixie flipped her hands over and shooed Tori down the long hallway that led to the rear parking lot. "Don't you worry about a thing, Victoria. I was running this library long before you were even a twinkle in your daddy's eye."

And just like that, the shooing morphed into something much closer to shoving. "Perhaps you could take Rose out for coffee or even lunch after her appointment." Dixie cocked her head to the side in consideration of her own suggestion. "Come to think of it, I think that might be just what the doctor would order after having to be hooked up to that drip pole again."

"But I need to get back here—"

Yanking the employee door open, Dixie all but pushed Tori into the wall of humidity known as a South Carolina summer day. "Give Rose a kiss for me. And I'll see you this afternoon. Much, *much* later this afternoon."

Before Tori could formulate a coherent protest or last-minute plea, Dixie had shut and locked the glass-plated door, her slightly hunched form fairly skipping down the hall and back toward the main room.

With her unease at an all-time high, Tori turned to see a powder blue station wagon veer around the corner and screech to a stop less than six inches from her feet. A familiar face peered across the front seat. "Thank heavens you ain't left yet. Why, I nearly got me a ticket tryin' to get here in time." Reaching across the seat, Margaret Louise Davis unlocked the door, plucked her tote bag off the passenger seat, and threw it into the back. "Hop in."

"You want to go with us?"

"Got nothin' better to do today. Melissa took the youngins to see her folks, Debbie's got things covered at the bakery, and Leona took Paris to get his tail fluffed."

"Your sister took Paris to get his tail fluffed?"

"And this surprises you?"

She couldn't help but laugh as an image of her self-appointed southern coach—emerging from a beauty shop with a perfectly coiffed garden-variety bunny in her arms—filled her mind. "Actually, no. It doesn't."

"Well then you understand why I'm bored."

Poking her head through the open window, Tori studied her friend. "All we're going to be doing

16

is sitting there for two or three hours while Rose gets her IV drip. It's really not all that exciting."

"You're gonna be there, right?"

Tori nodded.

"And Rose is gonna be there, right?"

Again, she nodded.

"That's good enough for me. And besides, I've got something to talk 'bout with the two of you once we get Rose settled. Now get in."

Tori finally did as she was told, the tension caused by Dixie's odd behavior dissipating at the thought of spending the morning with two of her dearest friends—women who were some thirty- and fifty-odd years her senior yet as close to her as anyone her own age could ever be. And it was all because of a common love of sewing.

A love that, for Tori, had been passed down from her late great grandmother and then restoked by Rose Winters and the rest of the members of the Sweet Briar Ladies Society Sewing Circle.

Margaret Louise stepped down on the gas, showering the back parking lot with a cloud of dirt. "Woo-wee, it's a hot one today, ain't it?"

Dropping her tote bag and purse onto the floor, Tori grabbed her seat belt and clicked it into place. "And that's different than yesterday because . . ."

Margaret Louise's deep belly laugh echoed

around the car. "It's a good thing Leona didn't hear you say that or else we'd be listenin' to her spoutin' crime statistics 'bout Chicago."

And it was true. Ever since Tori had moved to Sweet Briar, she'd been subjected to Leona Elkin's endless sales pitch on life in a small town—friendlier people, charming shops, and less crime. Though, considering the way Leona lamented the joys of traveling to such cities as Paris, London, and New York—citing their fine cuisine and vast cultural amenities every chance she got—one had to wonder if there was more to the story.

Tori leaned her head against the passenger-side window and watched the trees whiz by en route to the outpatient treatment facility on the western edge of town. "At least you know what you're getting from Leona. Dixie, on the other hand, is a complete mystery to me."

"Dixie? Dixie Dunn? Are you pullin' my leg? That woman is 'bout as predictable as Sally when it's time to take a swallow of medicine."

Turning her head, she studied the proud grandmother of seven behind the steering wheel. "Little Sally is predictable, I'll give you that. But Dixie? Not even close."

Margaret Louise met her gaze. "You feelin' okay, Victoria?"

She nodded. "I'm feeling fine. But my nerves? That's another story."

A knowing smile spread across Margaret Louise's rounded face. "Still frettin' over Milo's proposal?"

Tori blew a pent-up whoosh of air from her lungs. "Not really. Not any more than normal, anyway."

"You should just say yes."

Oh, how she wished she could. She wanted to. More than anything. But she was afraid.

"I bet that man is missin' you somethin' fierce right now."

As she was him.

Milo Wentworth was everything she'd ever dreamed about and nothing she'd ever thought she'd find. Especially after the catastrophe that was her former fiancé, Jeff. In fact, at times, it was almost hard to remember ever having loved the man who'd celebrated their engagement party in a coat closet . . . with one of Tori's own girlfriends. Yet, at other times, the pain and humiliation was still so fresh it made her second-guess her own judgment.

Sure, she wanted to marry Milo—more than anything else in the world, actually. But to accept his proposal meant exhibiting a measure of courage she was having trouble finding where her heart and an engagement ring were concerned.

"I miss Milo, there's no doubt about that. But the nerves aren't about him. They're about Dixie and what she's planning to do to the library while I'm gone."

"Oh. *That.*"

She stared at her friend. "What? You know about these changes?"

Margaret Louise waved her hand. "She wants to set up a coffeepot and stick a few pillows on some chairs."

"Am I the only one who sees the irony in this coffeepot suggestion?"

"She's different now."

"How?"

Letting up on the gas just a little, Margaret Louise turned into the driveway just beyond the main hospital. "She has hope. Nina going on bed rest has given her hope."

"But—"

"And a second chance of sorts."

Ahhh. It made sense now. She said as much to Margaret Louise.

"That's all this is, Victoria. Dixie is tryin' to show everyone that she still has some spunk left in her."

Tori unfastened her seat belt as the station wagon came to a stop. "You mean like the spunk she showed when she lambasted me for allowing patrons to drink coffee in the library shortly after I got here?"

Margaret Louise pulled the key from the ignition, reached into the backseat for her tote bag, and dropped her keys inside. "Sort of, I reckon. Only this time she's tryin' to prove somethin' about her age."

"Her age?"

"That she's not dead yet. I think this stuff with Rose has unsettled her a bit. Makes her realize that she's gettin' to be old, too."

Tori considered her friend's words as they set out across the parking lot on foot, their arms laden with everything from crossword books and sewing magazines to photographs and the invisible weight of the latest gossip making the rounds of Sweet Briar. Anything and everything they could think of to make Rose's latest treatment more bearable for the elderly woman.

"Give her a chance to show you she's changed. That she still has something to offer the library, too."

Margaret Louise was right. Dixie Dunn might be prickly, even downright rude at times, but she adored the library just as much as Tori did. It was the one common ground, beyond sewing, that bound them together. "Okay. I'll try."

"Good. Now let's find Rose—oh, there she is." Lifting her hand into the air, Margaret Louise wiggled her fingers back and forth. "Woo-hoo, Rose, we're here."

"Woo-hoo? Woo-hoo?" Rose rolled her eyes skyward and blew out a frustrated exhale. "I may be shrinking, Margaret Louise, but I don't need to be confused with one of your grandbabies, you hear?"

Tori felt the corners of her mouth lifting upward as she closed the gap between the entrance and the waiting room. Leaning forward, she planted a kiss on Rose's cheek, the feel of the woman's frail body transitioning her residual tension into worry. "Are you up for this today?"

"Doesn't seem as if I have much of a choice, now does it?" Patting the empty cushion beside her, Rose met Tori's smile with one that trembled ever so slightly. "I'm glad you're here, Victoria."

Surprised by the rare admission, Tori settled into the seat beside Rose, noting the colorful flower arrangements and inspirational wall hangings around the room. "I like the pictures with the little sayings. Helps with the positive thoughts, you know?"

"If you're fit enough to climb a mountain or to sail around the world, I suppose they do," Rose mumbled. "But if you're here, you're probably not."

Tori studied her friend closely, the woman's downtrodden demeanor catching her by surprise. "You're climbing a mountain right now, Rose. Everyone in this room is. And you'll get to the top. Soon."

"You want to know what the worst part of being here is?"

"What's that?"

"It makes me feel old. And weak."

Tori reached for Rose's hand and patted it gently. "You're one of the strongest women I know, Rose Winters, you really are. And remember . . . the nurse said it'll only take a few hours. The same goes for everyone else in here."

Rose pulled the flaps of her cotton sweater close. "I'm not sure some of these folks can *spare* a few hours."

Following the path made by Rose's bony finger, Tori turned toward the opposite end of the waiting room, her gaze falling on a woman in her mid-to-late fifties with a bandana wrapped around her head and a small pillow on her lap. Any trials the woman had endured were overshadowed by the determination that lit her eyes.

"I don't understand. She looks like she's been through a lot but she doesn't look like she's about to—"

"Not her, Victoria," Rose hissed. *"Her."*

Anxious to appease her friend, Tori pulled her focus from the cancer patient and trained it, instead, on the gray-haired woman seated two chairs to the left—a woman hunched at the waist and staring at Tori as if . . .

She heard the gasp of disbelief as it escaped her lips, felt Margaret Louise's hand on her arm and Rose's breath on her cheek as her gasp was echoed from the other side of the room—a gasp that brought the hospital staff running.

Chapter 2

She knew they were staring. She could feel it as surely as Rose could feel the nurse rooting around her hand for a vein. But like her elderly friend, Tori said nothing.

The fact that Rose's silence came from courage and hers came from utter disbelief was something that needed to be addressed. Especially in light of the worry she could see tucked around the edges of Rose's bravery.

"Finally," Tori mumbled as the nurse declared victory over Rose's vein. "For a moment there I thought she'd become a human pincushion."

The nurse nodded a smile and then reached for the drip pole that stood poised and ready to administer relief to Rose's arthritis-ravaged limbs. "It happens sometimes. Especially for our elderly." Hannah—as her name tag stated—opened Rose's line and then gave her a gentle pat. "This'll take about two or three hours. If you need anything, press the button right next to you."

"Thank you, Hannah, but I'll be fine. I have some angels with me today . . . even if one of them looks as if she's seen a ghost."

Tori swallowed.

Hannah's hand moved to Tori's upper arm. "Ms. Calder has been sick for quite some time. Weak heart."

Tori closed her eyes and willed her breathing to steady.

"Would you like to talk to one of our chaplains? I know that watching someone go into cardiac arrest like that can be upsetting. Even if it's a stranger."

"But she wasn't a—" She stopped and opened her eyes, the nurse's kind face coming into focus once again. "I'll be fine. Really. Margaret Louise and I will look after Rose."

"If you're sure . . ."

"She's sure." Slowly, Rose lifted her hand and pointed down at the bag by her feet. "Victoria? Can you hand that to me?"

"Of course." She leaned over, scooped the lavender bag from the tiled floor, and handed it to Rose. "Do you need something?"

Rose reached into the bag and extracted a small notebook and pen from inside. Holding it toward Hannah, she gestured her chin toward the woman with the bandana. "Would you give this to Lynn over there? She said she'd jot down the directions for her pillow for me today. Might get her mind off things."

"I don't know, Rose," Margaret Louise protested. "She looks like she's sleeping to me.

Besides, I think she might have known that woman out in the waitin' room based on the things she was sayin' to the nurses as we were bein' ushered out of the way."

Tori followed Margaret Louise's gaze to the woman now reclined in a cubicle directly across from theirs. Try as she could, she couldn't place the woman's face from any photograph she'd ever seen or any party she'd ever attended . . .

"Nonsense. She's resting her eyes is all. Besides, life goes on and she—more than anyone else—realizes how important it is to keep on living."

"She has some sort of cancer, doesn't she?" Tori asked.

Rose nodded. "Breast cancer."

Silence engulfed them as they peered, once again, at the woman seated across from them, a pale pink pillow nestled between her arm and her chest. Finally, Margaret Louise spoke, her normally strong voice somewhat muted. "That pillow helps her, don't it?"

Again, Rose nodded.

"Is that something we can make in our circle?" Tori asked, the reason behind Rose's notepad and pen becoming clear. It was, after all, one of her favorite parts of the Sweet Briar Ladies Society Sewing Circle.

Rose watched Hannah cross the open space between the cubicles and set the notepad and pen beside Lynn's chair. "I'll answer that *after* you tell us what went on out there in the waiting room just now."

She gulped. "You mean the part about the woman going into cardiac arrest in front of us?"

"No. She means the part about you darn near hyperventilatin' when you saw that woman," Margaret Louise offered from her spot on the patient recliner in the empty cubicle directly next to Rose's. "And the part about that woman hyperventilatin' herself into bein' admitted when she saw you."

A chill shot down her spine. "You don't think Vera—I mean . . . you can't seriously think seeing *me* caused *that,* can you?"

Rose's eyes, illuminated to nearly twice their size behind bifocal lenses, bore into Tori's. *"Vera?"*

"I knew it! I knew it! I told you she knew her, didn't I?"

Ignoring the woman to her right, Rose simply waited for Tori to come clean.

She toyed with the notion of waiting Rose out, hoping against hope that the medicine dripping into the woman's too-thin arm might lull her friend off to sleep. But even if, by some miracle it did, she'd still have the woman on the other side of Rose to contend with.

And Margaret Louise didn't give up.

Ever.

Not that Rose did, either.

"So tell me about your friend's pillow."

"No," Rose and Margaret Louise echoed in unison.

Surrounded on all sides, Tori lifted her hands into the air in surrender. "Okay. Okay. Yes. I know her."

Rose rolled her eyes. "We may be old, but dumb we're not."

"Good thing my twin isn't here. She'd protest that statement."

"If Leona was here, Margaret Louise, I'd have left off the part at the end."

It felt good to laugh. It helped to relieve some of the tension that had started with Dixie and grown exponentially at the sight of Vera Calder.

"So how do you know her?" Margaret Louise prodded.

Tori glanced up at the IV bag hanging from Rose's pole and took a long, deep breath. "Would you believe she's Jeff's great-aunt?"

"Jeff?" Margaret Louise pushed the green button on the side of her chair and reclined as far as she could go, a look of contentment settling across her face. "Jeff who?"

With her gaze locked on Tori, Rose offered the clarification Tori wasn't up for giving. "Victoria's former fiancé."

Ignoring the button that would reverse her original decision, Margaret Louise bolted upright, the afghan she'd secured around her body falling to the floor. "You mean the one who was tomcattin' around on you while your family was toastin' your engagement in the next room?"

In an instant, Tori was back, standing in the hall her family had rented to celebrate her upcoming nuptials. She could still hear her cousins laughing . . . her grandfather's stories . . . the songs her brother had compiled as a sort of musical time line of her relationship with Jeff.

And, of course, her friend's giggle from a nearby closet as Jeff—

Closing her eyes against the memory, she forced a carefree smile to her lips. "One and the same."

"You never told us she lived in Sweet Briar," Margaret Louise accused.

"That's because I didn't know she—"

"She doesn't live in Sweet Briar. She lives in Lee Station."

Tori's head snapped up as Lynn reached forward and grabbed a white Styrofoam cup from the snack table beside her chair. "Lee Station? You mean the Lee Station that's five miles south of here?"

"That's right. It's the summer home she had with Garrett's dad, the one she moved into permanently after her husband passed away about two years ago." Lynn took a sip of her water then set it back down.

Garrett.

Tori remembered that name.

"Who's Garrett?" Margaret Louise inquired.

"My soon-to-be ex. And Vera's—"

"Stepson." The relationship rolled off Tori's tongue with barely a pause, bringing Margaret Louise's attention squarely back on Tori.

"You know this Garrett person, Victoria?"

"I met him. Once." She heard her voice morphing into a mumble but she couldn't help herself. Painful memories were painful memories no matter how much time had passed.

"Yes you did," Lynn confirmed. "At your engagement party."

Rose waved away Lynn's statement. "They broke it off."

"I remember." Lynn tucked her pillow close to her chest and released a soft cough, a grimace of pain marring her otherwise pleasant features. "And I'd have sent my condolences only we'd never met and, well, Vera wouldn't have been too pleased with me if I had. But I knew you were better off. The apple doesn't fall far from the tree in that family."

"Is that why this woman's stepson is your *ex?*"

"My wish-to-be-ex, actually." With her gaze still trained on Tori, Lynn addressed Margaret Louise's inquiry with a wry, yet tired, smirk. "Every day I sent him off to work to count pills, believing he was tired at night from standing on his feet dealing with sick and cranky people all day long. But I was wrong about him just like *she*"—Lynn lifted her needle-pierced hand off the armrest and pointed in Tori's direction—"was wrong about Jeff."

Margaret Louise made a face. "He was cheatin' with one of your friends, too?"

Lynn shrugged. "Was, is, it's all the same. She's one of his little pharmacy techs. Young, pretty . . . you know the drill."

"Then why not make it official and give him the old heave-ho like he deserves?" Margaret Louise retrieved the afghan from the floor and tossed it over Rose.

"Because Garrett's money management skills leave much to be desired and without money and his health insurance, I'm kind of trapped." Lynn looked down at the clear, narrow tube that penetrated her leathery skin. "It's either stay or die."

"I'm sorry." And Tori was. She hated to hear of people struggling financially. Especially when they were sick. It seemed overly cruel. "But I see you've managed to accomplish something I couldn't."

"What's that?" Lynn asked.

"Your tension with Garrett didn't put you on Vera's Most Hated List the way my breakup with Jeff did."

Lynn nodded, a knowing smile twitching at the

corners of her lips. "You know the reason for that as well as I do."

"What's that?" Margaret Louise inquired as curiosity pulled her left eyebrow upward. "What are you leavin' out, Victoria?"

She shrugged. "Nothing really. Except that Jeff could do no wrong in his great-aunt's eyes."

"Not even carryin' on with another woman durin' his own engagement party?"

"Not even that."

"Then she ought to have her head examined if you ask me," groused Rose.

"I suppose. But when you've practically raised someone since childhood I guess you don't want to see their faults. Human nature." Still, it was hard to keep the sting out of her words. It wasn't that she'd expected Jeff's family to abandon him completely, because she hadn't. But a little empathy might have helped at the time. Something, anything, to let her know they'd understood her need to call it quits on the spot.

"More like ignorant stupidity if you ask me." Lynn looked up at her chemo drip then closed her eyes, her voice little more than a whisper. "Have you seen him since that night?"

"There's been no reason to see him. Our lives took two separate paths from that day forward and I don't foresee them ever having to cross again." And for that, Tori was grateful. The clean break had allowed her to move on—in her career and in her life.

"I wish I could say the same," Lynn mumbled.

"There must be a way for you to get along on your own. Isn't there?"

The woman addressed Margaret Louise's question without so much as raising her eyelids. "That's not the cards I've been dealt."

"Cards?" Rose asked.

"That's right." Lynn pulled her pillow to her chest and released a cough that nearly shook the room. "But that's okay, the ace of spades has to turn up sometime. Everyone is entitled to at least one in life, right?"

Her words were cut short by the hesitant pitter-patter of Hannah's shoes on the linoleum between their cubicles. "Mrs. Calder?"

"Yes?"

The nurse's face paled to a near perfect match of the uniform she proudly wore. "Mrs. Calder. I'm sorry. It's just that—"

"She's gone, ain't she?"

Hannah took hold of the woman's hand and nodded her confirmation as the meaning behind their brief, yet public exchange hit Tori with a one-two punch.

Vera Calder was dead. Of that, Tori was certain.

But it was the part that followed—the part that had her stomach clenching, the room spinning, and Margaret Louise running to her side—that she simply couldn't understand.

Chapter 3

Somehow she'd gotten through the next two hours, the position of her head alternating between the back of her chosen chair and dangling between her knees in an effort to keep from passing out.

Convinced she was still in shock from watching Vera code, Hannah had repeated her offer to locate a chaplain in short order.

Margaret Louise, on the other hand, was certain the mere notion of someone dying had upset Tori's stomach and had placated her with crackers hijacked from the health center cafeteria every five minutes until Rose's drip was complete.

Even Rose seemed to pin Tori's reaction to Vera's death on something it wasn't.

Yet Lynn, the one woman who should have known better, had thought nothing of asking Tori to contact Jeff about his great-aunt's demise. It would be easier that way, Lynn had explained, especially since Garrett despised the very ground on which Jeff walked . . .

Dropping her head onto her desk, she moaned. She always knew family dynamics had the potential to be tricky business, especially after spending two years in close proximity to Jeff's. But still, hadn't her obligation to that crew ended that fateful night over two years ago?

It had if she had half a brain in her head.

Which, unfortunately, she did not.

What she *did* have was a heart that had been shaped by her late great grandmother—a woman who had put what was right over what felt good every single day of her life.

And what was right in this particular situation meant her path was about to cross with one she'd vowed to steer clear of for the rest of her life.

"So much for vows," she mumbled.

"Oh, I don't agree. Not at all. Vows are the difference between doing and not doing." Dixie breezed into the office Tori shared with her bedridden assistant, Nina Morgan, and claimed the folding chair to the side of Tori's desk. "Would you believe my luck? I found this in the basement during a break in patrons."

Tori mentally counted to ten then lifted her head to see the obviously ancient coffeemaker the woman held in her hands. "It was in the basement because it's old."

Dixie waved her objection away. "Old, schmold. Just because something isn't twenty doesn't mean it's outlived its usefulness, Victoria."

"In coffeemakers it does."

"Don't be silly. I've already plugged it in and it heated up like a champ." Placing the coffeemaker on the desk, Dixie narrowed her eyes at Tori. "What happened? You look positively awful."

"That's because, once again, our dear Victoria, didn't pay enough attention to her makeup application this morning," proclaimed an all-too-familiar voice from the open doorway. "But just because one's sweetheart is out of town doesn't mean one should get lazy, now does it?"

Tori's earlier moan morphed into an exasperated groan. "Leona, please."

Margaret Louise's twin sister pranced into the room, her perfectly manicured fingers wrapped tightly around the brown bunny nestled in the crook of her arm. "Please what, dear? Please help you with your makeup? Please get rid of those atrocious circles under your eyes? Please guide you in making this office look"—Leona gazed around the room—"*inviting* to those of the opposite sex?"

"Oooh, I could help with the office, too," Dixie offered, the same frightening look from earlier that morning returning to her eyes in spades. "Perhaps I could find a coffeemaker for us, too."

"Us?"

Jumping to her feet, Dixie marched over to Nina's spotless desk and sat down with an unmistakable air of authority. "Of course. If I'm to cover for Nina while she's out on bed rest, I'll need a place to plan and prepare."

"P-plan and prepare?" she stammered.

"Precisely."

Leona froze in the middle of the room. "Dixie? Did you hear that?"

Dixie looked up from her newly acquired desk. "What?"

"I think I hear someone seeking your expert assistance in the main room."

"I'll take care of that right away." Dixie stood, crossed the office with several quick strides, and disappeared into the hallway. "If you need anything, you know where to find me."

Feeling the first twinges of a smile, Tori let her gaze travel from her friend's salon-softened gray hair to the pale pink linen suit that hugged her surprisingly toned body, and back again. "You heard no such noise, did you?"

Leona shrugged then lifted the bunny to her plump lips for a kiss. "How else was I supposed to rescue you from that insufferable woman?"

Tori knew she should protest Leona's unkind description of their fellow sewing circle member, yet all she could do was laugh. If only for a moment.

"So what brings you by?" she asked as she pulled a pencil from its holder and turned it slowly between her fingers.

"I wanted to hear your thoughts on my sister's

little plan. See if I could prevail on your good taste."

She stilled her pencil. "What are you talking about? What plan?"

Leona shifted from foot to foot. "Margaret Louise didn't tell you?"

"No. I—"

"What's wrong, dear?" Leona asked. She sat down, claiming the same folding chair that Dixie had graced before the pull of Nina's desk had relocated Tori's perpetual thorn across the room. "You look . . . torn."

And just like that, her personal coach on all things southern had summed up her mood with one simple word.

"I have to contact Jeff."

Ever so gently, Leona nestled Paris back into her arms, stroking the bunny's soft fur with a loving hand. "Time to gloat?"

She stared at her friend.

Flipping the fingers of her free hand over her palm, Leona inspected her barely hours-old manicure. "Because, if you ask me, he could stand to hear that you've not only found your prince charming, but that your prince charming has also asked you to marry him."

"Why would I do that?"

"To make him jealous."

Tori felt her mouth gape open and worked to close it. "I could care less what Jeff knows about my life and even less what he thinks about it. I'm with the right person now, that's all that matters."

"Suit yourself, dear." Leona crossed her legs at her ankles and cast a pointed look in Tori's direction. "Then I give up, dear. Why else would you need to call him? Are you planning on inviting him to the wedding?"

"I'd have to say yes in order to have a wedding to invite him to, remember?" But even as she said the words, she knew she was being cryptic. Leona had freed her of Dixie's overeager plans and for that she should be grateful. Toss in the fact that she valued Leona's sometimes insightful, sometimes infuriating opinion on most matters and, well, it only made sense to come clean about the stifling weight that had been thrust upon her shoulders. "Jeff's great-aunt died of a heart attack this morning. Virtually in front of my eyes."

"Was she overweight?"

"A little, I guess."

"Did she smoke?"

She thought back to her encounters with Vera Calder during her relationship with Jeff. "She did."

"Well there you go." Leona gestured toward Paris with her chin. "He's been such a good boy lately. He got out by accident about two-and-a-half weeks ago and he found his way back home all by himself. And then, just last night, when I was planning my attire for today, I asked him which purse I should use and he twitched his little nose at this one." Leona lifted an off-white beaded clutch from her lap and held it up for Tori to see. "He has impeccable taste for one so young."

"And rabbit-like," Tori added before steering the topic back to Jeff. "I have to call Jeff to tell him about his aunt."

"Why?"

"Because his stepcousin won't do it."

Leona's recently waxed eyebrow rose in curiosity. "Why not?"

"Jealousy, I guess. Vera was crazy about Jeff and merely tolerated her late husband's child, Garrett. And Lynn is right . . . if I don't make the call, it might be months before Jeff finds out."

"Who on earth is Lynn?"

"Garrett's soon-to-be ex-wife. They lived with Vera."

"You're making my head ache, dear."

"Then it must be contagious." Leaning back in her chair, Tori spun around to look out at the grounds of the library, the view of the hundred-year-old moss trees failing to provide the sense of peace and comfort they normally did. "I saw them both—Lynn and Vera—while I was with Rose this morning. Lynn happened to be having a chemo appointment across from Rose's cubicle. I guess Vera was there to lend Lynn some support."

"I don't see how having a heart attack is giving support, dear."

"Lynn said she had a weak heart and Hannah, the nurse, concurred."

"So you call Jeff and tell him. What's that, maybe ten or eleven words? 'Jeff, it's Tori. Vera kicked the bucket this morning. Call Garrett.' See? That's not too bad."

Tori stared at the leafy branches as they swayed in a rare summer breeze. Was Leona right? Was she making it harder than it needed to be? After all, once the news was delivered, she could forget all about Jeff once again, couldn't she?

"Now, can we go get some lunch?" Leona prompted. "Deirdre over at the diner called to say a truckload of firefighters from down south just stopped in for lunch and I want to extend a warm southern welcome while they're here."

"'A warm southern welcome'? Is that what they're calling it now?" She allowed the momentary image to ease some of the tension that had hovered around her body like a suffocating storm cloud all morning. And it felt good. Really good.

"If they stay because of my welcome, we'll decide what to call it then."

Tori rolled her eyes, then stood. "Did Deirdre happen to say how old these firefighters are?"

"Age doesn't matter, dear. I can tame a twenty-year-old just as surely as I can tame a sixty-year-old. It's all in the presentation." Leona rose to her feet and led the way to the door, stopping to give Tori a once-over. "Which is why I must insist you put on a little lipstick before we leave. We don't want your warm southern welcome to be met with cringing, now do we?"

Tori rolled onto her back and stared at the ceiling. She'd put off the call for as long as she could, using everything and anything she could find as an excuse for waiting—lunch with Leona, shelving books, re-shelving books, re-re-shelving books, making dinner, cleaning up after dinner, alphabetizing her junk mail before tossing it in the trash, et cetera. Yet now there were no more excuses to be found.

Except perhaps the fact that it was approaching nine thirty in the evening. If she waited much longer she'd be off the hook.

For about twelve hours anyway.

No, getting it over with was a better option.

Without taking her focus off the ceiling above her bed, Tori reached for her cell phone and flipped it open, her fingers instinctively finding the number she'd once called as often as four times a day.

There's always the chance he's moved . . .

Buoyed by the hope the thought provided, she

held the phone to her ear and listened to the rings. One. Two. Three. Four—

"Hey, this is Jeff."

Her stomach lurched at the sound of his voice, the familiar and friendly tone momentarily throwing her off her game. "Uh . . . Jeff? Um . . . uh . . . it's Tori."

"Tori? Oh my gosh, baby, how are you?"

She closed her eyes against the term of endearment she'd once treasured, yet now despised as the farce their entire relationship had been. "I have some bad news."

"Are you okay?"

She nodded.

"Baby . . . you still there? Are you okay?"

Realizing her mistake, she put words to her unseen action. "I'm fine. But I have something to tell you." Inhaling every ounce of courage she could muster, she proceeded. "It's your great-aunt. Vera. She passed away."

"What?"

"They think she had a heart attack." There. The words were out. Her duty was over.

"Where? When? How did you find out?"

"I—I was at a clinic in my town with a friend. Vera was there with Garrett's wife. It happened in a matter of minutes."

Silence filled her ear. "You live in Lee Station?"

"No, actually, one town over. It's called Sweet

Briar." The words trailed from her mouth as she realized she'd given more information than she'd intended. Leona had been right. She should have stuck to the eleven-word script.

"Sweet Briar. Sweet Briar, South Carolina," Jeff repeated as a telltale tapping overtook his words. After a few seconds, his voice returned in her ear. "I can get a flight into Columbia first thing in the morning. Any chance you can pick me up?"

She bolted upright in her bed. "Pick you up? Jeff, I can't do that."

"C'mon, Tori. I don't want to be trying to navigate an unfamiliar area in my grief. And Lord knows that good-for-nothing stepson of Vera's isn't going to offer his assistance."

Fisting her free hand at her side, Tori willed her head to win over her heart just this one time. Surely her great grandmother would have understood . . .

"Just get me where I need to go and I won't bother you ever again. Please, Tori. Just this once."

Damn.

"What time does your flight arrive?" she asked in a voice that could only be described as wooden.

I am an idiot.

"Tori, you're the best. I don't know how I ever let you get away."

Chapter 4

I am an idiot . . .
   I am an idiot . . .
   I am an idiot . . .
Even the roar of passenger airplanes as they took off and made their approach just yards above the roof of her car couldn't drown out the four-word mantra that had been running in a continuous loop for nearly fifteen hours. In fact, it had gotten louder and more persistent over time, peppered only by Leona's inquiry about Jeff's looks.

She knew she shouldn't have called after talking to him, but she'd been desperate. Leona, of all people, would have a way for her to get out of the biggest blunder she'd made since falling for Jeff in the first place, right?

It had been a sound thought.

Until Leona had learned of Jeff's single status—a tidbit Tori hadn't sought yet Jeff had given nonetheless. After her initial outrage that the woman could even think of pursuing her mortal enemy, she'd come to accept the notion Leona had laid out. Payback was a—

The sound of her cell phone broke through her

woolgathering and forced her thoughts back to the present. The number on the display screen merely kicked the fifteen-hour-long mantra into overdrive.

I am an idiot . . .

I am an idiot . . .

I am an idiot.

Flipping it open, she held it to her ear and simply waited, a tree-shadowed station wagon parked in a far corner of the cell phone lot providing a vague distraction from the voice in her ear.

"Tori? My plane just landed. All I'm doing now is waiting for the horde of idiots milling in the aisle to actually locate their bags and get the hell off the plane."

A flash of movement pulled her focus from the station wagon to the line of trees behind it as an unidentified figure bent at the waist and ran—or, rather, shuffled—its way to the backseat. She narrowed her eyes and leaned over the steering wheel for a closer look just as a pair of binoculars, held by someone in the front passenger seat, turned in her direction.

"Baby? You there?"

Tori waved at his voice like a pesky firefly as she narrowed her eyes still farther and continued to observe the flurry of activity getting in and out of the station wagon. A station wagon that looked an awful lot like—

"Margaret Louise," she gasped as the three separate forms she could make out in and around the car took on decidedly familiar features . . .

There was Rose's hunched body . . .

Leona returning to the car from the potty break that no doubt meant Paris was near . . .

Margaret Louise filling the front seat in what appeared to be a lime green workout suit . . .

"Margaret, who?"

And, of course, Jeff in her ear.

Shaking her head against the reality that those were her friends, she forced her attention onto the one person she wished she could forget. "I'm sorry, Jeff. I was distracted there for a moment. I'll meet you at the curb outside baggage claim in ten minutes."

"Make it five. I can't wait to see you."

She looked again at the threesome across the parking lot, their efforts at being sneaky pathetic at best. "Actually, make it *fifteen*." Closing the phone with a flip of her hand, Tori turned the key in the ignition and headed straight for the blurry-turned-crimson faces on the other side of the lot.

With a quick crank of her hand, she popped her head out the side window. "What on earth are the three of you doing here of all places?"

Rose coughed and looked at the ground.

Leona shifted from one stylish pump to the other.

Margaret Louise stepped out of the car, looked

down at the binoculars tethered to her neck, and pointed at her twin sister. "It was Leona's idea."

Tori pinned Leona with her eyes. "Is that true?"

Red-faced, Leona looked around wildly. "Frankly, dear, I don't know what you're talking about. The only reason I'm here is to reminisce about an encounter I had in this very spot with a pilot I met during a trip to Bali."

Rose rolled her eyes then muttered something under her breath.

Leona turned a penetrating glare of her own on the elderly woman. "Is something wrong, you old goat?"

"I'd rather be an old goat than a common, everyday streetwalker."

A gasp escaped Leona's mouth. "Streetwalker?"

"Though most streetwalkers prefer motel rooms, I believe."

Leona bit the second and louder gasp off with her teeth. "Rose Winters, you take that back!"

"When you take back *old goat!*"

Margaret Louise stepped in front of the unexpected sideshow and shrugged her hefty shoulders. "I've been wantin' to talk to you 'bout somethin', Victoria, and now seemed as good a time as any."

She pointed at the binoculars. "Planning on bird-watching after we talk?"

The woman released a loud sigh. "Okay, okay.

I give up. We heard what you're doin' and we reckon it's got to be hard. Milo or not, that man broke your heart and seein' him again has got to be like stickin' your hand in a light socket and havin' someone flip the switch. So, we just wanted to be here in case you needed reinforcements."

"Reinforcements?" she echoed as a lump sprang up in her throat.

"That's what I said," Margaret Louise bellowed as the roar of a jet threatened to drown out her words. "Make you soup when you're sick, fight off the wolves when they're circlin', hold your hand when your knees are a-clackin', help dig the hole when you're spittin' mad . . . that's what friends do."

Tori laughed away the urge to cry. "And the three of you have done all of those things at some time or another over the past eighteen months and I'm grateful. Truly."

"We ain't dug a hole for you yet," Margaret Louise reminded. "Though, dependin' on how today goes, that might be fixin' to change, I imagine."

The roar of the jet dissipated overhead. "I'm not sure I follow."

Rose peeked around Margaret Louise. "You need a hole to bury a body, don't you?"

"Bury a body?" she echoed.

With a sniff, Leona cut through Tori's inquiry.

49

"That's what we do with dead bodies in civilized places, dear. Leaving them to litter the sidewalks as they do in Chicago is simply not done here."

Tori's laugh echoed over the sound of the next jet as it hurtled its way down the runway just beyond the bank of trees that framed the back edge of the parking lot. "One of these days, Leona, I will get to the bottom of your issues where Chicago is concerned."

"Issues?" Leona groused. "I have no issues."

Rose snorted.

Leona stamped her foot. "Rose Winters, enough!"

Tori held up her hands. "Ladies, ladies, please. I'm . . . I'm touched that the three of you made the drive out here just to make sure I'm okay. It means more than you could ever know. But I'll be okay. Really."

"Of course you will be. Your sweet Milo would have our heads if you weren't."

Milo.

Inhaling the much-needed sense of calm that invariably came with the mention of his name, Tori leaned her head against the seat.

"He would if he *knew*."

Just like that, Leona's public summation made mincemeat of Tori's calm.

"Milo doesn't know that tomcat is in town?"

She closed her eyes against the disbelief in Margaret Louise's voice.

"Our dear Victoria didn't want to upset him."

So much for confiding in Leona . . .

In a flash, Margaret Louise was around the car and sitting in Tori's passenger seat. "It's not 'bout being upset, Victoria. It's 'bout sharin' your troubles with the man you love."

Was Margaret Louise right? Had she made a mistake in not telling Milo about Jeff's trip to South Carolina?

Leona tsked under her breath. "Twin, get with the program, will you? Victoria didn't tell him because she didn't want to get him all green-eyed. Though, if you ask me, every man could stand to have his hold on a woman shaken from time to time. Keeps them more attentive."

"I'm not worried about him being jealous," Tori protested.

"Then why didn't you tell him?"

She met Rose's questioning eyes, saw the uncertainty in her own reflected in them.

The ring of her cell phone saved her from having to offer an answer she didn't have. Peeking down at the display screen, she felt her mouth go dry.

Jeff.

Suddenly, the distraction her friends had provided with their unexpected appearance was over. She could no longer ignore the reason she was there in the first place.

"It's him, ain't it?" Margaret Louise asked.

She inhaled deeply, then nodded and reached for the phone.

"He can't hurt you no more, Victoria. Remember that."

Margaret Louise was right. The days of trying to piece her life back together again were long gone and she was better than ever.

"I can do this," she mumbled before flipping the phone open and holding it to her ear. "I'll be there in two minutes."

She could feel his eyes inspecting every nuance of her body just as surely as she could see Margaret Louise's pale blue station wagon tailing her from three cars back. "So . . . um . . . how was your flight?"

It was the safest question she could think of at the moment—something relatively innocuous to keep her from giving him a similar once-over. Besides, she already knew the way his dark blond hair curled at the point where it met his ears. And she already knew the way he used his emerald green eyes to wow the female population.

It was how to *forget* him that she'd fought so hard to learn only to throw it all away in a moment of misguided kindness.

I am an idiot . . .

"It was good. But sitting here now, next to you, is even better." His deep voice tickled her ear and she tightened her grip on the steering wheel in response. "You look great. Amazing, actually. The south certainly agrees with you."

"It does." Swinging her gaze upward, she noted the way Margaret Louise sped up as Tori approached an upcoming traffic light. "I love my job, my friends . . . my life. Moving here was the best decision I've ever made."

"Hurting you was the worst decision *I* ever made."

She felt her mouth gape open and her heartbeat accelerate. Why was he doing this?

Jeff reached across the center console and grabbed hold of Tori's right hand. "I've regretted it every single day since it happened."

As evident by the hundreds of times my phone never rang in the months that followed . . .

To Jeff, though, she shrugged what she prayed was a carefree shrug. He didn't deserve anything else. "Sometimes things happen for a reason." Pulling her hand from his, she placed it firmly on the steering wheel and said a preemptive mental prayer for forgiveness. "I—I'm engaged now. And I'm happy. Happier than I've ever been. His name is Milo and he teaches third grade at the local elementary school."

Silence filled the space between them as the light turned green and Margaret Louise's car lurched forward behind them. "Milo, eh?"

She nodded.

"I don't see a ring."

"It's, um, being sized," she lied.

"Well"—he reached for her hand once again—"until it's on that beautiful finger of yours with a wedding ring planted right there next to it, there's still a chance."

She felt her stomach churn. "A chance? A chance for what?"

"C'mon now, baby. You know what I'm saying."

"No, I actually don't," she said. "Enlighten me."

"There's still a chance for *us,* Tori." His hand struck again, this time coming to rest on her thigh. "Engaged is just engaged. It's not a done deal. Nor is my relationship with Julia—I mean, Kelly. Hell, Julia only came to pass because . . . I don't even know anymore. She just did. But then Kelly came along and, man, did she look cute in the overalls she was wearing when she came with her dad to fix a faulty circuit breaker at the club. But I don't owe them anything any more than you owe this Milo guy until the day you're actually married."

Jerking the car onto the shoulder, she slammed on the brakes, the roar of anger in her head nearly drowning out the answering screech behind them. "An engagement is merely a *statement* of intent to the rest of the world, Jeff. The commitment between the two people is already there. That's the part you seemed to miss two years ago." Gulping back the sobs that threatened to stop her tirade in its tracks, she continued, her voice rising to a pitch capable of shattering glass. "You took everything I knew to be true at that moment and yanked it from under my feet. And you know what? I was drowning in your betrayal . . . absolutely drowning."

"I—"

Movement outside Jeff's door cut his response short, replacing it instead with a loud knock and the sight of Leona and Paris peeking in the passenger-side window. Motioning over her shoulder, Leona stepped to the side to reveal a simmering Rose and a shovel-wielding Margaret Louise.

"Who—who the hell is that?" Jeff mumbled.

"The life raft that pulled me to shore."

Chapter 5

They were waiting for her when she arrived at the funeral home, their unmistakable elbow jabs and expectant stares more than a little unnerving.

Sure, there was a part of her that was grateful for their moral support. How could she not be? Reinforcements were always good.

But it was the unanswerable question in their eyes that negated any positive that came from their presence.

Willing herself to remain calm, Tori took a deep breath and inched her way toward the receiving line positioned at the entrance to the viewing room. One by one, each mourner took a moment to offer his or her condolences to Vera's family members while those who awaited their opportunity took precious moments to compose similar sentiments or simply survey the next of kin with slightly morbid curiosity.

First, there was Garrett—the resentful little boy who'd come into Vera's life via marriage when he was just ten years old. Now in his late forties, the perpetual childhood scowl he'd worn in photographs was nowhere to be found, replaced, instead, by a confidence that was impossible to miss.

Beside him stood a woman Tori didn't know. Though, if she were a betting woman, she'd take a chance on it being Garrett's pharmacy tech girlfriend. A good fifteen years his junior, the woman's too-tight dress and matching red lipstick made her an ill fit—if not a stereotypical midlife crisis.

On the girlfriend's other side was Garrett's estranged wife, Lynn, her balding head hidden by a tasteful black scarf. Any indication she was bothered by the presence of her husband's mistress was hidden from view, the nature of the event winning out over any hurt and resentment she may have been experiencing.

And, finally, there was Jeff—the epitome of the grieving great-nephew right down to the impeccably pressed navy blue suit, starched white dress shirt, and red-rimmed eyes.

She swallowed over the sympathy-induced lump that sprang into her throat and stepped forward, Garrett's hand closing over hers a full second before any sort of recognition dawned on his face.

"Wait. I know you. It's—" Garrett snapped his finger in rhythmic fashion as he searched Tori's face for clues. "Kylie, right? From the Mid American Professional Pharmacists' convention? But what are you doing *here?*"

His girlfriend dropped the hand of the mourner she was receiving and focused squarely on Garrett, her fake red fingernails planted firmly on her impossibly narrow hips. "You met a *Kylie* at the conference? You never told me that!"

Pulling her hand from Garrett's grasp, Tori thrust it in the girlfriend's direction. "My name is Tori. Tori Sinclair. I knew Garrett's stepmom through her great-nephew, Jeff."

The girlfriend cocked her head and cast a puppy-dog look in Jeff's direction. "Garrett? Is that true?"

Ignoring her, Garrett clapped his hands. "Ahhh, Tori. That's it." His dark brown eyes slipped downward as he took in Tori's black pantsuit, white cami, and open-toed heels. The naked appreciation at what he found warmed her face. "Wow, you look fantastic. Absolutely, positively fantastic. Wow. Not only is that stepcousin of mine a perpetual thorn in my side, he's also an even bigger idiot than I realized."

She bit back the urge to agree, opting, instead, to offer a graceful shrug. "I'm so sorry about your loss."

Garrett matched her shrug with one of his own. "Thanks. But I've had time to prepare. She was a heart attack waiting to happen just like everyone else in her family."

Her gaze slid to the end of the line as a long-ago conversation filled her thoughts. "That's how Jeff's grandfather died, right?"

"His grandfather, his father, his uncle, his cousin, you name it." Garrett leaned forward, his breath warm against her ear. "He did you a favor in the closet that day, Tori. He really did."

Feeling the piercing blue daggers from his mistress, she stepped back. "It took awhile . . . a very long while . . . but I've come to believe the same thing."

"Oh?" he asked before a knowing sparkle lit his eyes. "Who's the lucky guy?"

"Milo. Milo Wentworth."

Slipping his arm around his mistress, Garrett let his gaze slip down Tori's form once again, the blatant visual inventory more than a little unsettling. "Indiscretion isn't always bad, huh?"

Feeling her Jeff-induced anger resurfacing, Tori looked from Lynn to the mistress and back again before resuming deliberate eye contact with the buffoon in front of her. "When it saves a beautiful woman from continuing to worship a first-class jerk, I couldn't agree more."

Without waiting for a response, Tori stepped two people to the right and took hold of Lynn's gently trembling hand. "I wish we didn't have to meet again under these circumstances."

The corners of the woman's mouth lifted. "Victoria, I'm touched you came. Especially with"—Lynn jerked her head to her immediate left—"you-know-who here and all."

"Sometimes you have to do what's right over what's easy. Though, from what I see here, you don't need me to tell you that, do you?"

Lynn took in the spectacle that was her husband and his mistress and released a soft laugh. "No, I suppose you don't."

She squeezed Lynn's hand. "When the receiving line is over, Rose and I—along with a few of our friends—will be sitting over there." Tori pointed in the direction of her gaggle of sewing buddies gossiping away in the back corner of the viewing room. "We'd love it if you'd join us."

"Thank you, Victoria. If I'm feeling up to it, I will."

And just like that, she noticed the woman's pale face and clammy skin—features she'd been too preoccupied to notice thanks to her exchange with Garrett and the swell of nerves that came with knowing she was one step away from yet another face-to-face with Jeff. "Are you okay? Is there anything I can do?"

"Short of handing me a winning lottery ticket and/or wiping my philandering husband from the face of my own personal world, no. But thank you for asking. It means a lot." Without waiting for Tori to fully register her words, Lynn flashed a weak smile. "Really, I'm okay. Just a little tired and a little nauseous. All par for the course at the moment."

Tori met the woman's smile with one of encouragement. She liked Lynn, liked her spunk.

"The offer stands." Tori glanced over her shoulder at the dwindling line. "Hang in just a little longer. Looks like you're almost done here."

Then, out of respect for the person behind her, she stepped forward, stopping in front of Vera's final family member—the biggest pothole standing between her and the safety of her friends. Careful to avoid any unnecessary contact, she simply bowed her head quickly. "Jeff."

Her former fiancé's face lit in its familiar charming way. "Baby, I'm so glad you came. I was hoping you would." Grabbing hold of her shoulders, he pulled her forward and planted a kiss on her lips.

"Jeff, please," she hissed, backing away. "There's no need for that."

A taunting smile spread across his still damp lips. "Oh trust me. There's a need."

A jingling behind her made her turn, the anger that gripped her heart taking a backseat to confusion as a woman about Tori's age breezed into the viewing room and sidled up on Jeff's open side. "Sweetheart, I'm so sorry I'm late. My flight was delayed getting out of Chicago, the stupid rental car company didn't have my car ready, and apparently they don't believe in road signs in the south."

Jeff pried the woman's fingers from his forearm and rolled his eyes. "I didn't know you were coming, Kelly."

"How could you think I wouldn't?" With a flick of her wrists, the fair-skinned blonde fanned her long tresses across her diminutive shoulders. "If you'd given me half a chance, I'd have flown in with you this morning."

"I didn't want to take advantage of Tori's offer to pick me up."

Kelly's eyes narrowed to near slits as she turned and took in Tori. "Tori? You mean, *the* Tori?"

Tori swallowed and took a step back only to have her progress thwarted by Jeff's strong hand. "Tori, I'd like you to meet my current girlfriend, Kelly Walker. Kelly, this is Tori Sinclair . . . the one I let get away."

Feeling her mouth gape open, Tori rushed to craft a response that would remove some of the sting from Jeff's words. But before she could speak, Lynn took the ball and ran it into the end zone. "Don't you mean the one who wised up and took off without so much as a glance backward, Jeff?" To Tori, she said, "Rose is looking a little peaked, don't you think you should check in on her?"

Whipping around, Tori spotted Rose sitting in the corner, her pallor no different than normal. She turned back to Lynn and gratefully acknowledged the exit offered during an intensely awkward moment. "Oh Lynn, thank you. You're right. I better go check on her."

Jeff's face fell.

Kelly's eyes continued to shoot daggers in her direction.

She squared her shoulders and took a long, deliberate breath. "Kelly, it's nice to meet you. And Jeff . . . again, I'm sorry about Vera."

And with that, she was gone, her feet leading her across the room and into the welcome arms of her most loyal friends. "Margaret Louise, Leona, Rose . . . you have no idea how good it is to see you here."

"What a difference a few hours—and the presence of a little competition—makes," Leona mused from her spot on an upholstered wing chair, flanked on either side by Rose and Margaret Louise in cushioned folding chairs.

Drawing back, she stared at her most ornery friend. "Competition? What competition are you talking about?"

Rose lifted a too-thin finger into the air and pointed across the room. "That little thing next to your Jeff."

She winced at the choice of pronoun. "He's not *my* Jeff."

"You seemed mighty protective of someone you don't consider yours, dear."

Grabbing hold of an empty chair, she pulled it over to complete the makeshift circle. "First of all, Leona, death by shovel is not really my thing. Nor is the notion of visiting the three of you in jail. Jeff is simply not worth that."

"See?" Margaret Louise smacked the backside of her hand into her sister's shoulder. "I told you, Twin. That whole 'things are fine' thing wasn't about Victoria havin' feelings for that man. She just don't want us meddlin' where we don't belong."

Was that it? Was that really why, back at the airport, she'd rolled down Jeff's window and told them to go home?

It certainly made sense.

Even if it wasn't true.

"Okay, then what's the second reason, dear?" Leona inquired while folding her arms.

"Second reason?" she repeated.

"You said not wanting to see us kill Jeff and be sent to prison was the first thing," Rose reminded. "What's the second reason for your protectiveness?"

She swallowed. "I don't know how to answer that."

"Why not?"

Shrugging, she met Rose's question with as much of an answer as she could give. "I've been trying to figure that out since I dropped Jeff at his hotel. And I still don't have an answer other than he's not entirely to blame for what happened between us."

Margaret Louise's gasp was put into words by Rose. "He broke your heart, didn't he?"

She nodded.

"And he did it in as despicable a way as possible, didn't he?" Margaret Louise asked.

Again, she nodded.

"Then who else is there to blame, dear?"

She met Leona's pointed gaze. "Me."

"You?" her friends asked in unison.

"Me," she repeated.

"How on earth could you come up with that?" Rose demanded.

"Easy. It's what every woman wants to know when the man they love dumps them in such an awful way."

Tori jerked her head up at the sound of Lynn's voice, a lump forming in her throat at the understanding on the woman's face.

Rose huffed. "That's preposterous. Absolutely preposterous."

"No it's not," Lynn countered as she, too, pulled up a chair. "Their cheating was surely a reaction. A reaction to some sort of shortcoming in us. At least that's what we think . . . for a while."

Leona folded her perfectly manicured hands in

65

her lap. "Tell me this isn't true, dear. Tell me I've taught you better than this."

Oh how she wished she could.

Yet she couldn't.

"It's not that I think I deserved what he did, Leona. Because I didn't. No one does. But that doesn't mean there wasn't something about me that made him lose interest. And maybe, if I find out what that something was, I could keep from making the same mistake with . . ." The words trailed from her mouth as the reason she was stalling on Milo's proposal hit her between the eyes with a resounding thump.

Leona uncrossed her ankles and stood, pure disgust evident in every cosmetically altered feature on her face. "I've heard enough. Margaret Louise, I think it's time you let Victoria in on your little plan. Because as much as I'm aghast at the notion of spending an entire weekend away from men, I think it might be the only chance we have to knock some sense into this one's head."

Chapter 6

Tori stepped to the left to avoid Sally's Big Wheel and to the right to avoid smudging Lulu's chalk masterpiece, the sound of giggling laughter from the backyard magically loosening the knots in her stomach.

For much of the day, she'd discarded the notion of attending the evening's meeting of the Sweet Briar Ladies Society Sewing Circle. Her mood was simply too dour. Yet somehow, someway, she'd allowed a phone call from Margaret Louise to persuade her otherwise.

Then again, Margaret Louise was a master at getting Tori to do what she wanted. And Tori knew why.

Margaret Louise Davis was the kind of friend everyone wished they had. She was loyal and true, encouraging and supportive, a giver in every sense of the word, and she didn't expect anything in return for her efforts. Ever.

That fact alone was enough to make Tori set aside her personal pity party and heed the woman's request. And, now that she was there, she was glad. The weekly sewing circle meeting had always been a way to recharge her battery after a busy week at the library. It was an opportunity to catch up on her friends' lives as well as the gossip making the rounds, and it gave her permission to sit and sew—the one tangible connection she still had to her late great grandmother.

The fact that this week's meeting was being held at the home of fellow circle member and Margaret Louise's daughter-in-law, Melissa, was simply the icing on the cake.

In her mid-thirties, Melissa was only one of two other circle members whose age was within a few years of Tori's. And while Melissa was at a different stage in her life with a husband and seven children, she could empathize with certain circumstances in a way some of the older members couldn't.

Toss in the opportunity to get hugs from Melissa's entire brood—including the always precious Lulu—and, well, she was exactly where she needed to be. The stuff with Jeff could wait.

"Victoria, you made it!" Melissa stuck her head out the front door and tugged Tori inside. "Margaret Louise has been telling me about everything going on and I just assumed you'd be hankering for a quiet night to yourself."

"I've been having that all day. Now it's time to let something besides second-guessing to the forefront for a little while." Tori breathed in the scent of sugar cookies, talcum powder, and bubbles that clung to her friend's hair as she passed.

"Second-guessing?" Melissa asked as she took the covered dessert plate from Tori's outstretched hand and placed it on the counter. "Second-guessing about what?"

She tugged her tote bag higher on her arm then waved off the question with her free hand. "Am I the last to arrive?"

Melissa's eyes narrowed momentarily only to return to their normal round shape, with a warm smile to boot. "Rose will be along soon. She got sidetracked in some woman's garden. You know how she is about that sort of thing."

Tori did. "She's just like I am with a book and your mother-in-law is with those grandbabies you and Jake have given her."

"You can't forget the way that twin sister of mine is with whatever uniformed male has caught her eye at the moment," Margaret Louise bellowed from the hallway that linked the kitchen with the rest of the house. Stepping all the way into the room, she strode over to Tori and planted a kiss on her forehead. "I'm glad you decided to come. We've got a lot to talk about if we're going to head north at the end of the week."

Melissa clapped her hands. "Are you going?"

"I—I'm not sure just—"

"Of course she's going," Margaret Louise interjected. "Dixie has already offered to stay behind and man the library so everything is set. It'll be me, you, Leona, Rose, Debbie, Beatrice, and Victoria."

"Margaret Louise, I'm not really sure I—"

"Debbie's bringin' chocolaty treats . . ."

A gurgle sounded from somewhere deep inside Tori's stomach.

"And I'm goin' to be making supper both nights . . ."

She slapped a hand over her abdomen as Margaret Louise continued.

"And it's not goin' to cost you so much as a nickel."

"How do you figure that?"

A smile spread across Margaret Louise's face like wildfire through dry prairie grass. "You 'member that prize money I got for my sweet potato pie recipe last summer?"

Tori nodded as a matching smile appeared on Melissa's face.

"I set some of that aside for somethin' special. I didn't know what that was or when it would come, but I knew I wanted to wait until it did. And it's time now, Victoria. Time for one of those girls-only weekends I read about in one of my sister's travel magazines a while back."

She looked from Margaret Louise to Melissa and back again. "So that's where that whole cabin in the woods thing you mentioned last night came from?"

"Sure as shootin'. Though, if you'd been listenin' to everything I said at the funeral home, you'd have known this then."

Touché.

"Margaret Louise, I'm sorry. I really am. I guess I just had a lot on my mind."

"I know, dear. That wasn't meant as an accusation. Just a fact . . . like you comin' to the cabin this weekend."

There was a part of her that knew she should protest—the part that was more than a little terrified at the notion of leaving Dixie in charge of the library for two whole days, front and center.

But the things that could go wrong in a forty-eight hour time period were *possibilities*. The fun she'd have with her friends in a remote mountain cabin for one whole weekend was all but an absolute certainty.

"You know you want to," Melissa teased.

"Jake is okay with all of the kids?"

The woman's dirty blonde ponytail bobbed up and down. "Everyone except the baby. I mean, he said he'd keep her but I can't leave her behind. She's too little."

She couldn't help but smile. Melissa was truly an amazing mother. "And Leona is okay with this?"

"If she don't want to be left out of the fun, she's gonna have to be." Margaret Louise pushed off the linoleum floor with her toes and swiveled around, the squeak from her sneakers nearly lost in the sound of Rose's knock. "Well look at you, Rose Winters, aren't you quite the sight."

Rose peeked through the screen door and scowled. "What are you talking about, Margaret Louise?"

Melissa nudged the door open and gently wiped a smudge of dirt from the elderly woman's wrinkled face with a practiced hand. "Don't you pay my mother-in-law any mind, Rose. You look as beautiful as always."

"What? What did you just rub off?" Rose groused.

"Just a little souvenir from an evening of fun you've sorely earned after the treatments you've been having."

Tori stepped forward, brushed a kiss on Rose's cheek, then mouthed a thank-you in Melissa's direction. "So? Who's the lucky recipient of your gardening know-how this time?"

In a flash, any and all embarrassment disappeared from Rose's demeanor, pushed aside by the pride and joy she displayed every time her expertise in the garden was referenced. "I'd like to say I was able to help Lynn, but I think it's safe to say she taught me a thing or two I hadn't known."

Tori's mouth gaped open in time with Melissa's. "*Lynn* taught *you* something about gardening? Is that even possible?"

"I thought I was versed in all the flowering plants that can be grown in this part of the country, but she introduced me to a few I hadn't known." Rose pushed past Margaret Louise to place her own contribution to the circle's dessert lineup on the counter. "It's just like I've always said . . . it's never too late to learn new tricks."

"You're right." Linking her arm through Rose's, Tori gestured toward the hallway. "Well? Shall we join the others?"

Rose patted the bulging bag on her arm. "I brought Lynn's pillow to show everyone. She let me borrow it for the evening."

Slowly, Tori matched Rose's steps down the hallway, Margaret Louise and Melissa following behind at a respectful distance. "This pillow. Does it have a purpose other than providing a small reminder of home during outpatient procedures?"

"It's called a comfort pillow and it's used primarily by women who have had a mastectomy . . . like Lynn. When they're driving, it protects the incision from impact with the steering wheel. When the surgery is recent, it can lessen the pain when they cough or sneeze."

"Wow. I didn't realize there was an actual use

for them." They rounded the corner into Melissa's family room, the welcoming smiles from the rest of the circle members confirming, once again, the wisdom behind Margaret Louise's gentle shove. Already, Tori felt better, the stress Jeff's presence in town had created all but disappearing into the land of it-doesn't-matter.

"Victoria! Rose! We're so glad you came." Debbie Calhoun patted the empty sofa spots on each side of her body. "I saved a place for both of you."

Rose lurched forward, extricating her arm from Tori's grasp in the process. "I'll take the end closest to the lamp. Makes threading my needle a bit easier."

"You can thread a needle faster than I ever could." Debbie scooted a hairbreadth to the side set aside for Tori and allowed Rose to get situated. When she had, Debbie scooted back. "Victoria, I heard Jeff is in town. I imagine that's making you miss Milo all the more. You holding up okay, hon?"

It was just like Debbie to know that buried beneath the happiness Tori derived from being there was the cloud of Jeff's presence and Milo's absence. It was one of many reasons the thirty-something wife and mother of two was the successful business owner she was. That innate sense had served her well in getting her bakery off the ground and into everyone's mind as *the* place to go in Sweet Briar.

Needles and machines stilled around the room as all eyes turned in Tori's direction. Waiting.

"I—I'm doing fine, I guess."

"What's this bloke like?" Beatrice Tharrington, the youngest of the group, inquired from her chair beside the hearth. Other than Tori, Beatrice was the only non-southern voice in the room. The fact that the nanny's accent reflected her ties to England made her stand out even more.

"I don't understand the question." It was a lame response, but it bought her time. Time to take a few deep breaths and search for the calm that was suddenly playing a game of cat and mouse.

"What does he look like?" Beatrice clarified.

A safe question. One she could answer with simple facts. "He's tall, about six-foot-two." Tori pulled her wooden sewing box from her tote bag and set it on the coffee table, then reached back into the bag for the pink and blue material she'd brought along. "His hair is sort of dirty blond, I guess, and his eyes are a dark brown."

"With that odd little sparkle that the truly dangerous ones have," Leona interjected. "You know the kind. They lure you in with their charm and then wreak havoc on your life."

She looked from Leona to the onesie pattern

she'd selected for Nina's baby-to-be and back again, the woman's spot-on description catching her by surprise. "You say that like it's happened to you, Leona."

An unfamiliar tint of red blanched across Leona's face right before it sunk behind the magazine designed to keep her busy while everyone else worked on sewing projects.

Intrigued, Tori opened her mouth to lure Leona back into the conversation only to shut it again when Margaret Louise cast a look of warning in her direction.

Hmmm . . . Could this be why Leona had never settled down? Was this life-wrecking charmer the reason behind her friend's hatred of Chicago? She had to wonder. And wonder she did—

"What's the rest of him like?"

Beatrice's soft voice cut through the parade of questions flooding her mind, begging to be asked.

"Him?" she echoed absentmindedly.

"Jeff."

She swallowed. "There's not much to tell, really."

"What does he do for a living?" Rose prompted from her spot on the other side of Debbie.

It was a safe question. "He's a fitness trainer. For the biggest gym in Chicago."

"A fitness trainer?" Debbie asked as the corners of her mouth nearly rose to her eyes. "A *fitness trainer?* And the two of you were *engaged?*"

A chorus of laughter rang up around the room.

"Hey!" she protested. "I'm in shape!"

Margaret Louise shook her head slowly. "And that is one of the many questions I'll have when I'm standin' before those pearly gates."

She shot a questioning look at Leona's twin. "You've lost me."

Gesturing from her plump form to Tori's slender body, Margaret Louise grimaced playfully. "Don't get me wrong. I know I like to eat. Goes along with the cookin' and all. But I don't believe I've ever seen you turn down a second helpin' of dessert in all the time I've known you, Victoria."

"My metabolism is just fast. That's all."

"It's okay, Victoria, I adore you too much to despise you." Margaret Louise cast a wink in her direction. "But I must say, I'm with Debbie. Seems kind of funny a fitness trainer would fall for a girl with such a sweet tooth."

Tori leaned forward, opened her sewing box, and scanned her various thread colors for a pastel pink and a pastel blue. Finding the perfect shade of each, she pulled them out and settled back against the sofa. "Trust me, he was always trying some new health food out on me. And I, being the quick-to-please girlfriend I was, went along with it."

A slight nod from behind Leona's magazine didn't escape her notice, but she let it go. There would be time to question her friend later. In private.

"Then I hope you pigged out on every decadent delight you could find after he hurt you the way he did."

She had to smile at Beatrice. Barely into her twenties, the young woman rarely said much let alone something even vaguely resembling a derogatory statement in another person's direction. "Once I was able to eat again, Beatrice, I did exactly that."

Leona lowered her magazine just long enough to steal a glimpse in Tori's direction. "How long were you unable to eat, dear?"

"Too long," she answered honestly. "But that's all behind me now. Moving here . . . to Sweet Briar . . . was the smartest thing I've ever done."

"I bet that little moppet he had with him at the wake last night is glad you moved." Rose pulled a comfort pillow from her own bag and rested it on her lap. "Was she the one he was canoodling with at your engagement party?"

She thought back to the blonde who'd seemed more than a little intimidated by Tori's presence at the funeral parlor, then contrasted it with the never-far-from-her-mind image of the statuesque brunette she'd once considered a friend. Shaking her head against the memory, she forced a smile to her lips. "No. I guess Julia got the old heave-ho somewhere along the line, too."

"Once a cheat, always a cheat," Georgina, the town's mayor and founding member of the Sweet Briar Ladies Society Sewing Circle mused from her chair beneath a gooseneck lamp. "Which is why I say, good riddance. You're far better off with Milo Wentworth."

Like clockwork, the mere mention of the third grade teacher's name started the familiar butterfly brigade in Tori's stomach. The man had, single-handedly, restored her faith in the opposite sex. And true love.

"I bet you're missing him something fierce."

She nodded at Debbie. "It seems like he's been gone forever instead of just a week."

"When will he return?" Beatrice inquired.

"Not soon enough."

"Does he know Jeff is in town?"

Tori dropped her gaze to her lap.

Georgina repeated her question. "Does he know Jeff is in town?"

"No." When everyone leaned forward, she repeated her answer. "No."

"Good heavens, Victoria, why not?"

Why not, indeed.

She struggled to put words to the reasons she'd yet to explain to herself. "I know that I'm holding off on accepting Milo's proposal because of Jeff. Because of the insecurities his cheating stirred up inside me. I guess I'm hoping that maybe I can find a way to banish them once and for all while Jeff is here."

For a moment, no one said anything, each woman seemingly lost in her own little world. Finally, though, Leona spoke, her words clipped and to the point. "You can banish them, dear, by putting him out of your mind once and for all."

"I suspect it's not that easy, Twin."

"It most certainly is," Leona snapped at her sister, her eyes fiery behind her stylish glasses.

Tori narrowed her eyes and studied her friend, a flash of something besides fire suddenly bringing answers to the questions she hadn't been able to ask. Leona knew the kind of hurt Tori had experienced with Jeff. Of that, she was absolutely certain.

"No man—I repeat, *no man*—is worth second-guessing your worth." Lowering her magazine to her lap, Leona met Tori's gaze. "You hold the power in your own life, Victoria. Don't ever, *ever,* hand that over to anyone else."

"You mean like you do, old woman, every single time an attractive man crosses your path?" Rose taunted.

Leona clenched her teeth. "Make no mistake about it, Rose Winters, I always hold the power. Always."

A domino of disbelief fell across the room as Leona's failure to take Rose's infamous age-related bait hit them at the same time. Even Rose, herself, looked shell-shocked. And thoroughly defeated.

"I, well . . ."

Margaret Louise pointed to Rose's lap. "Why don't you show everyone the pillow, Rose."

"I, well . . ." Rose's words trailed off once again as she looked down at her lap. "I, um, have, um, an idea for a group project if everyone's interested."

Leona disappeared behind her magazine once again.

"Tell us," Debbie said, her focus shifting between Rose and Leona and back again.

Rose lifted the pillow into the air with trembling hands. "This here is a comfort pillow for women who have had mastectomies. Helps protect their incision when driving. My friend, Lynn, from the treatment center swears by hers."

"Are they hard to make?" Beatrice inquired, as she, too, stole a glance in Leona's direction.

"Not at all." Margaret Louise took hold of the conversation. "In fact, if we take everything we need with us on Friday, we can get a good number of 'em done at the cabin. In between our hootin' and hollerin', of course."

And, just like that, the conversation turned to the mountain cabin that would play host to the Sweet Briar Ladies Society Sewing Circle's first-ever girls' weekend. A weekend of sewing, good food, and endless gossip . . . all against the stunning backdrop of the Smoky Mountains featured in Leona's travel magazine.

But even as her friends oohed and aahed over the photographs and Margaret Louise's accompanying sales pitch, she couldn't shake Leona's words from her thoughts long enough to focus on anything besides the mistake she'd agreed to meet in a little over two hours.

Chapter 7

He was waiting on her front porch when she arrived, his tall muscular frame sprawled out with confident ease on her wicker rocker.

"I was beginning to wonder if you'd stood me up. But then I remembered who I was waiting for and I knew that would never happen." Jeff pushed off the chair and sauntered over to the top step, blocking her admittance with a playful smile. "You see, Victoria Sinclair is sweet and she would never make plans with someone and not show up."

Tori tugged her tote bag higher onto her shoulder and ducked her way around Jeff's waiting arms. "Considering this is my home, that's probably a safe bet."

He laughed. "You'd come even if we'd set a park bench as our meeting place."

Oh, how she wished he were wrong.

"Jeff, I don't—"

A ring from Jeff's pocket cut her off mid-sentence. Instead, she found herself watching as he pulled out his cell phone, made a face at his caller ID, then flipped it open and held it to his ear. "Yeah Kelly, what do you want? I told you, I had something to do . . . what difference does it make . . . okay, fine, I'm with Tori right now . . . yes, Tori . . . no, I haven't told her yet . . . look, I don't owe you anything . . . I told you I was going out to celebrate and that I'll be back to Vera's when I'm done . . . find a movie to watch or file your nails . . . I gotta go."

Shrugging, he shoved the phone back into his pocket and flashed his most charming smile at Tori. "Sorry about that. It won't happen again. Now where were—ahhh, yes, I know. I was commenting on how true you are to your word. And how I knew you'd show up simply because you said you would."

At least one of us is true to our word . . .

"So, what did you want to see me about?" She made a beeline for the stationary chair a good twenty feet from the rocking chair he'd claimed just moments earlier. "It's getting late and I really need to get some sleep."

Pulling the rocker to within mere inches of her knee, Jeff sat down. "I want you to give me a second chance."

She stood up. "I don't have time for this. I told you, I'm committed to someone else. Someone caring, and sweet, and funny, and—"

"Broke."

"What are you talking about?"

He grabbed hold of her hand and tugged her back down to her chair. "You said he teaches, right? Which means he's broke. While I, on the other hand, am now in a position to lavish you with diamonds, and trips, and whatever your heart desires."

"My heart desires a man who knows what commitment means. And you and I both know that isn't you, Jeff."

"It could be."

She couldn't help but laugh at his refusal to see reality. "You mean like you're doing right now by being here and talking like this? Don't you think Kelly might disagree?"

He waved his hand in the air. "Kelly means nothing."

"Like I apparently did."

"That's not true. You meant the world to me, you really did. I just wanted to get a few last-minute gulps of air before we got married."

She stared at him. "Gulps of air?"

"You know . . . of freedom."

And in that moment every insecurity she'd carried from the moment she'd found him in the closet with Julia disappeared, chased from her heart by anger and repulsion. "You saw marriage as an end to your freedom?"

"Who doesn't?"

"Those of us who see marriage as the beginning of something beautiful, that's who," she hissed through clenched teeth. "I think it's time you leave."

He stepped in front of her as she stood. "I'm ready now, Tori. I really am. I can have"—he pointed toward her front door—"this place packed in less than twenty-four hours and we can be on our way back to civilization."

"Civilization?"

"I'll get us an apartment on Lake Shore Drive. You can even have a room that's just for you and all of your books."

"Did you rob a bank?" she asked.

He snickered. "Something like that."

She pushed past him and glanced down at her watch.

Nine thirty.

There was still time to call Milo.

Whirling around, she faced Jeff for what she hoped was the very last time. With a heart that was suddenly free of everything except the knowledge that her broken engagement was nothing short of a blessing. "I wouldn't give up what I have with Milo for a thousand apartments on Lake Shore Drive. And you want to know why?"

"Why?" he asked with a voice that was suddenly bored.

"Because you can't put a price tag on things like loyalty and honor. And you sure as heck can't *buy* them, either."

Jeff rolled his eyes and meandered over to the steps. "I'm staying at Vera's place for another day or so before I head back to Chicago. Either way, you know how to reach me when you change your mind." Looking back over his shoulder he blew her a kiss. "Or, shall I say, when *he* changes *his* mind."

Her face warmed at the implication. "I'd watch it if I were you, Jeff. I really would. One of these days you're going to get what's coming your way."

She was just reaching for the phone when it rang, the unexpected noise doing little to calm her already unsettled nerves. Checking the name on the screen, she felt the smile it brought to her face and the instantaneous way it disappeared.

Did she tell Milo that Jeff was in town? That she'd been the one to summon him and pick him up at the airport? That he'd been there, on her front porch, less than twenty minutes earlier? And, if she did, how did she explain the days-long delay in telling him to begin with?

She took a deep breath and answered. "Were your ears ringing or something? I was just getting ready to—"

"Why didn't you tell me he was in town?" Milo's voice, uncharacteristically sharp, made her tighten her grip on the phone. "Why did I have to hear it from Leona?"

Something akin to ice water washed over her. "*Leona* told you? Why? When?"

"She called me about a half hour ago. Said she was worried about you. And after I heard the things that jerk had to say, I can see why. Are you okay?"

"But how could you have heard?" she stammered. Dropping onto the edge of her bed she stared up at the ceiling. "I—I just spoke to him."

A weighted silence made her pull the phone from her ear and check its connection. "Milo?" she asked as she held the phone against her cheek once again. "Are you still there?"

"Yeah. I'm here. I just don't want to get Leona in trouble. She did the right thing."

She counted to ten silently.

"What right thing would that be? Butting in where she doesn't belong?"

"No. Looking out for you. Like a friend does."

She knew he was right. She really did. It's just that she didn't like him finding out in this way. It made her feel dishonest, somehow.

"I'm not going to ask why you didn't tell me he was in town sooner. I'm just going to assume you had your reasons." His voice softened momentarily, allowing her to imagine him lying on his hotel bed. As he continued, though, his tone took on an unfamiliar edge. "But he had no right, no right to speak to you the way he did earlier. I swear, if I could have reached my hand through the phone and wrapped it around his neck, I would have."

"Reached through the phone?" she echoed in a whisper. "What are you talking about?"

"Leona had me on speaker so I could hear the whole thing."

Tori sat up. "On speaker? But how? Where was she?" She closed her eyes, recalling every sound she'd heard while on the porch with Jeff. But aside from a few crickets and the occasional barking dog, there'd only been a quick rustle or two from the bushes during Kelly's call. Was Leona, elegant Leona, in the bushes?

"I don't know and I didn't ask. It wasn't important. What was important was making sure you were okay. Though, I have to tell you, I almost threw my stuff in my bag and checked out while that was going on."

"You can't," she protested. "You're at those workshops for a reason, remember?"

"I've heard enough. And besides, I've met a few peers that could take notes for me."

"No, Milo. You've been looking forward to this conference all summer. Stay. Please. I'll be fine." Tori pushed off the bed and wandered over to the window, Leona's suspected hiding place in full view. "I *am* fine."

And she was. Whatever self-doubt Jeff's past actions had stirred inside her subconscious was gone, cured by the realization he wasn't the man she'd once thought. What that said about her judgment on the other hand, certainly left room for greater self-examination in the very near future.

"I'm not that far away, Tori. I could be home in a matter of hours . . ."

She couldn't help but notice the way Milo's concern chased any lingering chill from her body. It was as if his words were an extension of his arms—holding her close, keeping her safe.

"I'm fine. Really. Talking to you, right now, makes everything better. Knowing you left your conference early for me would only make me feel worse." She rose onto the balls of her bare feet and pivoted, her gaze coming to rest on her favorite picture of Milo. "I'm sorry I didn't tell you sooner . . . about Jeff being here and all. But I didn't know what *I* was thinking let alone how to share it with you."

"That's okay. Leona filled me in. Though trying to decipher what that woman is saying when she's clenching her teeth and going off on a verbal rampage is a lot harder than one might imagine."

"A verbal rampage about what? You lost me."

"About this clown being in town and making you doubt yourself."

She crossed the tiny room to her nightstand and lifted the silver frame from its surface. The picture had been taken nearly a year earlier, after they'd been dating for a few months. Even then, the love Milo had for her had been written all over his face—writing that had only grown more clear in the ensuing months.

If she was honest with herself, Jeff had never looked at her that way. Sure, his eyes had held desire and intrigue at times, but the same complete love she saw on Milo's face every time he looked at her? Not even close.

"The doubt didn't start when he arrived in Sweet Briar. It's been there for a while."

A sigh filled her ear. "It kills me to know you've been harboring this crazy notion that you somehow pushed that jerk into cheating on you. You're the most amazing woman I've ever met. With no disrespect intended toward Celia, of course."

Celia, Milo's late wife. The woman he'd been married to over a decade earlier, only to have her taken from his life by cancer within the first six months.

"Milo, you don't have to say that."

"What? The truth? Of course I do. Because you need to hear it. And you need to believe it. The fact that this guy, this—this *Jeff whatever-his-name-is* threw you away so cavalierly just proves he's an idiot."

She couldn't argue that last point. Not anymore, anyway.

"In fact, if you want to know the truth," Milo

continued, "he doesn't deserve to breathe the same air you do . . ."

She opened her mouth to speak, to thank him for his heartfelt words, but she didn't get a chance.

"Or even *breathe at all* for that matter."

Chapter 8

For as far back as she could remember, books had always been Tori's go-to of choice for any number of reasons. If she'd had a tough day at school, she sought refuge in her bedroom with a book. When her beloved great grandmother passed away, she'd pulled out favorite titles they'd read together and sobbed. When she'd been sick with whatever was making the rounds of her friends, she'd bypass the soup and head for her personal to-be-read pile. And when her engagement to Jeff had ended, they'd provided a way to hide from the world until she was ready to face it again.

Today was no exception. Though, at the moment, that go-to reaction had to be satisfied by merely touching rather than reading.

"I think it's wonderful that your weekend off is coinciding with Margaret Louise's little trip." Dixie followed behind Tori as she moved from aisle to aisle, straightening and re-shelving. "Of course, I won't be able to join in the fun, but that's okay. I said I would cover you this weekend and I will."

She tried not to read too much into the

overeager tone in the elderly woman's voice but it was hard. Dixie Dunn was practically salivating at the prospect of running the show for an entire weekend. The fact that Tori would be a few hours away during that time was simply the icing on the proverbial cake.

"Are you really sure it's okay? You've been part of the sewing circle for years, Dixie. Seems only fair *you* should go." Tori pulled a science fiction novel from the mystery shelf and carried it to its proper home. "If we did that, then I could take off next weekend, instead . . . when I can be close by in the event of a problem."

"No!" A deep red spread across Dixie's face as a patron on the other side of the room turned an angry glare in their direction. Dropping her voice to a more suitable volume, Dixie shook her head vehemently. "I put this weekend on my calendar when you first told me about Nina's bed rest. To switch now would mess up my, um . . . my plans for next weekend."

Plans?

Dixie Dunn had plans?

Before Tori could respond, the woman's cold hand grabbed hold of her shoulder and ushered her toward the information desk and the lunch sack she'd been ignoring for the past thirty minutes. "Now, no more talk about switching weekends. I've committed to working here and you've been given a lovely way to spend your time off. There's nothing left to discuss."

She knew she should be grateful for Dixie's help. Without it, she'd be working nonstop to cover for her assistant's leave of absence—a less than appealing thought under any circumstances, virtually unfathomable in light of the stress of the last few days.

There was no doubt about it, spending a weekend in the mountains with seven of her closest friends sounded as close to perfect as she could imagine. The only thing that could make it better would be Milo.

She'd stared up at the ceiling for hours after they'd talked, thanking her lucky stars for his presence in her life. He was creative and funny, supportive and trustworthy, and he made her strive to be a better person whenever he was near. Surely Jeff's misstep two years earlier had been orchestrated by a chorus of angels hell-bent on making sure life turned out as it should . . .

With Milo Wentworth by her side instead of Jeff.

"Victoria? Are you alright?"

Shaking her thoughts back to the present, Tori tried to remember where they were.

The weekend. The girls-only-getaway-while-Dixie-runs-the-library weekend . . .

Dixie brought her hands to her hips. "You do realize I ran this library for more years than you've been alive, don't you?"

She held up her hands. "I know. I know. It's not you, Dixie, it's me. I have a hard time turning over—"

"The reins. I know. Trust me, I know." Dixie marched around the information desk and plucked Tori's lunch sack from the bottom shelf. "But sometimes you have to . . . whether you want to or not. Now here, go. Eat."

Nodding, she took the bag from Dixie's hand and turned toward the door. "I'll be back in thirty minutes."

"Take an hour and go for a walk, too. The fresh air will be good for you. Helps clear your head."

Clear her head . . .

As if that was going to happen anytime soon.

She waved, then pushed her way out into an August day in Sweet Briar, the stifling heat almost bearable thanks to a gusty breeze the local weather forecasters hadn't predicted. If she was smart, she'd head back inside, eat her lunch in her air-conditioned office, but the notion held little appeal. Somehow, being outside with the serenity of the town square in front of her and the familiarity of the library at her back just seemed right. Calming, even.

Summer had always been one of her favorite seasons. As a child, it had signaled the start of uninterrupted time with her great grandmother— time spent reading, sewing, baking, talking. When college came, it afforded her time to volunteer at her local library, preparing her for the career she'd been dreaming about for years. And now that she was an adult, she loved what it represented even more. Suddenly, the school-aged children came through the doors because they wanted to, adults came in search of the perfect vacation read, and Milo was off for nearly three months.

Maybe that's why she'd been so antsy the past week. She missed having him around—watching movies, taking long walks, eating dinner together on his deck or hers.

But it was more than that.

It was Nina's absence and Dixie's presence, it was worry about Rose and the diagnosis of rheumatoid arthritis that seemed to creep up on her elderly friend with little to no warning, it was Jeff's re-entry into her stratosphere, and her inability to give Milo a firm answer to his months-old proposal.

Sighing, she made her way to the bottom of the steps and over to one of two wooden picnic tables that had been a gift from the Friends of the Library after their annual spring book fair. In spite of the noon hour she had the table to herself and she was glad. Her lunch was lacking in all areas except sugar and she wasn't in the mood for any comments it might bring. Restless nights simply demanded sugar-infused days.

A flash of movement behind a nearby tree

caught her attention and she bobbed her head to the left to afford a better look. Seconds later, a plumpish brown bunny sporting a miniature black bow tie hopped into the clearing.

"Paris?" she asked as she released her death grip on the chocolate bar inside her bag and stood. "Is that you?"

The bunny stopped, turned back toward the tree, and made a beeline toward the bejeweled hand that tried to wave it back in Tori's direction.

She rolled her eyes and sat back down. "Are you trying for a second career as a psycho stalker, Leona?"

A huff emerged from behind the tree followed by the slender, stylish sixty-something dressed to the nines in a baby blue Donna Karan suit. "A psycho stalker? Really, dear, must you be so, so, I don't know . . . *dramatic?*"

"Okay. A spy, then?"

"Of course not. Though, I did date a spy once. He was very charming and so very creative when it came to finding unique places to—"

Tori held up her hand, successfully cutting off a parade of details she didn't want to hear. "Then how do you explain your fascination with trees as of late?"

"Trees?" Leona brought her non-Paris holding hand to the base of her neck. "I don't know what you're talking about, dear."

Reaching into her lunch sack once again, she

plucked out the candy bar, unwrapped it, and took a bite. "I know you were listening in on my conversation with Jeff last night. And I know you took it upon yourself to include Milo in that conversation as well."

"I did no such thing."

She stared at Leona over the top of her candy bar. "Leona . . ."

A tinge of crimson rose in the woman's cheeks just before she lifted Paris into the air and held him in Tori's direction. "Did you notice his little bow tie? Isn't it precious?"

"Adorable. Truly." She pointed at the vacant picnic bench on the other side of the table and watched as Leona sat down. "Now tell me why."

"I think he has a little friend in the neighborhood. I just want him to look dapper."

She shook her head. "No, why did you involve Milo without telling me?"

Leona tilted her head downward and peered at Tori across the top of her glasses. "Because I figured someone had to talk some sense into you where that sorry excuse for a man is concerned."

"Sense?" she echoed.

"Sense," Leona repeated. "I was talking with him on the way to your place after the circle meeting with the intention to simply hand you the phone when I got to your house. But then, when I got there, and I realized you were talking to Jeff . . . and I heard the awful way he was talking . . . I guess I turned the phone so Milo could hear, too."

"You shouldn't have." She took another bite. "It wasn't your place."

"That man was making you doubt yourself. I wanted it to stop."

"His actions two years ago made me doubt my worth. It made me question myself. His being here now has finally enabled me to see the facts."

Leona set Paris on the picnic table and tented her manicured fingers beneath her chin. "Such as . . . ?"

"Well, first of all, his cheating had nothing to do with me and everything to do with him."

"Haven't I been trying to tell you that since we met?"

She shrugged. "I guess I needed to figure it out for myself."

"Will you accept Milo's proposal now?"

It was the same question she'd asked herself again and again throughout the night. Would she? *Could* she?

Something resembling pain flickered in Leona's eyes. It was fleeting, and she tried her best to hide it, but Tori caught it nonetheless.

Seconds later, Leona dropped one of her hands and patted Tori's. "Whatever you do, dear, don't let a man like Jeff keep you from someone as wonderful as Milo. You will regret it one day. You truly will."

She studied Leona closely. "You had a Jeff once, too. Didn't you?"

A few beats of silence morphed into a combination head nod and mumble.

"He's why you establish the upper hand in relationships and never stay in one for long, isn't he?"

A second nod.

"And he's why you despise Chicago, isn't he?"

Leona looked down at the silver link watch on her wrist. "Oh, would you look at the time? Paris and I have an appointment. Leeson's Market just got a new shipment of carrots this morning and I promised him he could have one if he wore his bow tie like a good boy all day."

She watched as her friend rose to her feet. "You're not going to tell me, are you?"

"There's nothing to tell, dear." Swooping forward, Leona lifted Paris into her arms. "We'll see you Friday, yes?"

"Friday?"

"The trip to the mountains, dear."

"Oh, that. Yes, I'll be there." She looked from Leona to her half-eaten candy bar and back again. "I'm sorry. For the heartache this man caused you, Leona."

"Then heed my advice, dear."

And with that, Leona was gone, her off-white pumps making soft clicking sounds against the sidewalk as she made her way toward the center of town, her beloved Paris clutched protectively in her arms.

She couldn't stay mad at Leona. She just couldn't. For as infuriating as the woman's actions could be at times, there was something always bubbling beneath the surface hinting at softer edges and genuine feelings. Everyone knew it. Even, perhaps, Leona herself.

Looking back at the remnants of her candy bar and the secondary bar still housed in her lunch sack, Tori couldn't help but sigh. Sugar wasn't cutting it. Not at the moment, anyway. Instead, she gathered up her belongings and headed toward the sidewalk, determined to wake herself up once and for all. Besides, it was the first day below a hundred degrees in weeks—a fact that only strengthened the merits of a brisk walk.

She tossed her wrapper into a nearby trash container and strode toward the sidewalk that would, eventually, lead her around the town square. But three steps into her quest for exercise, her feet rooted themselves to the ground.

Two years may have come and gone, but the three prior to that were enough to commit Jeff's shape to memory. A shape she'd recognize anywhere, anytime. Including at that very moment—a moment that saw her ex-fiancé, clad in black running shorts and a Chicago Cubs

T-shirt, taking his afternoon jog right through the center of Sweet Briar.

Her Sweet Briar.

Suddenly, the notion of a walk seemed utterly repugnant. Sugar would have to do. At least until Jeff and his girlfriend were safely back in Chicago where they belonged.

She tightened her hand on her lunch sack and spun around to face the library that had become so much more to her than simply a place of employment. In fact, the building that most people equated with books symbolized all that was good in her life at the moment.

He'll be gone, soon.

Slowly, she lapped her way around the building—once, twice, three times before finally heading toward the stone staircase and the second home they led to, images of her upcoming weekend chasing all things Jeff from her mind. Monday night sewing circle meetings were one of the highlights of her week. Having an entire weekend of that dynamic could only be better. Especially with Margaret Louise manning the kitchen—

The wail of a police siren cut through her fantasy, making her stumble on the first step. Reaching outward, she steadied herself against the railing just in time to see a Sweet Briar police car race down the block and turn left, its blue and white lights flashing.

Pedestrians stopped in their tracks as the department's rarely used second car went zipping by, too, its siren blaring and lights flashing in perfect copycat fashion.

"What on earth," she mumbled only to have her words wiped from the air by a third and even louder siren—this one belonging to the ambulance she'd never seen outside the confines of a town parade.

Feeling her heart begin to pound, she retraced her steps out to the sidewalk and the ever-growing group of Sweet Briar residents hell-bent on being among the first to uncover the details that would later be whispered across every picket fence in town.

"How goes it, Victoria?"

She couldn't help but smile. Mr. Downing was one of her most loyal patrons at the library. His gentle spirit, soft-spoken demeanor, and inquisitive nature made his twice-weekly visits something to be treasured.

"I'm doing fine. We just got a new book on World War II. It's got some spectacular pictures I think you'll really love."

The elderly man nodded. "I'll head in there in a little bit and give it a look." He gestured toward the green. "Always cuts right through your chest when something like this happens, don't it? Especially when it's a young person."

"Do you know what happened?"

Mr. Downing swung his hand to the right and pointed at a young man she recognized as a bagger from Leeson's Market. "Mary Fran's grandson here does. Saw it with his own two eyes, didn't you, Douglas?"

The freckle-faced redhead nodded. "I was finishing up my lunch break in the gazebo when this dude went jogging by. Guess the heat got to him or somethin' because he dropped to the ground like a brick . . . Bam!"

"Did you say *jogging?*" she stammered.

"Yeah. In the middle of the afternoon . . . in August, if you can believe it." Douglas unraveled a piece of navy cloth between his hands and secured the Leeson's Market apron around his neck. "Between that and the Cubs shirt he was wearing, I'm pretty sure he's not from around here."

"Cubs shirt?" she echoed as the ground began to spin under her feet. "I—I . . . I've got to go. I've got to make sure he's okay."

"Victoria?" Mr. Downing asked. "Victoria, what's wrong?"

She took a step forward, dizziness giving way to a rush of darkness.

Chapter 9

Her eyes flew open as the side of her head vibrated against the cool glass. Bolting upright, Tori grabbed the map from Margaret Louise's hand and pointed at the road.

"*You're* supposed to be driving and *I'm* supposed to be navigating, remember?"

Margaret Louise's pudgy hand returned to the steering wheel. "I didn't have the heart to wake you, Victoria. You looked downright angelic with your head on the window and all."

"I can sleep later." Tori looked out the window, the interstate that had lulled her to sleep a thing of the past. "Where are we?"

"I turned off the exit 'bout twenty miles ago. Saw a sign back yonder for the cabin company but haven't seen another since." Margaret Louise gestured toward the map. "That's why I was tryin' to take a look. See if I'd gotten off track somehow."

Tori looked down at the handwritten directions she'd clipped to the North Carolina map. "Did you take a left at the bottom of the ramp?"

"I did."

"Did you turn right at Fill 'er Up?"

"I did."

"Did we get to the fork in the road with the big windmill in the center?"

"Haven't seen that yet."

"Then we should be fine." She settled back against her seat and took in the scenery as it whizzed past her window, the lush forest and roadside creeks bringing a much-needed smile to her lips. "Oh, Margaret Louise, you have no idea how badly I need this weekend away."

"I reckon I can imagine, but I'd sure like you to fill me in. Leona, Rose, and me, well, we've been worried 'bout you, Victoria. Real worried." Margaret Louise pulled her gaze from the narrow two-lane country road and fixed it on Tori. "I tried to call, and so did Leona. Rose, too. But you didn't answer."

She took a deep breath then let the air swoosh out between her lips. "I know, and I'm sorry I didn't return any of your calls. I meant to but I—" She glanced out the window once again. "I guess I didn't know what to say. I mean, I'm not *supposed* to be upset about what happened."

"Who says you're not supposed to be upset?"

"I don't know . . . Magazines, talk shows . . . nobody . . . everybody."

Margaret Louise jerked the car onto the shoulder and pulled to a stop. Popping the gear-shift into park, she took the keys from the ignition and opened her door. "C'mon. Let's go for a walk."

Tori watched her friend as she ambled around the car. When the woman showed no sign of returning, she opened her own door. "Margaret Louise, we can talk in the car."

"I need to stretch. I've been drivin' for miles."

"But we're in the middle of nowhere."

"That sign right there"—Margaret Louise pointed at a green metal pole sporting the back side of a sign—"says there's a hiking trail right here and—oh, here it is." With absolutely no acknowledgement of her age, the grandmother of seven swept her hand in the direction of a leaf-strewn path that disappeared down a hill. "C'mon, it'll do us both good."

"Both?" she asked as she took point.

"It'll give you a chance to get what happened off your chest and it'll give me a chance to burn a few calories and quiet the worry once and for all."

She spun around to face her friend. "Is something wrong with one of the kids?"

"No. They're all good and not a one of 'em even has a runny nose if you can believe it."

"Then what are you worried about?"

Margaret Louise slipped her arm inside Tori's and gave a gentle tug. "Why, you, of course."

"Oh." They meandered down the sun-dappled path, a year's worth of leaves crunching beneath their feet as she traveled back in her memory to the last moment she saw Jeff. "I know I should hate Jeff for everything he did to me. He made me fall in love with him only to rip my heart from my chest in front of all of our friends and family. He turned my world upside down and made me doubt myself and my worth for far too long. Yet, with all of that, my heart still aches at his loss."

She felt Margaret Louise's hand on her shoulder and looked up, a blast of sunlight nearly blinding her as it reflected off a small lake in a nearby clearing. "Oh, Margaret Louise, it's beautiful."

"An unexpected gem, isn't it?" The woman tugged on Tori's arm once again, leading her to a large rock on the bank. "Now sit. And listen."

She sat.

And she listened.

"Jeff broke your heart. Jeff made you doubt yourself. But you're not Jeff, you're Victoria. And your heart was broken because you gave it . . . fully. You doubted yourself because you have an open heart and you were unwilling to let him shoulder all the blame even though that's where it belonged." Margaret Louise plopped herself onto the rock beside Tori and rolled her shoulders forward and backward, a soft moan escaping her full lips as she did. "It makes perfect sense that you'd be sad over what happened. You'd given him your heart. And even though he treated you horribly, he still had it. You're not built to turn your feelings on and off with the flip of a switch. It's one of the things that makes you special."

Reaching down, Tori plucked a small flat rock from the ground and threw it across the lake, the familiar plunk as it hit the water bringing a smile to her lips. "It's not that I still had feelings for him, because I didn't . . . I don't. I know that. But I knew this man. I knew his likes and dislikes, his strengths and his weaknesses, and his goals. And now he's dead."

Dead.

Jeff.

"Georgina said he was thirty-two." Margaret Louise pushed off the rock and paced back and forth. "Heck, my Jake isn't much more 'an that."

She stood and reached for her friend's hand. "I know what you're thinking, Margaret Louise, I really do. But Jeff's death isn't as much of a fluke as you might think. Sure, he was young— too young—but he had a history of heart problems throughout his family. Jake doesn't have that."

The woman's posture noticeably relaxed. "I reckon. But still, it makes you think."

"Don't let it. Really." She walked to the water's edge and closed her eyes, the distant sound of quacking and chirping loosening the knots in her shoulders. Oh, how she needed this time with her friends—time to unwind, time to sleep, time to talk, time to laugh, and, if need be, time to cry.

"Victoria, can I ask you a question?"

She opened her eyes and studied her friend. "Sure. Shoot."

"Did you decide not to go back to Chicago for the funeral simply because of this trip?"

She tried the question on for size. Had she? After all, she had looked at flights . . .

But, in the end, she gave the only answer she could give.

The truth.

"I've not heard any specific details about a funeral yet, but, even when I do, I won't go. I said my good-bye to Jeff on my front porch the night before he died. I don't need to say it again in front of people I no longer know."

"You don't feel any guilt?"

She stared at her friend. "Guilt? For what?"

"For turning him down? For his having a heart attack the very next day?"

Stepping back, she dropped onto a neighboring rock. "You can't be serious. You can't think I had anything to do with that."

Margaret Louise waved her hands in the air. "Of course I don't. But I know you, Victoria. I know how your mind thinks."

She pulled her knees up to her chin and rested

her cheek against them. "Okay, it went through my mind. Briefly."

The woman's left eyebrow rose. "Briefly?"

Busted.

"Well, how could it not? Men his age don't just drop dead while running." The words streamed from her mouth in rambling fashion. "I mean, he was in shape. He was a fitness trainer, for gosh sake. Was it really that hard of a stretch—even for a little while—to think the stress of our conversation the night before might have had something to do with what happened?"

Reaching over, Margaret Louise brushed a strand of hair from Tori's face. "But you don't still think that, do you?"

Did she?

She was trying not to . . .

As a second strand of hair was pushed from her face, she smiled up at her friend. "No, not really. As I said, there were heart problems in Jeff's family. In fact, I hadn't realized just how extensive it was until last weekend, at his great-aunt's funeral."

"Well, do you see? There's nothin' for you to feel guilty about. Nothin' at all, Victoria."

Margaret Louise was right.

She lifted her head and looked back at the lake. "Then it's one down, two to go."

"Why, Victoria, you lost me. What are you talkin' 'bout now?"

"Things keeping me up at night."

Margaret Louise folded her arms across her ample chest. "What else is troublin' you?"

"Milo, for one. Dixie, for two."

"No wonder you have such dark circles under your eyes. You're worryin' 'bout everything under the sun, aren't you?" Margaret Louise left her rock in favor of Tori's. "Tell me about Milo."

"He heard everything Jeff and I said to each other Monday night."

"That's good, ain't it? That's better than avoidin' him the way you've been."

She winced at her friend's description. "I wasn't *avoiding* him. Not really, anyway. I just didn't know what to tell him about Jeff being here."

"Least you finally called and talked to him."

If only that was the way it had happened.

But it wasn't.

"I didn't call him," she finally said.

Margaret Louise shrugged. "Doesn't matter who called, just so long as you talked."

"That's what Leona seems to think, too."

"Then my twin is smarter than I give her credit for."

"I think *sneakier* is a more fitting description, frankly." She raked her hand across the top of the rock then let the tiny pieces of gravel and dirt sift through her fingers.

"Wait. What did my sister do?"

"She hid in the bushes next to my front porch and held her phone out so Milo could hear my conversation with Jeff."

All nature noises stopped as Margaret Louise's near sonic gasp echoed around them. "You're foolin' me, right?"

Tori shook her head. "I wish I was."

"Why, I—I don't know what to say. I'm simply speechless. And madder than a hornet gettin' swat at."

She couldn't help but smile. "Don't be. Really. Milo and I spoke and things are okay. He understood my reluctance to talk and he was as supportive of me as he has been from the beginning."

"Then why the worry?" Margaret Louise asked.

"Because he was angry," she whispered. "So very, very angry."

"At you?"

"He turned it toward Jeff, but I have to wonder if it was really aimed at me. I mean, think about it, my former fiancé comes into town while he's gone and suddenly I don't call for a few days?" A lump of guilt formed in her throat. "Not exactly the kind of thing you want to see from the woman you've asked to marry you."

She felt Margaret Louise's arm slip across her shoulders. "We're talkin' 'bout Milo Wentworth,

114

Victoria. *Any* anger exhibited from that man would seem like a lot."

"There was no *seem* about it. He was furious."

"He was probably just bein' protective is all. Men do that, you know." Margaret Louise looked down at her watch, then stood. "We better be headin' back to the car. I don't want everyone arrivin' at the cabin before we do."

And just like that, any residual tension weighing on Tori's shoulders dissipated. In its place was pure, unadulterated anticipation.

Pushing off the rock, she hurried to catch up with her friend. "Everyone's still coming?"

"Everyone's still comin'," Margaret Louise echoed between huffs and puffs as they made their way up the very path they'd descended thirty minutes earlier. "Everyone 'cept Dixie, of course."

She trudged ahead of Margaret Louise, careful to point out any discrepancies in the trail that might pose a tripping hazard. "I'm trying not to worry about being so far away from the library this weekend but it's hard."

"You've left Nina in charge, haven't you?"

"But we're talking about Dixie, here."

Margaret Louise snorted. "You mean the woman who ran the library for four decades before you took over?"

She rushed to explain as they reached the side of the road and Margaret Louise resumed the lead. "It's not that I don't think she's capable . . . because I—I do. It's just that, well, she was talking about making those changes the other day and I guess it has me a little nervous."

"So she moves a few chairs and rearranges a few shelves. You can always change it back when you return, right?"

"I guess . . ."

Margaret Louise yanked open her car door and sat down, swiveling to the left just long enough to grab her seat belt and snap it into place. Tori did the same.

"So what's there to worry 'bout?" Margaret Louise asked as she slammed her foot down on the gas and peeled out of the gravel turnoff. "It's not like she's gonna burn the place to the ground while we're gone."

Chapter 10

All her life, Tori had pictured cabins as simple wooden structures tucked away in the woods, housing groups of men intent on hunting, fishing, and various other outdoor pursuits.

These cabins—as she imagined them—had little more than a tattered and lumpy couch, a mini-refrigerator in the so-called kitchen, and a fire pit out front for cooking whatever food had been caught earlier in the day. An outhouse, similar to the ones she remembered from Girl Scout camp, would be nestled among the trees out back.

How wrong she was.

Each room of the four-bedroom cabin was nicer than the one before, the log walls and wood floors gleaming with a rustic charm befitting one of Leona's travel magazines. The family room alone was worthy of gaping mouths thanks to its vaulted ceiling, stone fireplace, and hand-hooked rugs. Scattered around the room was a series of seating options that ranged from the coziest couch Tori had ever seen to rocking chairs and recliners.

"Oh my, isn't this just the prettiest place

you've ever seen?" Georgina dropped her suitcase at her feet and pulled her trademark straw hat from her head. "Why, I thought that lovely little brook that meandered along the driveway was something special, and now this?"

"Can't you just imagine a fire blazing away in that fireplace?" Debbie added, a look of wonder on her face.

"Not in this heat, I can't," Margaret Louise replied. "Fortunately, the man I rented this place from said the air conditioner runs like a champ so we'll be good."

"We can't keep it too cold." Beatrice stepped cautiously through the room and lowered herself to the edge of one of the rockers. "Rose won't like that."

Margaret Louise opened a door in the far corner of the room and pulled out a pile of colorful afghans. "Which is exactly why I requested a few blankets."

"You thought of everything," Tori mused.

"You ain't seen nothin' yet." Margaret Louise returned the blankets to the closet and shut the door. "Just wait until we have dinner tonight."

"I can hardly wait," said Georgina. "I've been so busy with meetings the past few weeks I can't tell you the last time I had a home-cooked meal."

Tori smiled at the mayor. "I've been cooking and I'm still looking forward to Margaret Louise's concoctions."

"Between the eight of us, maybe we can get Rose to eat more than a mouthful." Beatrice lowered her already quiet voice to a near whisper. "She has me worried."

She laid a hand on the young woman's shoulder and gave it a gentle squeeze. "We're all a little worried, Beatrice. But the treatment she had last week should help with the flare-up of her arthritis for a while."

"We can hope." Georgina lifted her suitcase once again. "Margaret Louise? Where should I put this?"

Margaret Louise gestured for Georgina, Beatrice, Debbie, and Tori to follow as she led the way into the first of the four bedrooms. "Georgina, I have you in here with Beatrice. Does that work?"

Georgina smiled at Beatrice. "It's perfect."

Beatrice agreed.

Waving at Tori and Debbie, Margaret Louise stepped back into the hall and led the way to the second bedroom. "Debbie, I thought that, perhaps, you and Melissa would enjoy this room."

Debbie nodded and looked at her watch. "When is she expected to be here?"

"Any minute now. She's bringing Rose and Leona."

Margaret Louise turned to Tori and gestured toward the third doorway off the hall. "Tori, I was kind of hoping you'd be okay rooming with Rose for the weekend. Just being around you seems to give her a lift."

"As it does for me as well." And it was true. The prickly older woman had become a real treasure in Tori's life, reminding her, at times, of her own late great grandmother—a woman she missed terribly.

"Perfect. Leona and I will be in the room down the hall."

Tori couldn't help but laugh. "You sure that's going to be okay?"

"We shared a womb for nine months, we can certainly share a room for two nights." Margaret Louise spun on her soft gray Keds, leaving Tori alone in the room she'd soon share with Rose.

Running her hands along the maple dresser and dual headboards, she couldn't help but feel the excitement for their weekend building to an all-time high. There were simply no other women on the face of the earth she would rather spend the weekend with than these women. Each and every one of them had brought something special to her life in the nearly two years she'd known them.

Georgina Hayes had taught her about courage and strength in the wake of the murder of Sweet Briar resident, Tiffany Ann Gilbert. Despite the effects of the crime on her own life, the small-town mayor had kept her head held high.

Beatrice Tharrington was sweet—the kind of

sweet that made Tori want to be a better person. Rarely, if ever, had she heard an unkind word about anyone or anything out of the British nanny's mouth.

Debbie Calhoun was the epitome of someone who had it all and had worked hard to make it happen. Her lifelong dream of opening her own bakery had not only come true but had become Sweet Briar's favorite "it" place, serving up decadent treats all day long. Yet she hadn't let the achievement of that dream get in the way of an even bigger one—to be the best wife and mother she could possibly be. Another dream she'd hit out of the ballpark if the smiles on the faces of her husband and children were any indication.

Melissa Davis, Margaret Louise's daughter-in-law, was the kind of mom everyone wished they had. She was fun, encouraging, supportive, and beautiful inside and out. When and if Tori became a mother one day, she wanted to be exactly like Melissa.

Leona Elkin had been by Tori's side since her first day in Sweet Briar, teaching her the ways of the south. Any detours Leona had taken along the path of their friendship had been short-lived. And despite her overbearing tactics and over-the-top nosiness, Leona would do anything for Tori.

Margaret Louise Davis was Margaret Louise Davis—open, loyal, kind, generous, funny, and truly one-of-a-kind. The woman was, without a doubt, the reason Sweet Briar had gone from merely a place to live to Tori's true home.

And then there was Rose. Despite getting off to a semi-rocky start at the onset of their relationship, Rose had grown to be one of Tori's dearest and most loyal friends. Her take-charge attitude and vast knowledge of everything under the sun were to be envied, while her surprisingly gentle heart was to be cherished.

In short, Tori's life was richer for having moved to Sweet Briar. And the thought of spending two whole days surrounded by her friends was exactly the pick-me-up she needed.

"Hello? Anyone here?" Melissa's voice, happy and almost song-like, echoed against the walls of the cabin.

Tori stepped out of her room and joined the others in the family room to greet the last of the group to arrive. Melissa stood just inside the entryway to the kitchen, one arm casually linked through Rose's, the other wrapped around a sleeping Molly Sue. Behind them, stood Leona.

"I told you, Twin, pets aren't allowed," Margaret Louise said, pointing to a bow-tied Paris in her sister's arms.

"Paris isn't a pet. He's part of the circle."

Rose snorted.

"He is?"

Leona shot a look at Georgina. "He most certainly is."

"I guess it goes to show they're right—old people really *do* lose their minds, don't they?" Rose grumbled before extricating herself from Melissa's grasp and heading for the rocking chair beside the fireplace.

Paris's ears shot straight up as Leona stamped her foot. "Are you calling me old, Rose?"

"If the shoe fits." Rose lowered herself to the chair then pulled the flaps of her cotton sweater close against her body. "Did anyone see the flower garden at the end of the driveway? It's beautiful."

Tori felt the smile as it spread from one side of her face to the other. "I'd like to if you're up for a walk later."

"Of course I'll be up for a walk. What do you think I am? An invalid?"

"That's not what *I'd* call you," Leona said before resuming her self-imposed sulkathon.

"Oh shut up, Leona." Rose pushed her foot against the wood floor and began to rock, her large eyes taking in their surroundings. "You've done good, Margaret Louise. Real good."

Heads nodded around the room.

Margaret Louise beamed.

"It's a shame Dixie can't join us."

Rose held up a frail hand. "Melissa, trust me, Dixie is exactly where she wants to be right now.

She's more excited than I've seen her in years. And it's all because of Tori here."

Tori met Margaret Louise's eyes, saw the twitch at the corner of the woman's mouth. "Technically it's because of Nina."

"How is she feeling?" Melissa asked, expertly shifting her one-year-old from one shoulder to the other without so much as earning a blink from the still-sleeping little girl.

"Ready to have her baby, that's for sure. Duwayne is waiting on her hand and foot. And I'm counting the days until she comes back. The library just isn't the same without her."

"How are *you* feeling, Victoria?" Rose stilled her foot long enough to cough and then resumed the easy pace she'd found.

Tori waved her hand. "I'm okay. Really."

Debbie shook her head. "I still can't believe your ex-fiancé is dead. You just don't expect to hear of a thirty-two-year-old man who works out for a living dying of a heart attack."

Feeling the calm of her surroundings beginning to erode, Tori rushed to change the subject back to safer topics.

"So what sort of culinary treat do you have planned for us tonight, Margaret Louise? Anything I can help with?"

Margaret Louise squared her shoulders. "As to your first question, you'll see when it's on the table. And as for your second question, no. I just want everyone to unpack and relax. We've got a long night of sewin' and gossipin' ahead of us."

And with that, six bodies went off in six different directions—Margaret Louise toward the kitchen, Melissa and the baby back out to the car, Beatrice toward the restroom, and everyone else to find their assigned bedrooms.

When they were gone, Rose cleared her throat and looked up at Tori. "How about that walk now?"

She studied her friend. "Are you sure you're up for it? You had a long drive."

"I'm fine," Rose snapped. "Just help me up, will you?"

Tori reached forward and gently helped Rose to her feet. Once the woman was steady enough, they walked through the kitchen, amid Margaret Louise's protests, and stepped outside in time to see a hummingbird dash across the yard.

"Oh how they love foxglove," Rose mumbled, shuffling down the stairs beside Tori. "Almost makes me want to grow some myself."

"Why don't you?"

"It's too late for this season, they're already flowering. But now that Lynn has told me about them, I plan to add them next year." Rose stepped carefully onto the gravel driveway and fairly tugged Tori toward the garden. "They used to just be a purple pink color but now, thanks to cross hybridization, they come in other colors, too. At least that's what she told me."

Slowly, they made their way down the driveway to the flower garden at the end. Fragrant climbing plants, old-fashioned roses, and hollyhocks completed the garden.

"It's beautiful, Rose. I can see why it caught your eye."

"Didn't it catch yours?"

She shook her head. "I guess I was busy bending Margaret Louise's ear when we drove in."

"About what?" Rose bent forward and re-situated a rose branch against its trellis.

"I don't know, nothing special. Just talking."

Rose turned her head and pinned Tori with a stare.

Tori swallowed. "Sorry. I don't know, Jeff . . . Milo . . . Dixie, you name it."

"That's better." Rose straightened up only to bend over once again, her hand lovingly cupping a dying rose. "Flowers are so much like people. They have their season to be alive and beautiful."

She felt her shoulders slump. She hated when Rose talked that way. "Some flowers are meant to last longer than others."

"I suppose." Rose gently released the flower and slowly stood upright. "I heard what you said in there. About that young man dying of a heart attack."

"Rose, I really don't want to talk about that right—"

"What would you say if I told you it might not have been a heart attack after all?"

She stared at her friend. "Wh-what are you talking about?"

Rose's shoulders rose and fell beneath the cotton sweater she wore. "Jeff wasn't well liked."

"By me, maybe. For one very specific reason. But—"

"By a lot of people, Victoria. For a *million* reasons."

Chapter 11

Cattle had nothing on the Sweet Briar Ladies Society Sewing Circle when it came to eating.

They weren't as eager.

They weren't as fast.

And they weren't nearly as pushy.

Then again, they didn't have Margaret Louise preparing their meals.

If they had, there would be no need for a bell to call them home. The aroma of their dinner would be enough to start a stampede.

"Ladies, ladies, may I have your attention, please?" Margaret Louise bellowed through the pockets of chatter taking place in and around the kitchen. "Tonight, I'm treating all of you to a true southern cookout in honor of our roots."

The buzz around the room heightened as seven sets of eyes trained on the group's culinary master.

"Any sweet potato pie?" Rose asked through the screen door. "After all, that pie is why we're all here right now."

Margaret Louise's ever-present smile grew even wider. "I considered it, I really did. But, in the end, I decided to try out some new recipes . . . for a cookbook I'm thinkin' about writin'.'"

Debbie clapped her hands. "Are you serious?"

"I am. Don't know it will ever make it beyond that old portable typewriter I pulled out of the basement but I'm sure gonna give it a whirl." Margaret Louise looked at each woman before catching Tori's eye through the screen door. "I also know a home-cooked meal can cure just about any ill known to mankind, even stress."

Tori shifted from foot to foot under the well-meaning scrutiny.

"I can think of things far better than food to cure stress," Leona drawled from the other side of the kitchen. "And until Milo gets home from his conference, Victoria will have to wait for that."

She felt her face warm. "Leona!"

Rose wrapped her hand around the narrow handle and yanked the door open, shoving Tori through the opening and stepping in beside her. "Put a sock in it, will you, Leona? Your sister is trying to talk and your overactive hormones could use a rest."

Leona stamped her foot, only to be drowned out by laughter as it spread its way across the room.

Margaret Louise held her hands up, reclaiming the attention of seven hungry women. "To start things off, I've prepared hush puppies with

Green Zebra tomato jam and a chopped salad with quick pickled vegetables."

Seven mouths dropped open.

Paris's nose twitched.

"After that, we'll move onto my crispy buttermilk fried chicken and grilled corn on the cob with roasted garlic and herbs."

Georgina fanned herself with her hand. "Am I the only one getting a hot flash listening to this?"

"I haven't had a hot flash in twenty years," Rose countered. "But I can tell you this, I'm glad I grabbed one of my old lady diapers before I got in the car with Melissa."

Leona rolled her eyes. "For the millionth time, Rose, no one wants to hear . . ."

Tori knew Leona was still talking, could sense the way Rose's posture tensed in response, but all she could think about were the things the elderly woman had said out in the garden—things she'd wanted to question yet hadn't been able to thanks to Margaret Louise's harried request for an extra gallon of milk from whatever market Tori could find.

A well-placed elbow to her ribs snapped her back to the present. "Huh? What?"

She felt Rose's stare as she found a smile for Margaret Louise. "Did you, um, get to dessert yet?"

"I was just about to say that, Victoria." Reaching below the center island that had served as her podium thus far, Margaret Louise lifted a pie into their field of vision. A collective hush fell over the room. "In keepin' with my southern theme, I whipped us up a peach shortcake with vanilla whipped cream."

And just like that, the stampede began—Georgina and Debbie leading the way with Beatrice, Leona, and Rose on their heels.

"I don't know how she does it, I really don't."

Melissa's hushed voice in her ear brought Tori up short. "Who?"

"My mother-in-law. Her energy level is never ending."

She couldn't help but laugh. "Isn't that kind of like the pot calling the kettle black?"

A touch of crimson spread across Melissa's face. "Trust me, I get tired."

"When? At two in the morning after all seven kids are in bed and you've washed, dried, folded, and put away all of their laundry?" She slipped an arm around her friend and pulled her close. "I'm glad you came. I was afraid you'd change your mind at the last minute."

Melissa shrugged. "I almost did. Jake Junior had a makeup baseball game added to the schedule at the last minute but Jake insisted I go. Said I needed a little fun that's just for me. Or as me as I can get with Molly Sue in tow."

Bobbing her head first left, then right, Tori searched the floor for any sign of Melissa's seventh child. Just a little over a year, Molly Sue was a little bundle of walking, smiling, gabbing energy.

"Where is she?"

"She's in her portable crib playing with some blocks Margaret Louise brought."

Tori glanced toward the woman who'd made the weekend possible. "She thinks of everything, doesn't she?"

"And then some." Melissa rested the side of her forehead against Tori's and dropped her voice to a near whisper. "Are you okay? You seemed really distracted when you got back with the milk."

"I'm sorry. I'm happy to be here, I really am. It's just—well, Rose said something earlier that caught me off guard and I haven't had a chance to ask her to elaborate."

Melissa straightened up. "You mean about your former fiancé?"

Tori grabbed hold of Melissa's arm. "You mean she told you?"

"We rode up here together, remember?"

"What did she say—"

"Maaaa Maaa!"

Molly Sue.

"I'm sorry, Victoria, I've got to go." Melissa spun around and headed toward the family room only to glance over her shoulder as she reached the doorway. "We'll catch up later, okay?"

Margaret Louise held a plate in Tori's direction. "Aren't you going to eat?"

She looked up, noted the absence of the rest of her friends and the sizeable dent in each of the featured menu items. "Ahhh, yeah . . . sure."

Leaning against the refrigerator, Margaret Louise watched her move from platter to platter, filling her plate as she went. When Tori reached the corn on the cob, the woman finally spoke. "I was hopin' that bein' here was gonna wipe those lines from your forehead but that doesn't seem to be happenin'."

Slowly, she took in a breath of air and then let it escape through her nose. "I'm sorry, Margaret Louise, I really am. This place is"—she lifted her plate-holding hand into the air and gestured around the room—"amazing. It really is. And I love being here with everyone. It's just that . . . well, Rose said something outside about Jeff's death that took me by surprise and I haven't had a chance to ask her about it."

"Then let's ask her." Margaret Louise grabbed a plate from the pile at the end of the island and breezed through the buffet style setup. "As I see it, there's no sense frettin' 'bout somethin' that might not be worth frettin' 'bout."

She trailed behind as Margaret Louise led the way into the family room. "I'm not sure I need to ask in front of everyone else."

"Fiddlesticks. We're all friends here." Crossing

the circular hook rug housed between the sofa and one of the recliners, Margaret Louise pointed toward an open chair for Tori before staking claim on one of her own. "So what does everyone think?"

Rose chewed and nodded.

Georgina gushed.

Beatrice smiled shyly before going back for another mouthful of salad.

"It's delicious," Debbie said between bites. "Absolutely delicious."

Margaret Louise beamed.

Leona leaned across the arm of the couch. "The hush puppies are to die for, Victoria."

Popping one into her mouth, Tori had to agree. Margaret Louise had outdone herself once again. "Mmmm, this is amazing."

"So, tell us, Rose," Margaret Louise prompted over a piece of fried chicken. "What's this about Jeff's heart attack that has Victoria all distracted?"

Rose looked up from her plate. "Doc said his heart was doing fine at his last checkup."

Georgina's head rose in time with Tori's. "But Daryl said it was a heart attack."

"Who's Daryl?" Beatrice asked softly.

"The paramedic." Georgina plucked a carrot from her salad and offered it to Paris. "And Daryl said it was confirmed by the hospital."

"He came from a long line of heart attacks,"

Tori offered even as Rose's words looped their way through her thoughts. "Most recent, of course, was his great-aunt."

Rose shrugged. "Perhaps. But when you take into account his sudden and unexpected windfall, you can't help but wonder about the timing."

Tori's mouth dropped open.

"Windfall?" Margaret Louise asked. "What kind of windfall?"

"Seems his great-aunt Vera was rather wealthy."

"She was," Tori confirmed.

"And, apparently, Jeff was her pride and joy."

"He was."

Rose shrugged. "So he was left all that wealth. To the tune of one million dollars."

"Jeff got some of her money?" She moved her plate to the end table beside her chair, the food virtually untouched save for the one hush puppy that was now a distant memory. "When?"

"He found out Monday, I believe."

Suddenly his ploys to win her back with lavish gifts made perfect sense.

Tori felt her stomach churn.

"So what does that have to do with his heart attack?" she finally asked. "Or, rather, the notion that it *wasn't* a heart attack?"

"Money doesn't buy friends," Rose mused. "It buys enemies. And that young man had a lot."

"Beyond me, I can't say that for certain. And I wouldn't even call myself his enemy."

"You should have been." Leona, too, set her food down. "He certainly deserved to be hated by you."

She shook her head. "I didn't hate him, either. He hurt me and that's it."

Leona lowered her chin and stared at Tori above her glasses. "That's enough to make *me* hate him."

Rose nodded. "Me, too."

"Me, three," Margaret Louise added.

"That didn't make you his *enemies*."

Rose stilled her chicken-holding hand mere inches from her lips. "Maybe, maybe not. But I suspect Kelly was one after Monday night."

"Kelly?" Tori leaned forward in her chair. "Why?"

"Because after he left you, he contacted another ex-girlfriend. Julia something or other."

A wry smile tugged at her lips. "I know Julia . . ."

Margaret Louise's ears perked up. "You do?"

She nodded. "Julia was the one in the closet with Jeff."

"Seems he tried to rope her back in, too," Rose said.

"And?" she asked, hating herself for even wanting to know.

"She told him to take a hike, too."

"And this Kelly woman knew this?" Leona inquired.

"From what Lynn said, yes." Rose set her chicken bone on her plate and started in on her corn.

"So what's that got to do with Jeff's—"

"And she wasn't the only one gunning for him." Rose stopped talking long enough to take a bite of corn, her eyes nearly rolling back in her head as she did. "Garrett was pretty angry, too."

"Garrett?" she echoed.

"Jeff didn't just get *some* of Vera's money, Victoria." Rose spun her corn between her buttery hands. "He got all of it. Every last dime."

Ouch.

"This is certainly interesting news but it's all moot. The man died of a heart attack," Georgina reminded everyone. "To imply anything else would be nothing short of foolish."

"Foolish?" Rose dropped her corn onto her plate and wiped her mouth with a napkin. "You mean like writing off the man's clean bill of health as nothing more than a mistake?"

Touché.

Chapter 12

She tried to concentrate on the pillow taking shape in her hands, tried to lose herself in the reason behind the project, but it was hard. Especially when Rose's comments were still so fresh in her mind.

Could she be right?

Could Jeff's death have been something other than a heart attack?

No. He fell over while running. People saw it happen.

"London's getting fat," Rose mumbled from her spot on the rocking chair, her trembling hands curiously quieted by the presence of a needle and thread. "I'm surprised you haven't looked into that stomach stapling procedure."

Heads lifted around the room, a medley of confusion and worry etched in each and every face. It was Beatrice, though, who finally spoke, her calm nanny-voice aimed solely at Rose. "I believe the prime minister has advocated a program throughout the schools to address that very concern. And as far as any surgical procedures, I would guess it's like it is here . . . Those who can afford, do. Those who can't, don't."

Rose's eyes narrowed behind her bifocals. "What on earth are you talking about, Beatrice?"

The nanny's face drained of all color. "I—I was addressing your comment about London. How they're trying to address that issue through a combination of education and exercise."

Without taking her focus off Beatrice, the elderly woman pointed at Leona. "And *I* was talking about that old goat's rodent."

Leona's mouth gaped open.

Margaret Louise chuckled.

"You take that back, Rose Winters!" Setting her travel magazine on the coffee table, Leona leaned forward, plucked Paris off the ground, and set him in her lap. "I will not have you insult him like that. And his name is *Paris,* not London."

"Then let me rephrase . . . *Paris* is getting fat."

"He's not getting—wait." Georgina set her square of white fabric in her lap and bobbed her head first left, then right. "Actually, Leona, he does seem to be getting a bit, um, pudgy."

Leona stamped her foot on the ground. "He has a healthy appetite as a man should, but that does not make him pudgy." Elevating the bunny into the air, Leona looked into his large eyes. "Don't you listen to a word these women are saying, Paris. You are handsome just the way you are."

"I like his bow tie, Leona. He looks very cute

with it around his neck," Debbie interjected. "The brown really brings out his eyes."

"I agree," Beatrice whispered. "Luke and I saw him with you at Leeson's the other day and it was all he talked about on the way home. He wants a bunny now."

"Sally and Lulu want one, too." Melissa held a sleepy Molly Sue against her shoulder and rocked back and forth. "But they say it has to be just like Auntie Leona's bunny."

"He's still *fat,*" Rose mumbled.

"So, Victoria, tell us about Milo's conference." Georgina flipped the lid on her sewing box and rooted around inside for a thread that would match the pink and white cover she was making for Margaret Louise's pillow. "How is it going?"

"Okay, I guess."

"This was for math?" Debbie asked.

"It's touching on various subjects and teaching styles. New methods, new approaches, that sort of thing."

"What's been his favorite part so far?"

She felt her face warm with embarrassment. She knew it was a question she should be able to answer, yet she couldn't. And it was her fault. She'd been entirely too preoccupied with her own stuff the past two weeks—too preoccupied to show interest in Milo's trip let alone listen to any updates he may have divulged on his own.

"I don't know." She knew it sounded lame. Pathetic, even. But it was the truth.

Margaret Louise reached across the gap separating their seats and patted Tori's hand. "You've had a lot on your mind, Victoria."

"I imagine Dixie being at the library has been a help."

She met Georgina's gaze. "You're right, it should be. Except that I'm beginning to think I'm a bit of a control freak."

Debbie laughed. "Who of us in this room *isn't?*"

"But I worry about silly things like whether she's remembered to lock the doors at night even though she's locked them more times than I have." She stared down at the pale blue fabric still folded neatly in her lap. "I guess I'm just more familiar with Nina's work ethic than I am Dixie's."

"Dixie will do just fine." Rose adjusted her glasses to sit more squarely on her nose. "I promise. Not everyone becomes incompetent as they age."

Tori sucked in her breath. "Rose, I never said— I mean, I wasn't trying to insinuate that Dixie is incompetent. It's really more a case of me and my reluctance to hand over the reins."

"Do you think that's why you haven't given Milo an answer yet?" Melissa brushed a kiss across Molly Sue's temple and then stood, closing the gap between the rocker and the baby's travel crib with soft, even steps.

She tried on Melissa's words for size. Was that why? Was she afraid to hand over control? Was she afraid that if she did, she'd somehow lose control over her own destiny?

"She handed them over once and got her heart broken. It's really no wonder why she'd be afraid to do it again." Leona stroked Paris again and again, the pads of her fingers disappearing into the animal's soft brown fur. "Fortunately, Victoria is a very smart girl and she realizes what happened with Jeff has everything to do with Jeff, and Jeff alone. It has absolutely no reflection on her at all."

Rose nodded her approval in Leona's direction. "I couldn't have said that better myself."

Feeling her eyes begin to burn, Tori searched for the safest topic she could find. "So how many pillows are we trying to make?"

"The more the merrier." Rose winced and dropped her needle.

Tori pushed off her seat. "Rose? Are you okay?"

"I'm fine. My hand just aches."

"Do you think last week's treatments helped at all?" Margaret Louise asked.

Rose shrugged, her frail shoulders rising ever so slowly only to drift back down with just as much care. "Maybe. A little. But I still don't feel like I want to feel, or like I used to feel."

She rested her hand on Rose's shoulder and gave a gentle squeeze. "I'm sorry, Rose."

Rose waved her sentiment aside. "It's hard to feel sorry for myself when there's people like Lynn who are fighting a much harder battle than I am. Especially when they haven't had as many years as I've been blessed with on this earth."

"Your friend has had a rough time, hasn't she, Rose?" Beatrice looked up from the pillow taking shape under her portable sewing machine.

"She has," Rose confirmed. "Though you wouldn't know it from talking to her. Sure, she worries about the mounting treatment bills and the chance of losing the battle, but she seems determined to stay positive."

"Makes you almost want to dust off them shovels from last week and use 'em on that good-for-nothin' she's married to, don't it?"

"There's no *almost* about it, Margaret Louise." Rose held her hand toward Tori, allowing it to be massaged. "But it's not my place. All I can do is be a friend. Show interest in her gardening and her books and her soap operas so she knows someone cares."

Gently, she kneaded Rose's hand in an attempt to ward away some of the pain and stiffness that was slowly but surely threatening to rob the woman of a beloved hobby. "I'm glad she has you, Rose."

"I'm glad I have her, too. She keeps my frustration and self-pity in check."

Leona cleared her throat. "Do you really think Paris is, well, eating too much?"

Margaret Louise took Paris from her sister's arms and turned the bunny onto its back in the crook of her arm. "He's a little bigger 'n he used to be, that's for plain sure, but I think Lulu might have been givin' him table scraps the last time we stopped by for a visit."

Melissa's eyes widened. "Oh, Aunt Leona, I'm so sorry."

"It's alright. That's the day he managed to escape and I was beside myself with worry. Then . . . poof! He came when Lulu opened the back door. At that moment, I'd have given him caviar if he hadn't been so smitten with the pretzel in Lulu's hand."

"And the one in her pocket," Margaret Louise added.

"And the one in her pocket." Leona pushed off the couch and carried Paris across the hardwood floor en route to the bedroom she was sharing with her sister. "He's looking a little peaked right now. Perhaps a little rest would do him good."

Rose opened her mouth only to slam it shut in response to Debbie's stern eye.

When Leona was gone, Melissa let out a soft laugh. "If you'd told me two years ago that Aunt

Leona would be gaga over a bunny, I'd have said you were crazy."

Heads nodded around the room.

"I only give her a hard time about it because it's fun. He really is a sweet little animal." Rose tugged her hand from Tori's grasp and smiled. "If it brings her peace and makes her feel less alone, I'm happy for her. I really am."

It was the closest thing to affection she'd heard from Rose where Leona was concerned. Though even Tori knew it would be pushing it to ask her to repeat it when Leona was actually *in* the room.

Baby steps.

Tori returned to her seat as, one by one, heads bowed toward the project at hand, the whir of the portable machines and the snip of scissors the only audible sounds in the room as each member of the sewing circle slipped into their own thoughts.

Tori studied her friends, wondering what each was thinking as they set about the task of making comfort pillows for women like Lynn, women who were fighting for their lives.

Was Georgina pondering the next event on her official calendar or was she thinking about something more personal?

Was Rose in pain? Was she afraid of the age-induced changes that seemed to be overtaking her body almost daily?

Was Melissa thinking about Jake and the kids? Wishing she could kiss them all good night?

Was Margaret Louise dreaming up her next great culinary masterpiece? Or concocting her next outing with Jake and Melissa's brood?

Was Beatrice homesick for England? For people more like her?

Was Debbie juggling Colby and the kids' schedules while mentally reviewing the bakery's books?

It was anyone's guess, really. Private thoughts were just that. Private thoughts. Yet when she cared about a person as much as she cared about each of these women, it was hard not to wonder. And worry.

"You okay, Victoria?"

She paused her needle-pulling hand in midair and grinned at Margaret Louise. "You're amazing, you know that?"

"Why? What did I do?"

"Nothing. And everything."

Margaret Louise chuckled. "Well isn't that a mouthful of nothin' I can understand."

With her free hand, Tori reached across and patted Margaret Louise's arm. "Trust me, it's all good."

"Is it?" Lowering her voice still further, Margaret Louise continued. "Because I see that worry in your eyes. It's been there ever since

Rose said what she said 'bout Jeff goin' belly-up on the street."

Her stomach churned at the image. "Do you think she could be right? Do you think someone could have done that *to* him?"

"Don't see how they could. He was runnin' when it happened."

She considered Margaret Louise's words, reality hitting like a one-two punch. "Tiffany Ann Gilbert was walking when she died. And she didn't die of a heart attack, either."

"That was different. She was poisoned. To keep her quiet."

Tori closed her eyes against the image of the town sweetheart slumped against the Dumpster behind the library, the aftermath of the girl's murder her worst nightmare. But Margaret Louise was right. There was *motive* to kill Tiffany Ann.

Then again, if what Rose had said held any credence, there was motive to kill Jeff as well.

Motive *and* a list of possible suspects.

The theme song from *The Andy Griffith Show* wafted its way up from the floor, the familiar tune bringing a whistle to Rose and Margaret Louise's lips, and confusion to Beatrice's brow.

"What on earth?" Debbie asked.

"That's me." Georgina leaned over and pulled her cell phone from her purse. "Or, rather, my secretary. If it was one of our councilmen, it would have played 'Hail to the Chief.'"

Rose glanced at her watch. "Don't these people know it's Friday night?"

"They do. But it doesn't matter. Mailmen may walk through rain and sleet and snow to do their job, but *mayors?* In a small town like Sweet Briar? We're never farther than a phone call."

"Ever?" Beatrice stared at Georgina with disbelief.

"Ever," Georgina confirmed before consulting the now-silent phone and making a face. "Oh, fruit flies, I missed it." A second, shorter jingle followed, prompting the woman to flip the phone open and press a few numbers. "She left a voice mail."

Holding the phone to her ear, Georgina's smile slipped from her face as she listened to her secretary's message. "Oh no."

"What's wrong?" Margaret Louise demanded.

Georgina shook her head and pressed her free hand against her opposite ear to drown out any and all background sounds.

A hush fell over the room as Georgina continued to mumble the same words again and again until the moment she hung up the phone.

Rose leaned forward. "Georgina? What is it?"

Clutching the phone to her chest, Georgina

closed her eyes and took a deep breath. When she opened them again, she looked past Rose and locked gazes with Tori.

"What—what's wrong?" she stammered.

"It's the library. There's been a fire."

Chapter 13

She leaned her head against the seat back, the headlights of Georgina's car illuminating the way to Sweet Briar. The last fifteen minutes at the cabin had been a blur of heart-pounding disbelief, harried repacking, and tentative good-byes. Everyone anxious to help, no one able to speak.

It was as if Georgina's news had set life into a blender that alternated between slow motion and warp drive. Right now, it was on the slow setting and she could do absolutely nothing to change that fact.

Sure, Georgina could drive a little faster, probably even avoid a speeding ticket thanks to her title, but there was no sense swapping one tragedy for another.

Tori forced herself to take a deep breath, to ask the question she'd been dying to ask yet afraid to hear answered. "What happened? Do we know yet?"

"I felt so bad for Margaret Louise when we left. She'd had such high hopes for this weekend."

Pulling her gaze from the pavement in front of

them, she swung her head to take in the mayor. Had Georgina heard her question?

"She'll be okay. I'll call and give her a report after we see the situation for ourselves." A second deep breath paved the way for her question to be repeated. "Georgina? Do we know what happened?"

"All that food she brought? And those pillows we were supposed to make? No wonder she looked so sad when we were pulling out of the driveway."

She studied the woman behind the wheel, noted the set to her jaw and the determined lift to her chin. Georgina had heard the question; she'd bet good money on it. Why she wasn't answering though, was a bit less clear.

Unless she was avoiding the answer because . . .

"It was Dixie, wasn't it?" she finally said. "Dixie did something to cause this fire, didn't she?"

Georgina squared her shoulders, never taking her eyes from the road. "All my secretary could tell me was that the fire department was on the scene. Beyond that, your guess is as good as mine."

"Couldn't you call Fred? You are the mayor, after all." Her mind jumped to the library, to every possible fire cause she could think of. Was it the computers? The electric pencil sharpener at the information desk? A carelessly tossed cigarette that shouldn't have been smoked on the premises?

"He'll confirm when we get there. If he can even know this early in the game."

"Okay, I'm sorry I—wait! Did you say *confirm?*"

A pulse jumped in Georgina's neck.

"You know what caused it?"

"It's just speculation at this time, Victoria. It doesn't bear mention until we know facts."

"Facts?"

"As opposed to supposition. And supposition is all my secretary could offer."

She let Georgina's words roll around in her thoughts. "What was her supposition based on?"

"Please, Victoria. Can't we just wait? Let Fred do what he needs to do and then he'll be able to investigate your office more closely."

"My office?" she echoed. "It started in my office? Are you sure?"

Georgina nodded.

"But—but how? What could have caught fire in there?"

"Do you know that Margaret Louise was planning a Mexican feast for tomorrow night?" Georgina flicked on her blinker, despite the absence of traffic, and changed lanes. "I love Mexican."

It was official. The mayor of Sweet Briar was being evasive.

She pressed for an answer. "Georgina, please. I need to know."

A long sigh filled the air between them. "It was the coffeepot."

Tori drew back. "The coffeepot? But it can't be. The coffeepot isn't in my office. It's in the little alcove down the . . ." Her words trailed off as reality dawned.

It wasn't *her* coffeepot.

It was Dixie's look-what-I-found-in-the-basement coffeepot.

Dropping her head into her hands, she moaned. Loudly. "I wanted her to wait. Until we had a chance to talk her idea through from start to finish."

"For what it's worth, my secretary said Dixie is absolutely beside herself."

"How bad is the damage?" She knew she was being rude ignoring Georgina's statement, but she couldn't help it. Anger was rising inside her and she didn't want to unleash it on the messenger.

"She didn't say. She had more phone calls to make."

Tori trained her focus toward the road once again, the switch from the interstate to the familiar two-lane road that led in and out of Sweet Briar proof positive that the answers to her questions were only minutes away.

Her thoughts returned to the library. Only this

time, it wasn't to search for a possible culprit in the fire—that she already knew. No, this time it was more of a highlight reel containing her favorite parts—the comfy reading chairs, the hook rug where story time was held during her first few weeks of employment, the costume trunk and stage in the—

She smacked a hand over the gasp that sprang from her lips.

The children's room . . .

Georgina reached across the seat and squeezed Tori's arm. "It'll be okay, Victoria. Somehow, someway, it will be okay. Everything always is if you just wait it out. Nothing, other than death, is insurmountable."

She knew Georgina was right. She really did. But still, it was her library.

Her precious, beloved library.

They turned down one country road after the other until they crossed into the town limits of Sweet Briar, the rhythmic glow of emergency lights beckoning from the distance.

"I'm scared, Georgina," she whispered.

"I am, too." Georgina steered the car around the town square and toward the fire truck, the acrid smell of smoke seeping its way through the air vents. "Are you ready?"

Swallowing back the sobs that hovered in her throat, she nodded. "As ready as I'll ever be."

The second Georgina parked the car, Tori was

out and running toward the scene. Hoses from Sweet Briar's lone fire truck snaked across the grass, menacing in their presence yet comforting in their task.

"Whoa, whoa, whoa." Fred Granderson stepped into her path, his boots making soft squishing sounds in the wet grass. "Victoria, you can't go in there."

"But I have to see how bad it is." She heard the desperation and worry in her voice, knew the fire chief heard it, too.

"It could have been a lot worse. A lot worse."

The first sign of hope began to rear its head. She looked past Fred's shoulder to the familiar brick structure that looked as sturdy as ever. "Tell me," she begged. "Tell me."

He wiped a hand across his face, leaving a smear of soot across his forehead. "It's still early but we've got the actual fire under control."

She sagged against a nearby tree. "And?"

Fred looked toward the library. "And your office took the brunt. It'll be a while until you're back in there again."

"And the main room?"

She braced herself for his answer.

"Can't say for sure what kind of structural damage may or may not have occurred but, in terms of the right now . . . just smoke damage. Maybe some water, too."

They'd rebounded from water damage before,

despite Tropical Storm Roger's best efforts . . .

Closing her eyes, she mustered up the courage to ask the one question that still hung heavy on her heart. "And the children's room?"

"Same. Smoke, maybe a little water."

She followed his eyes back to the building, relief beginning to chase the knot of tension from her body. "But how? It has to be a virtual matchstick in there with all those books."

Fred shrugged beneath the weight of his gear. "Our saving grace was the fact that the building is old. The wood paneling on the ceiling of your office allowed it to burn there a little longer—buying us time to get in there and get it out before it extended into the roof and the rest of the building."

"When can I get inside?"

"We'll talk about that in the morning. If there's no structural damage, we can probably open the library and the children's room again in a matter of days. Your office, though, is going to be off limits for quite some time." Fred gestured toward the building. "I better go. We can talk again in the morning."

Pushing off the tree, Tori closed the gap between them with two quick strides. "Thank you, Fred. For everything."

He tipped his fire hat in her direction. "I'm sorry it had to happen at all."

"Me, too." She watched as he crossed the

lawn and headed toward the back of the building and the handful of volunteer firefighters who had donned their gear and left their families to save the Sweet Briar Public Library. When he disappeared around the corner, she turned and searched for Georgina, surprised the woman hadn't been by her side during the chief's report.

Bobbing her head first left, then right, she located her friend by the gazebo on the other side of the road. Carefully, Tori picked her way over the maze of fire hoses and crossed the street to share the latest news.

"Victoria, I'm so sorry. I really am." Dixie's face emerged from the shadow of the gazebo, the age lines around her mouth and eyes more pronounced than Tori had ever seen. "I—I just wanted to try and be hip, to put in place some of the things I've been reading about other libraries around the country."

She opened her mouth to speak, to remind Dixie of her very specific, very clear request to wait until Tori was back, but, in the end, she opted to shut it once again. Dixie loved the library every bit as much as Tori did. What happened was an accident and nothing more. Berating her, after the fact, served no purpose. Besides, there was hope now. Real hope.

"I plugged in the coffeemaker, turned it on, and went back into the main room while it got started," Dixie explained, her eyes never leaving Tori's face. "I intended to go right back, but I—I got distracted."

"By what?" It wasn't an accusation. Just a simple question.

Dixie looked from Tori to Georgina, and back again, the lines around her eyes deepening even more.

She, too, looked at Georgina. "What? What aren't you telling me?"

Dixie cleared her throat and then reached for Tori's arm. "Come. Sit."

She waved the elderly woman off, opting to stand, instead. "No. Just tell me."

"Chief Dallas came into the library."

"Okay . . . And so?"

"He was looking for you."

She stared at Dixie. "Why?"

"He—he had a few questions he wanted to ask you."

She felt Georgina studying her, felt the subsequent chill that shot down her spine. "What kind of questions?"

"Official questions."

"Official questions? About what?"

Georgina stepped forward, slipped an arm around her shoulders. "Can we save this for later? We've had enough drama for one night."

Drama?

She repeated her question through a mouth that

was suddenly bone dry. "Official questions about what?"

Dixie closed her eyes, took an audible breath, and then opened them once again. "I think Georgina is right. We can talk about this tomorrow . . . after we know about the library."

"I already know what I need to know about the library. Fred filled me in. So tell me. Please. What did the chief want to question me about?"

"Your ex-fiancé's murder."

Chapter 14

It was hard to believe just how much life could change in a matter of hours, even minutes, sometimes. Yet it could. And it did. Time and time again.

One unexpected surprise was enough to shake a person's world. But two? In the same day? It was too much.

Tori slipped the key into the lock and twisted her hand to the right until she heard the telltale click that had become synonymous with home. It was a sound that normally brought an immediate sense of peace. But not this time. No, it was going to take a lot more than a click to erase the tension from her shoulders and the dread from her—

"Tori? Is that you?"

She spun around, the key slipping from her hand and clattering against the wood planks beneath her feet. "Milo?"

"One and the same," he said before stepping from the shadows behind the wicker rocker that graced the far side of her porch. "I thought you were up north with Margaret Louise and the rest of the gang."

"I was but . . ." The words trailed from her mouth as she bridged the gap between them and ran into his arms. His warm, strong, loving arms. "Oh, Milo, you have no idea how good it is to see you."

His laugh rumbled against the top of her head. "Oh, I don't?" He took hold of her shoulders and backed her up a few inches so as to look into her eyes. "Are you kidding me? I've been counting the days until this conference is over just so I can get back to Sweet Briar for longer than ten minutes here and ten minutes there."

She lifted her head to the slight summer breeze and allowed it to whisper away the worry in her heart long enough to enjoy the unexpected reunion. "Why didn't you tell me you were going to be here? I would have passed on the weekend with the circle."

"That's why I didn't tell you." Dropping his hands to her waist, he pulled her in for a second, even tighter embrace. "I didn't want you to pass on the fun just to see me for a few minutes."

She leveled her palms against his chest and stepped back. "Then why are you here?"

Milo took hold of her hand and led her toward the porch swing that swayed ever so gently on its own. "Tomorrow we're sharing some of the innovative ways we've taught math in our classrooms and I realized I had the components of a game I created a few years ago back here at the house."

He lowered himself beside her and slung his arm across the back of the swing as he continued. "The drive isn't that bad, only a few hours. I figured I could do it again real quick. You know, get what I needed and still get back to the hotel in time for a little sleep."

Oh, how she loved Milo's passion for teaching. Some guys' eyes sparkled when they talked about football, others when they went fishing. But Milo? His eyes danced when he talked about his students and the many ways to excite them about learning.

It was just one of many things she adored about the brown-eyed, brown-haired man snuggled up next to her.

"Though, in all fairness, that was before I knew I was actually going to get to *see* you. Now I'm not so convinced on the getting back in time to sleep part."

His words broke through her woolgathering and she shook her thoughts back to the here and now.

"So, if you knew I was at the cabin with the ladies, what are you doing here . . . at my place?"

A hint of red sprang into his cheeks just before the dimples she adored. "I wanted to leave you a surprise. So you knew I was thinking about you." He pushed off the swing and made his way over to a cooler she hadn't noticed until that very moment. "There's a fudge factory about a mile from the conference hotel and, well, it screams out your name every time I see it."

He opened the cooler, extracted a tiny white bag from inside, and returned to the swing. "I got you a square of milk chocolate and a square of peanut butter chocolate swirl. Only the peanut butter one is a little smaller."

She took the bag from his hand and peeked inside. "Was it good?"

"It was awesome." Reaching for her hand, he pulled her off the swing and in for a kiss, his lips warm and firm against hers. "I missed you."

"I missed you, too." It was true. Despite everything that had happened since he left, he'd never been far from her thoughts.

"Now it's my turn."

"For what?" she mumbled as his arms closed around her once again. "More fudge?"

He laughed. "No, questions."

"Okay, shoot."

"First, why are you here? I thought you'd have left for the cabin by now."

And, just like that, everything she'd managed to shove to the background for several glorious minutes came rushing back. Hard.

She sunk back onto the swing and tugged him down beside her. "I did leave. Hours ago. Only I had to come back because of the fire."

"That was my second question."

"Second question?"

He nodded. "I wanted to know why you smell like a campfire."

A campfire.

If only she could be so lucky . . .

She looked into the bag once again and then set it aside, her stomach not the slightest bit interested. "It's not from a campfire. It's from a real fire. And it's why I came back."

Milo grabbed hold of her hand. "What happened?"

Suddenly, the tears she'd managed to stifle during the drive back to Sweet Briar came rushing down her face—only this time they were as much about relief as they were sadness.

"Tori? What is it?"

Swiping her fingertips across her cheeks, she willed herself to get it together. To answer Milo's question and wipe the worry from his eyes. "There was a fire at the library this evening."

Worry was quickly substituted for horror. "Oh no. What happened?"

The roar that had filled her ears an hour earlier, resurfaced, making it hard to think, let alone speak. "We won't know for sure until tomorrow at the earliest. But we suspect it was an old coffeepot Dixie found in the basement."

"How bad is it?" he asked.

"It could have been worse, that's for sure."

He pushed aside the last of her tears with his thumb. "Tell me."

Slowly, she filled him in on everything Fred Granderson had said—the part the wooden ceiling had played in slowing the fire, the quick response thanks to Chief Dallas being in the building at the time it started . . .

Chief Dallas.

She swallowed over the lump that threatened to cut off her ability to breathe. But if Milo noticed, he showed no indication.

"That's good, Tori. That's real good."

"I know. It is. But"—she pushed off the swing and wandered around the porch, Milo's gaze tracking her every step—"it could have been so much worse."

"But it wasn't."

She stopped, spun around, retraced her steps. "We don't know that for sure. There could be structural damage."

"And there might not be." Milo ran his hands through his burnished brown hair, tousling it at the top. "I always drive through the center of town when I come to see you. Always. Yet today . . . when something like that's going on . . . I opt for the back road. It figures, doesn't it?"

She shrugged. "It's okay. Georgina came back with me and Dixie was already there."

"Still, I wish I could have been there with you. So you didn't have to face that alone."

If he only knew.

Oh how she wanted to tell him the rest. Tell him that, once again, she was about to be the target of questions in a murder investigation. But before she could do that, she had to tell him Jeff was dead.

She could feel him studying her, waiting for more, yet she didn't know where to start. Or how to explain why she had, once again, opted to keep something Jeff-related from him.

"What is it, Tori? What else is on your mind?"

She took a deep breath and leaned against the porch railing, her thoughts traveling back to the moment she heard the news. "Jeff is dead."

She hadn't meant to say it so frankly, to dump it on him with such a resounding thud, but she did.

"And?"

What response she expected, she didn't know. But one thing was for sure, *that* wasn't it.

"You—you knew?" she stammered.

He nodded.

"But how? Who told you?"

"Not you."

She felt her face warm. "I'm sorry, Milo. I really am. I guess I was just in shock more than anything else."

He held up his hands. "There's no need to explain. I heard your conversation the night before it happened and I know how you felt about him. I considered calling to check on you but I figured you'd reach out to me when you were ready. Besides, I knew Margaret Louise would look after you."

Feeling like a complete heel, she crossed back to the swing and peered down at Milo. "I love you. I truly do."

Dimples appeared in his cheeks. "I know that. And I love you, too."

Everything was going to be okay.

It had to be.

She took a deep breath. "There's more."

"More?"

She nodded. "Remember how I said Chief Dallas was in the library when the fire started?"

Milo's eyebrows scrunched for a moment only to return to their normal position just as quickly. "Yeah, okay, what about it?"

"He wasn't checking out books."

He laughed. "I didn't figure he was. The chief isn't what you'd call well-read. He'd prefer to fish in his free time."

And make my life hell . . .

"He was there on more official business."

The laugh died on Milo's lips. "Official business?"

"That's what Dixie said."

He moved his finger in a rolling motion. "Okay . . ."

"Apparently, he's investigating a murder," she explained.

Milo's eyebrows scrunched again. "By asking *Dixie* questions?"

She closed her eyes and shook her head. All her life she'd been a placid person—the kind who avoided confrontation, opting instead to escape into the pages of a book. Yet here she was now, the target of yet another round of questions pertaining to yet another murder.

Jeff's murder.

"No. By asking *me* questions."

He sat up tall. "You? But why? Who was murdered?"

She met his gaze, her words wooden at best. "I guess because of our history together."

"History? What are you talking about?"

"I don't know all the details myself just yet. All I know is what I've pieced together from gossip at the cabin and what Dixie said just now."

"Okay."

"Well, it . . . well, it appears as if Jeff may have been . . . um, murdered."

"Okay."

It wasn't exactly the reaction she'd expected so she repeated it more succinctly. "Jeff may have been murdered."

"I heard that part. What I don't get is why *you'd* be questioned. The guy was a first-class loser. Surely there was a line a mile long with people wanting to wipe him from their existence."

She stared at Milo. "But don't you see why the police would come knocking at my door? We were engaged. He cheated on me. And then he shows up here . . . on my new turf."

Suddenly, the chief's desire to speak to her made sense. It really did. There was no conspiracy to try and link her to every wrongdoing in town. She had a connection to the victim, the kind of connection that couldn't—and shouldn't—be ignored.

"Is he still with the woman he messed around with when you were engaged?"

"No."

"Then maybe *she's* to blame. Or maybe her father decided to teach him a lesson once and for all. Or maybe one of the other women he surely hurt had finally had enough. Heck, maybe a whole group of them banded together."

"Rose said he got all of his aunt's—"

Milo continued on, oblivious to her efforts to speak. "Someone that vile, that selfish makes a lot of enemies along the way. And, eventually, they run up against someone who doesn't simply sit back and take it."

The sound of a car door made her look up, the identity of the driver all but certain even before she had visual confirmation.

"He's here."

Milo stood. "I'll take care of this."

She stopped him with her hand. "No. His questions need to be asked and answered before he can track down the person who did this to Jeff."

"Then I'll stay."

Chief Dallas crossed in front of his car and headed in their direction.

Rising up on tiptoe, she planted a kiss on Milo's cheek. "I've got this, Milo. I really do. Besides, you need to get back. I'll call you tomorrow and let you know what happened."

He looked from his watch to the chief and back again. "Are you sure?"

She nodded.

"Okay. But I don't want you waiting until morning. Call on my cell as soon as you can breathe again."

Breathe.

She watched as Milo stopped to shake the chief's hand before disappearing down the sidewalk, his last few words tickling something in her subconscious.

"Good evening, Miss Sinclair. I'm sorry I didn't have a chance to catch you in town but the fire had all of us in a bit of a tizzy."

"I understand."

"Now that we've both had a moment to breathe though, I'd like to ask you a few questions."

There was that word again—

"He doesn't deserve to breathe the same air you do . . . or even breathe at all for that matter."

Slapping her hand over her mouth, Tori sunk onto the swing and put her head between her knees.

Chapter 15

She could feel the chief studying her, waiting for her to say something, anything, yet she was at a loss. Milo Wentworth was the sweetest, calmest, most respectable man she knew. Yet there she was, *doubting* him in one of the worst ways imaginable.

"Miss Sinclair? You okay?"

Shaking away the fog that threatened to paralyze her, Tori forced herself to look up, to smile and be friendly. "I'm sorry. It's just been a rough night. At the end of a rough week."

Chief Dallas gestured toward the wicker rocking chair. "May I?"

"Of course. Please. Make yourself at home." She pushed off the chair and headed toward the still unopened door. "Can I get you something? Some soda? Coffee? Water?"

He shook his head. "Actually, I'd like to just have a few words with you if that's okay. Shouldn't take long."

Nodding, she turned around, retraced her steps back to the swing, and sat down. "What can I do for you?"

"Could you elaborate on what you said a

moment ago? About the rough night at the end of a rough week?"

She released a breath of air from her lungs. This question, at least, was easy. "Obviously the fire at the library was the last thing in the world I wanted to see. The drive down from the cabin was the longest two-and-a-half hours I've ever spent in a car." Pushing an errant strand of hair behind her ear, she continued. "All I knew was that there was a fire at the library. I, of course, envisioned a blazing inferno."

"Which could have been the case had I not stopped by to talk with you." Chief Dallas pulled a notebook from his back pocket and flipped it open before reaching back once again for a pen. "Another ten minutes and you might have had your blazing inferno."

Something about the inflection in his voice during his last statement made her stomach churn. He couldn't possibly mean what she thought he meant, could he?

"M-my blazing inferno?" she repeated.

He shrugged, his eyes locked with hers. "I just meant that worst-case scenario you had on the drive back to town."

"Oh." Nestling against the back of the swing, she willed herself to relax. No one in their right mind would ever think she'd want to see the library burn. The notion alone was simply proof that she needed a good night's sleep. Soon. "I'm so thankful you were there and able to get the call out to Fred Granderson so quickly."

"My pleasure."

He shifted his weight and uncapped his pen with his teeth. "Do you know of any reason someone might have wanted to set the library on fire?"

She froze, unable to speak.

He waited her out.

"Did the report come back already?" she finally managed to ask, her thoughts scurrying in a million different directions.

"No. We're hoping to have something in the morning."

"Then why would you even entertain the notion that someone deliberately set the fire?"

A smile appeared at the corner of his mouth. "I guess because I'm trained to consider various possibilities."

She resisted the urge to laugh out loud. As nice as Chief Dallas was at times, he tended to be rather narrow-minded. She, of all people, knew that firsthand.

"Well, as my great grandmother used to say, no sense borrowing trouble early."

"I prefer to stay a step ahead." The chief gave a quick wave of his notebook. "But let's get back to the reason for my visit, shall we?"

She lifted her hands to her head in an effort to stop the rush of noise that suddenly filled her mind. The last thing she wanted to do was play the cat and mouse game with this man. They'd played it one too many times. Instead, she took the proverbial bull by the horns. "You're here to ask me about my relationship with Jeff Calder. To see if, in someway, I might either be a) responsible for his death or b) know some tidbit of information that can help you figure out who *is*. Is that about right, Chief?"

He didn't even miss a beat. "That about sums it up, I suppose."

She swallowed. Hard. Sure, she knew it. She'd said the questions out loud all by herself. But having them confirmed was a slightly different story.

At least Dixie had given her a heads-up. Allowed her to prepare, at least on some mental level.

Dixie . . .

The elderly woman had looked so distraught when she saw her that evening, her large eyes looking over Tori's shoulder again and again, as if hoping the fire truck and acrid smell of smoke hovering around the library was some sort of bad nightmare.

"Miss Sinclair?"

The chief's voice snapped her back on track. "What? Oh, I'm sorry. My mind was elsewhere for a moment." She toed the porch floor, jump-starting the swing into a slow and gentle sway.

"Okay, as for the first item, I am not responsible for Jeff's death if, in fact, someone *is* responsible."

The chief's left eyebrow rose upward but he said nothing.

"Jeff and I broke off our engagement about six months prior to my moving to Sweet Briar. It was unexpected, it was heartbreaking, and it was cruel. But I didn't go after him at that time as I could have—*should have,* according to many of my friends at the time. And why? Because I was heartbroken. And unlike some people who lash out under those circumstances, I retreat. Into myself. Right or wrong, that's what I do."

"Go on," the chief said even as he jotted notes on his pad.

"After a few months of licking my wounds I realized it was time to stand back up. Only I wanted to do it somewhere new. Somewhere that didn't have memories in so many of the restaurants or theaters or streets I frequented."

"Which is how you came to Sweet Briar, yes?"

She nodded. "Exactly. I saw a listing in a library publication for the director job. I applied, I interviewed, and, obviously, I got the job. So I packed up my apartment and said good-bye to Chicago and Jeff, once and for all."

"How did he take that good-bye?"

"I wouldn't know."

His hand paused over top of his paper. "You wouldn't know?"

"I didn't tell him. I just moved. In fact, from the moment I left the hall where our engagement ended, I never spoke to, or saw, Jeff again."

"Until last week," Chief Dallas corrected.

He'd done his homework that was for sure.

"Yes. Until last week."

The chief's eyes narrowed. "Tell me about that."

She shrugged. "Not much to tell, really. I was with Rose Winters while she was receiving outpatient treatment for her rheumatoid arthritis. While I was there, I saw Jeff's great-aunt, Vera Calder. The woman died of a massive heart attack shortly thereafter."

"Shortly thereafter?" He snorted. "That's an understatement, don't you think?"

Feeling the first hint of anger rising to the surface, she willed her voice to remain steady. "It was a coincidence and nothing more. There's a substantial history of heart problems in Jeff's family. And Vera looked to be in very poor health."

"So you ran into Jeff when he was here for the funeral?"

She bit back the urge to challenge the question, to demand that the chief admit to what he knew, but she resisted, opting, instead, to walk him through the details she was confident he already knew.

The *how* behind that knowledge, though, was anyone's guess.

"Actually, I'm the one who called Jeff to tell him. I knew the relationship between Jeff and Vera's stepson wasn't always on the best footing and I was afraid he wouldn't find out any other way."

Like a dog in search of a bone, his ears perked. "Why the sudden concern for a man who'd broken your heart, humiliated you in front of your family and friends, and whom you hadn't seen in what? Two and a half years?"

Any speculation as to whether someone was feeding information to the chief had become fact. The humiliation comment tied it up in a nice little bow. The *who* behind the information, though, was still a mystery.

Not one to shirk from the truth, she faced his question head-on. "I wouldn't necessarily call it concern so much as the right thing to do. Two wrongs don't make a right, Chief. I knew Vera was dead. I suspected Jeff wouldn't be told. To say nothing would have placed me on a level of cruelty not much different than his."

"What happened when you called him?"

She pushed a little harder with her foot. "He asked if I would pick him up at the airport. Which I did. And then, other than dropping him off at his hotel, I didn't see him again until his great-aunt's wake."

"That was it?"

"That was it."

He pinned her with a stare. "Are you *sure?*"

Something in his tone made her stop. Think.

"Until the wake, yes. Then, a few days later, he showed up. Right here. On my porch."

"What was that about?"

She brought the swing to a stop and stood, desperate for an opportunity to move around, work off some of the stress she felt coursing through her body. "It was about Jeff being Jeff."

"Jeff being Jeff?" the chief echoed.

"Selfish. Egotistical."

"How so?"

"He wanted to see if I'd consider giving us a second chance."

"That doesn't sound selfish or egotistical to me."

She walked toward the stairs that led to the sidewalk and then spun around, her feet moving back and forth across the porch. "It does when you examine the motivations."

The chief followed her every move with eyes that seemed to never blink. "And what motivations would those be?"

"Jeff never showed one iota of interest in making things right after I caught him with a mutual friend during our engagement party. In fact, he never called to see if I was okay, never stopped by to say he was sorry."

"Would you have wanted him to?"

The question stopped her in her tracks. Would she have? Was that part of the reason she'd moped inside her apartment for so long afterward? Because she'd been waiting for him to come back?

The thought left a sour taste in her mouth.

"I'm simply saying he never tried—an indication he wasn't that upset over our broken engagement." She resumed her pacing. "Then . . . wham! He's here, because of a funeral, and he suddenly unearths this desperate need to reunite with me? Please."

"What do you think it was?"

"Jeff hated to lose. Hated to place anything but first in the runs he did, hated to be shown up at work by one of the other trainers at the gym, hated for someone to land a woman he didn't have."

"He already knew he didn't have you."

"But he didn't know I was involved with someone else until he got here and I told him."

The chief dropped his pen onto his notepad and crossed his arms. "You think he was motivated by Milo?"

"Absolutely."

"So what happened?"

"I told him to go. And he did."

The chief leaned forward in his chair. "And when did you next see him?"

She leaned against the porch railing and took a deep breath, her final image of Jeff filling her every thought. "On Main Street, lying facedown, with a ring of spectators standing around him."

"You didn't see him *before* that?"

"You mean between the time he left my porch and they found him dead in the street? No."

"Would you be willing to say that for a lie detector test?"

She didn't bat an eye. "Why wouldn't I? It's the truth."

A blanket of silence covered them as the chief seemed to consider her words, his eyes, his demeanor yielding no clues to his thoughts. When he did finally speak, his words were like a pinprick to a balloon, diffusing the tension between them in mere seconds.

"Which brings us to part B. Do you have any information that might be useful in finding out who *did* kill Jeff Calder?"

"Let me ask you a question, Chief. What makes you think someone killed him? I thought it was a heart attack. Just like so many in his family before him."

"His doctor in Chicago says he was in perfect health. That Jeff had only a minor hint of whatever flaw his family members had in their hearts."

So Rose was right.

Someone really did kill Jeff.

"Will they do an autopsy?"

The chief nodded. "It's being done as we speak."

"In Chicago?"

"No. Here."

"Oh." It was all she could think to say at the moment. Just the notion that someone may have taken Jeff's life was almost more than she could fathom. Sure, she knew he rubbed people the wrong way, but still, *Jeff?*

"If the autopsy points to foul play, as the doctor suspects it will, Mr. Calder's death will become a murder investigation."

"But he was running, right?"

The chief stood, then worked his notepad and pen into his back pocket once again. "He was."

"How could he have just keeled over if it wasn't from natural causes?"

The chief raked a hand through his hair and sighed. "In much the same way Tiffany Ann Gilbert dropped dead next to the Dumpster behind the library."

The chief was right and she knew it.

"So, do you have any thoughts? Any people you think might have wanted to see your former fiancé dead?" he asked.

Suddenly any arm's-length emotion she'd tried to employ since seeing Jeff's body disappeared.

This time, the victim wasn't someone she'd only heard about in stories. It wasn't someone she'd only seen in pictures.

She'd *known* Jeff.

She'd *loved* Jeff.

And regardless of the manner in which they'd parted ways, he'd been a very big part of her life. Sure, he'd been a jerk. Sure, he'd broken her heart—something that continued to affect her life even now. But that didn't mean he deserved to die by someone else's hand.

"Can I think on it, Chief? I don't really know much about his life over the past two-and-a-half years other than the abbreviated version he shared in the car on the way from the airport to the hotel. But maybe, if I think on it, something he said will be a trigger."

"Do you keep in touch with any of the friends you two had as a couple?"

She shook her head. "No. I retreated more than I should have when I lived there, and once I moved I guess I didn't want to look back."

The chief smiled. "I guess that's understandable." He walked toward the stairs only to stop at the top. "You know where to find me if anything—or anyone—comes to mind."

If there was something Jeff had said, or some connection they'd once had that could unearth his killer, she wanted to help.

She owed that to herself as much as Jeff.

"I'll do what I can."

"Thank you, Miss Sinclair." The chief nodded farewell. "For what it's worth, Chicago's loss was Sweet Briar's gain."

"Chicago's loss?"

"You."

She blinked against the sudden onslaught of tears that threatened to reduce her to a human puddle. It was the nicest thing the man had ever said to her. But before she could respond, he prattled on, any hint of emotion quickly erased by his back-to-business demeanor.

"As for Mr. Calder's possible murder, keep this in mind, Victoria. Sometimes the answer is where you least expect it."

Watching him descend the stairs and disappear down the street, Tori couldn't help but replay the man's parting words again and again, her unshared response coming quickly on its heels . . .

It wasn't the *where* she was worried about, but the *who*.

Her who.

Chapter 16

By the time the first traces of dawn peeked around Tori's bedroom curtains she was already dressed, her favorite sleep shirt still folded neatly on her nightstand. She'd intended to sleep, she really had, but her eyes—which had remained glued to the ceiling as everything from the library and Dixie, to Milo and Jeff, looped through her mind—had refused to heed her body's basic needs.

Part of that, she knew, was guilt. Guilt over not fulfilling Milo's request and calling him the second her chat with Chief Dallas had ended. Part of it, too, was the roller coaster of adrenaline and exhaustion she'd ridden from the moment Georgina's secretary called with news of the fire to the relief that had come when she'd finally gotten to speak to Fred Granderson. Yet, unlike most roller coasters, she hadn't been able to disembark from the ride at the end. No, she'd gotten a bonus second ride she'd neither sought nor appreciated—this one taking her from Dixie's shocking assertion that Chief Dallas was looking for Tori to being questioned in yet another possible murder.

A murder that just happened to have her ex-fiancé as the victim and, at least in her sleep-deprived mind, her almost-fiancé as a possible suspect.

All night long she'd replayed her last conversation with Jeff and the subsequent phone call with Milo. Try as she might, no matter how many times she hit the replay button, Milo's voice and words didn't change. He'd been angry, furious even over Jeff's treatment of Tori on the porch. Toss in whatever Leona may have said to stoke the fire even more and, well, there she was.

At a complete loss for what to say and do.

Under normal circumstances, she might be tempted to call Margaret Louise, bounce her wild notions off the levelheaded woman. But not today. Margaret Louise and the rest of the crew were still at the cabin, laughing and joking and sewing the hours away.

The hours away.

"Hours away . . ." Tori paused, her tube of lip gloss a mere inch from her lips, and stared at her reflection in the mirror. Milo had been *hours* away when Jeff died. Several glorious *hours* away, in fact.

And, just like that, the knot of tension that had taken root in her neck and shoulders and spread throughout the rest of her body during the night was gone.

Milo had been hours away. Which could only

mean one thing. If someone did, indeed, kill Jeff, it hadn't been her Milo.

Her Milo. Her sweet, caring, loving Milo.

Tension was replaced by disgust at herself as she looked past her own reflection to the photo of Milo in the Cubs shirt she'd bought him for Christmas last year, every facet of his face taking part in the smile his mouth formed as he pulled her close for the picture.

What kind of person suspected someone so caring and so sweet of nefarious things? What kind of person ignored the goodness that had been demonstrated to them time and time again in favor of suspecting something so despicable?

"Me," she whispered as she dropped the lip gloss onto her dresser and closed her eyes, grateful that she hadn't shared her worries with the chief. At least, in that sense, she'd done something right.

A familiar sound broke through her woolgathering and forced her into the present. Grabbing the phone from her nightstand, she flipped it open.

"Hello?"

"Why didn't you call last night?"

She backed against her bed and sat down, her thoughts racing for something that sounded better than the brutal truth. Especially when that truth was so glaringly false. "I guess I just crashed the moment my head hit the pillow. With the drive to and from the cabin, the worry about the library, my unexpected visit from you and Chief Dallas, well, I guess I was more tired than I realized."

His smile was audible through the phone. "I understand, though I missed hearing your voice. Did you at least sleep well?"

Tori sidestepped the question. "The talk with the chief went fine. He asked questions about my history with Jeff and he seemed to really listen. I don't think I'm on his radar."

"Is there anyone who is?"

"Not from what I can tell," she answered honestly. "He wants me to give it some thought, see if I can come up with anyone Jeff might have wronged along the way."

"From what I've heard, sounds like finding someone he *didn't* wrong might be the harder job."

She closed her eyes at the bitterness in his voice, her mind replaying her sleepless night and the nagging questions that had tossed her between fear and guilt with each passing hour.

"Can we talk about something else?" she finally asked. "Please?"

The warmth that was synonymous with Milo Wentworth returned in her ear. "Oh. Yeah. I'm sorry. So . . . are you going to head back up to the cabin today? Get in a little more time with Margaret Louise and the crew?"

A smile played at the corners of her mouth. She had to admit, the notion of delving back into the oasis her friends provided was more than a little tempting. Especially after the night she'd had.

"I want to talk to Chief Granderson first and see how things fared at the library. Maybe even get inside and look around."

"Do you want me to drive back up after my session today? I could go through the building with you if he'll even let us."

She leaned back against her pillow. "I couldn't ask you to make that drive again. It's too much."

"No it's not. It's mostly interstate the whole way and it goes fast. Trust me. We could give everything a once-over and then go out to eat."

As tempting as it was to take him up on it, to spend an evening together that didn't include a crisis, she had to decline. The conference would be over for good soon enough. Besides, she owed it to Margaret Louise to return to the cabin and finish up the weekend with the circle. She said as much to Milo.

"Okay." He released a playful sigh in her ear. "I'll wait until this conference is over to see you. But once it is, we have a date, okay?"

She laughed. "Okay." Glancing at the clock on her nightstand, she sat up. "Milo? Don't you have a class in a few minutes?"

A second of silence was followed by a rustling in her ear. "Oh. Wow. Yeah. I've gotta go. Talk to you later?"

"I'll talk to you later." She shut the phone inside her hand only to open it once again, scrolling through her personal directory in rapid fashion. When she reached Georgina's name, she pressed the green button. Her call was answered on the first ring.

"Good morning, Victoria."

"I take it I didn't wake you?"

She could hear the mayor smile. "Why do you say that?"

"Because you once told me that you're blind as a bat in the morning. Seems to me you wouldn't be able to read my name on your phone's tiny screen if you just woke up."

"That's why I have a different ring for everyone—my secretary, Chief Dallas, Chief Granderson, my accountant, even people I don't know."

Intrigued, Tori pushed off the bed and wandered over to the window, the early morning sun heating her room enough to kick off the air-conditioning she'd set at seventy-eight. "What do you have for Chief Dallas?"

"The theme song from *Hawaii Five-O*."

She couldn't help it; she laughed.

"And Chief Granderson?"

" 'Great Balls of Fire.' "

" 'Great Balls of'—wait, how come I didn't know this about you before now?"

"I didn't realize I could do it until my cousin came to town earlier this summer with her grandson, Bradley," Georgina explained. "You'd be amazed what kids these days can do with technology."

"What about your accountant?"

" 'Add It Up' by some group with a crazy name."

Tori nibbled her lower lip inward against the urge to snort. "The Violent Femmes?"

"Yes, that's it. It was Bradley's suggestion." Georgina stretched, loudly. "Shall we head back to the cabin this morning?"

"Wait. Not so fast," Tori protested. "What's mine?"

"Your what, Victoria?"

"The ring that let you know it was me calling just now."

"Oh. That."

She waited, only to be out-silenced on the other end.

"Georgina? Are you still there?"

"Yes, I'm still here."

"What's my ring?"

"I prefer not to answer that."

She turned from the window and walked to the center of the room. "Okay. But why?"

A long, drawn out sigh filled her ear, as if her

question was akin to a promise of torture. "If I tell you, I'll have to tell everyone else in the circle. And some of my callers may not be— well, let's just say they may not be amused with my selections."

"You do realize I'm a librarian, yes, Georgina?"

"Yes, of course."

"Which means I'm curious by nature."

"Then we shall be glad you're not a cat, Victoria, because my lips are sealed."

This time, it was her turn to sigh. "We can't make a deal? My silence in exchange for some answers?"

"No."

"Are you sure because I promise I won't—"

"No."

"Well, alrighty then." Looking around, she grabbed an empty laundry bag with her free hand and headed toward the front hallway. The smoke-filled clothes she'd stripped from her body the night before were right where she'd left them, the familiar campfire smell from her youth permeating the air around them. "Have you heard from Fred Granderson yet?"

"I'm meeting him at the site in thirty minutes."

She reached down, stuffed the clothes into the bag, and carried them out to the car. "May I meet you there?"

"Of course. And when we're done, we'll head back up to the cabin for the rest of the weekend."

Tori took a deep breath and allowed her thoughts to return to the cabin in the woods—a place that had seemed like heaven on earth until talk turned to Jeff . . .

"Margaret Louise is making Mexican tonight."

Jeff.

Maybe her friends could help her come up with possibilities for the chief. Or help get her mind off the whole business completely . . .

"Your bag is still in my trunk. And maybe now Dixie might consider coming up with us since she won't be able to work."

Dixie.

The word was like a slap across the face, the sensation bringing her back to the one-sided conversation taking place in her ear. "Can we just wait and see what Fred has to say? I don't want to head back to the cabin only to ruin everyone else's weekend by being in a dour mood."

"Alright. But, even if the news is less than ideal, I think the time away will be good for you. You've been under such stress these past few weeks."

She shut the trunk and leaned against the car, lifting her face to the sun's rays. Georgina was right. Between the business with Jeff's arrival in town and the shock of his death, she'd been living on a form of autopilot the past week. The fire at the library just ensured she'd be running the same way even longer. So, really, what harm could twenty-four hours away do?

"Okay. I'm in," she conceded. "But after we hear what Fred has to say about the library."

She could hear Georgina's smile through the phone. "Good. Margaret Louise will be pleased as punch."

"I'll meet you in front of the library in"—she pulled the phone from her ear and consulted the clock in the bottom right corner—"in twenty minutes, then?"

"That'll be fine. Oh, and Victoria?"

Crossing around the front of her car, she pulled the driver's side door open. "Yes?"

"Will it be okay with you if I actually call Dixie and invite her to come along? I think the change will do her good, too."

Tori leaned her forehead against the steering wheel and said a mental prayer for patience even as her stomach churned at the memory of the phone call that had brought her and Georgina running. "Yes . . . yes, of course it's okay."

Chapter 17

Tori slid the car into park and leaned against the seat back, the lingering scent of fire seeping its way through the open window. The unspoken hope she'd almost fooled herself into believing was gone, the victim of a yellow-taped reality.

She'd seen the Do Not Cross tape before—on TV shows, in newspapers, even in Sweet Briar. But strung around the trees and encompassing her beloved library because of a fire? Not in her wildest dreams. Or her worst nightmares.

Georgina tapped on her partially opened window. "Are you ready, Victoria?"

"I guess." She stepped from the car and followed Georgina toward the burly man standing sentry beside the library's back door. "Is Fred meeting us here?"

"He is. In fact . . . here he is now." Georgina adjusted her trademark straw hat atop her head and waved at the dark-haired fire chief as he emerged from the building. "Good morning, Fred, thanks for meeting us so early."

Fred Granderson waved the sentry from his post then extended his hand in Georgina's direction, nodding at Tori as he did. "My pleasure, Mayor. Are you ladies ready to get a look at the damage we sustained?"

She swallowed back the lump that appeared at the mention of the word *damage*. "You mean we're going to go inside?"

Again he nodded. "We can't go into your office, but we can tour everything else." A quick whistle brought the return of the sentry and a pair of hard hats. Fred handed one to Georgina and the other to Tori. "Put these on as a precaution and let's get to it."

They fell into step behind the chief as he pulled the employee door open and disappeared inside. Tori took a deep breath and followed, the campfire smell that had clung to her clothes the night before magnified a hundredfold inside the building.

"So what do we know so far?" Georgina asked as she picked her way down the hallway, sidestepping puddles and debris. "Do we know how it started?"

"We do. Though we've called in an arson investigator to take a closer look."

Tori froze. "An *arson* investigator?"

"Come with me." Fred led the way down the hallway, stopping outside the door of Tori's office. He gestured inside. "Take a look."

Tori sucked in her breath at the sight of the charred-out remains of what, just twenty-four hours earlier, had been her office. Hers and Nina's.

Her metal desk still stood, but it was merely a shell of its former existence, her pencil holder and papers gone. Nina's desk shared the same fate. The small sitting area she'd created was gone—the cushions she'd sat on with everyone from Lulu and Margaret Louise to Leona and various board members, gone.

"The fire started right there."

Tori followed Fred's finger as it directionalized her field of vision toward the tiny table in the southern corner of the room.

"How do you know?" Georgina asked.

"Do you see the V pattern on the wall? Right there around the base of the table?"

Sure enough, the darkest charring in the room was found in the area of the table—the table that had played host to the coffeepot Dixie had commandeered from the library's basement.

Georgina and Tori nodded in unison.

"The other indicator we have for the place of origin is that lamp over there." Fred shifted his finger to the right, leading their attention toward the charred lamp atop Nina's desk. "Do you see the bulb? The way it's bent toward the table? In the heat of a fire, those bulbs tend to melt a bit and bend toward the area of the heat source."

"So it truly was the coffeepot?" She heard the raspiness in her voice but could do little to stop it. Seeing the damage up close was nothing short of depressing.

"It was." Fred tucked his arm underneath Tori's elbow and guided her toward the main room. "Whether that coffeepot got a little help in starting the fire, though, is where the arson investigator will come in."

"Help?" she echoed.

Georgina stopped mid-step. "What do you mean *help?*"

Fred looked from Georgina to Tori and back again as a hood seemed to drop in front of his eyes. "It appears as if there was something in the outlet. Something that shouldn't have been there."

"But how?" Tori reached for her hair only to smack her fingertips into her hard hat. "I—I use that outlet all the time."

"That's what we're hoping to find out." Fred turned his complete focus on her. "Have you had any electrical work done in here recently?"

"No."

"Any workers of any kind in your office in the past few days?"

"No."

"Are you sure?"

"Of course I'm sure."

Fred prodded them forward once again. "Well, let's just wait and see what the investigator comes back with before we get into this any deeper, shall we?"

Unsure of what to say or even think, Tori

continued toward the library's main room, her feet growing heavier with each step. It was hard enough to see her office the way that it was, but the books? The shelves? The computers? She could only pray they'd fared as well as Fred had indicated the night before.

Georgina clapped her hands as they stopped just inside the room. "Oh, Victoria, it's fine!"

Fred released Tori's elbow and held his hand out. "Structurally, it appears sound to me, but the final verdict will come later today."

She felt the knot in her chest loosen its grip as she looked around the room. "I can't believe it . . . it looks . . . okay."

"The big window in your office and the back entrance allowed us to get in and tend the fire without needing to upset things in here too much. Though smoke damage is smoke damage and it will need to be addressed before the library can open again."

Her gaze ricocheted around the room—bouncing from section to section as a sense of peace settled over her. "We could be open in a matter of days."

"Again, if the structure is okay, that might be possible. But your office, of course, will be unusable."

Rising up on the balls of her feet, she swiveled back toward the hallway. "Can I see the children's room?"

Fred led the way. "The children's room fared pretty well, too, though there's some water damage on the floor. Probably affected some of the books on the lower shelves. But, all in all, it's okay."

She peeked into the room, her shoulders slumping momentarily.

"Water can be dried. A handful of books replaced," Georgina mused in her ear. "But what matters is the fact that the murals on the wall are still there, the majority of the books are fine, and we'll have an army of parents at the door the day we open to get everything in tip-top shape once again."

She knew Georgina was right, she really did. But still, seeing the water, the soaked books, the drenched hook rugs . . . it was unsettling.

"We got lucky, Tori. Real lucky."

Fred's words were like a slap to the side of the head, his honest assessment, born from experience with the devastating effects of fire, bringing her up short.

Floors could be dried.

Books could be replaced.

What mattered was the fact that the library was still standing. And standing well enough to open in a matter of days if the structural report came back as Fred anticipated.

She couldn't ask for anything better under the circumstances.

Pulling her gaze from the hand-painted murals on the walls, she fixed it, instead, on Fred Granderson. "Thank you, Fred. For saving our library."

A smile spread across the man's face, igniting a spark in his eyes. "If I was to show my face in front of my grandson again, I had no choice. He loves this room more than you can imagine. Made him love books even more than he already did."

She sagged against Georgina as relief's exhaustion grabbed hold of her body. "I'm just so, so grateful. I don't know what I would have done if—if . . ."

Georgina's arms were around her as the tears she tried valiantly to fight finally made their debut. "There, there, Victoria. Everything is okay. Your beloved library is okay."

Fred's waist-mounted radio squawked.

Pulling the device from his belt, he held it to his mouth. "Yes?"

"Arson is here."

"Roger." Fred replaced the radio in its holder. "Looks like our tour is over. I've got to get outside and get this investigation rolling."

Investigation . . .

Georgina pulled her arm from behind Tori and extended her hand to the chief. "Give me a call the moment you know anything. Victoria and I will be just a few hours north of here until sometime late tomorrow."

201

"Do you think we should still go? Maybe it would be better if we just stayed here . . . waited for Fred's call."

"The phone lines reach into the mountains, Victoria. Being here won't change anything. And besides, you need the break."

Fred gestured toward the back door. "The mayor is right, Tori. I'll let you know what I can as soon as I know what's going on."

They stepped around the chief as he pushed the door open, the brightness of the summer day nearly blinding them.

"Of course I'm right," Georgina stated. "*You* need this. *I* need this. And *Dixie* needs this perhaps even more than either of us do."

Suddenly, the tear-swollen face of the elderly woman who loved Sweet Briar Public Library as much as Tori did filled her mind. Dixie had been nothing short of devastated the night before, a combination of grief and panic adding years to a woman who'd seen seven-plus decades' worth already.

Accidents happened. They happened every day in homes and businesses across the country. Only *they'd* gotten lucky.

Very, very lucky.

There was no way either of them could have known the coffeepot would cause a fire. She knew that as surely as she knew Dixie was hurting.

She also knew there was nothing she could do to change the damage to her office. Only time and hard work could do that. But the weight Dixie was carrying on her shoulders because of her perceived part in the fire? That was something Tori could change.

"You're right, Georgina. Let's go get Dixie."

Chapter 18

By the time Georgina's late-model BMW pulled onto the gravel driveway that led to the cabin, Tori was spent. Part of that, she knew, was from her sleepless night and the nearly nonstop drama that had been her life the past few weeks. Margaret Louise had warned that it would catch up and she'd been right, as usual.

But it was more than that.

From the moment Dixie had gotten in the car, Tori had been trying. Trying to pick up the woman's spirits. Trying to offer hope regarding the library. Trying to make her smile. Trying to establish some sort of real connection.

Yet her efforts had fallen flat.

Dixie Dunn may have been in the car from a physical standpoint, but mentally? She was somewhere else entirely.

They'd given it the old college try, they really had. But even the rarely daunted Georgina had grown silent behind the steering wheel, lost in thoughts Tori could only imagine.

"It's beautiful, isn't it, Dixie?" She looked over her shoulder into the backseat. "Margaret

Louise couldn't have picked a more perfect place as a getaway."

"For her, maybe."

Tori studied her predecessor closely as the car bounced along the rutted ground. "I'm not sure I know what you mean."

Dixie's shoulders rose and fell beneath her pale pink cotton shirt. "It hasn't been much of a getaway for you or Georgina . . . thanks to me."

"It was an accident, Dixie. It could have happened to me. It could have happened to Nina. It could have happened to anyone." She waited for some sort of understanding to chase the sadness from the woman's eyes, some sort of tentative smile to nudge her lips upward, but there was nothing. Nothing except the same vacant look the woman had sported for the past few hours.

Georgina gave it one more try. "Do you know how many homes and businesses burn to the ground every year because of faulty wiring? It happens all the time."

"But *I'm* the one who brought the coffeemaker upstairs. *I'm* the one who was hell-bent on trying to be cool and fresh . . . to prove to anyone and everyone that I'm not the dinosaur the board thought I was two years ago." Dixie pressed her forehead against the window. "All I did, though, was make a mess. Of the library *and* your weekend."

"Dixie, it could have happened to me just as

easily," Tori countered as the car came to a stop beside Margaret Louise's station wagon.

"But it didn't."

Georgina yanked the key from the ignition and dropped it into her purse, her eyes seeking Dixie's in the rearview mirror. "If I drove you back to Sweet Briar right now, could you wiggle your nose and make the fire a bad dream?"

Dixie glanced down at her hands. "No."

"What's done is done, right?"

Dixie nodded.

"This weekend is not over yet." Georgina spat. "Was it dampened by the fire? Of course. But there's still a good twenty-four hours of fun yet to be had. Do you really want to ruin that by being a sourpuss?"

Tori nibbled her lower lip inward and stole a quick peek over her shoulder once again, Georgina's strong words and Tori's own reluctance to be confrontational leaving her torn between the urge to rubberneck and to run from the car with her hands over her ears.

For a moment, the silence that had claimed the backseat off and on for the past several hours returned, accompanied by an expression Tori knew all too well. An expression she'd once coined to Milo as the Don't-Look-Now-Dixie's-Gonna-Rip-Someone's-Head-Off expression. It was one she'd seen often during the past two years.

Only when it was trained in her direction, it didn't disappear quite as fast as it did for Georgina.

"You're right. I'm sorry. I'll do my part to make sure the rest of the weekend is better."

Tori's mouth dropped open as she looked from Dixie to Georgina and back again before checking the window for any indication of a sudden and severe ice storm. Or even a burst of flames to indicate they were at least in the right place when the deep freeze took place.

Grabbing her overnight bag from the floor, Dixie pushed her door open and stepped from the car, slamming the door in her wake.

Tori shook her head at Georgina. "H-how did you do that?"

"Do what?" Georgina asked.

"Get her to apologize?"

Georgina lifted her straw hat from the center console and positioned it on top of her dark brown bob. "I didn't hold any punches."

She leaned forward, visually following Dixie as she walked around the car and onto the cabin's front porch. "I see that. But . . . but that's *Dixie*."

"I don't care if it's the Prince of Wales . . . or the Queen of Spain. A wet blanket is a wet blanket and I'd had enough."

"Yeah but—"

Georgina shoved her door open and stepped from the car. "Let's go have some fun, shall we?"

Fun. The word alone was a foreign concept as of late. But Georgina was right. Tori couldn't control the stuff that had happened over the past few weeks. Nor could she wipe away the work now in front of her. But the rest of today and the bulk of tomorrow? *That* she could control. And *that* she could enjoy.

Tori followed Georgina down the path to the front porch, her thoughts racing ahead to the remainder of the weekend. If she had a chance to pull Margaret Louise aside and fill her in on the latest concerning Jeff's death, she would. If not, it would wait until they got back to Sweet Briar.

"I swear, Victoria, my mouth is already salivating at the thought of what Margaret Louise might be cooking for us tonight—"

"Goodness, gracious, great balls of fire."

She stopped short to keep from running into Georgina. "That's Fred's ring, isn't it?"

Georgina nodded, pulling the phone from her purse as she did. "Good afternoon, Fred, what can I do for you?"

Her heart began to pound in her chest as Georgina's brows rose, then dipped, and then rose again in reaction to whatever was being said in her ear. She tried to convince herself it was good news, that Chief Granderson had called simply as a courtesy, but she knew better.

Georgina's expression and string of hushed murmurs told her so.

"But why would someone do something like that?"

She heard the cabin's screen door open and then shut, knew Dixie had made her way inside, but beyond that she was at a loss for anything but Georgina's call.

"What's going on?" she whispered to Georgina only to have her question thwarted by an index finger.

"Will we still be able to open the library despite an active crime scene?"

"Crime scene?" she echoed.

Georgina's finger rose farther into the air just as the screen door opened for the second time.

"Dixie said you were out here." Margaret Louise stopped midway down the steps, her infamous face-splitting smile slipping away. "What's going on?"

Tori shrugged.

"Keep me in the loop. And yes, I'm sure Dixie will speak with you as soon as we get back." Closing the phone inside her hand, Georgina closed her eyes. "It wasn't Dixie's fault."

She stared at her friend. "What wasn't?"

"The fire." Georgina opened her eyes and gestured for Tori and Margaret Louise to follow her back to the car. Once there, she leaned against the shiny black finish and pulled her hat from her head. "It wasn't the coffeepot."

"It wasn't?"

"Well, it was . . . but only because that's what was plugged into that particular outlet."

Margaret Louise jumped into the mix. "So the outlet was bad?"

"Not exactly," Georgina said. "It was, for lack of a better word, tampered with."

Tori looked from Georgina to Margaret Louise and back again, confident she was hearing things. The expression on their faces told her otherwise. "Tampered with? What do you mean *tampered* with?"

Georgina pushed off her car, walked ten paces, and then came back, repeating the same sequence again and again. "I mean someone intentionally started that fire."

"How?" It was all she could think to ask in the absence of anything resembling a clear thought.

"By putting some sort of device inside the outlet that essentially caused a short the second Dixie plugged in the coffeepot."

"But how?" She knew she sounded like a parrot, but she couldn't help it. None of what she was hearing made any sense. "And why? And— and *when?*"

Georgina shrugged. "That's what the arson investigator will be trying to figure out."

"Did you let anyone in your office recently?" Margaret Louise asked.

She shook her head. "No. And I used that very

same outlet not more than a week or so ago. I wanted to make sure that old tape player I gave Lulu still worked before I got her hopes up. There was no spark, no fire then."

Margaret Louise's smile returned ever so briefly, the mere mention of one of her grandchildren enough to weather any storm. "It works like a champ. Why, Lulu's been usin' it to play school with Sally and they've been havin' a grand time with it."

"If the outlet worked fine then, that tells me the device must not have been there at that time." Georgina stopped in the middle of the driveway and turned around, determination evident where frustration had been just moments earlier. "Knowing that you used that same outlet within the past week or so should provide the investigator with a time line at the very least. That alone will give them a starting point."

A starting point . . . For figuring out who tried to sabotage the library.

"It'll be nearly impossible to figure out," Margaret Louise mused.

Georgina scowled. "Why is that?"

Tori looked to Margaret Louise for confirmation of the reasons that had occurred to her as well. "Because the hallway that leads to my office is the same hallway that takes patrons and delivery personnel to the children's room . . .

the bathrooms . . . and the back parking lot."

A groan escaped Georgina's lips. "But someone must have seen something."

"We can certainly hope." But even as the words left her lips, Tori knew she wouldn't be that someone.

She'd been much too distracted in the days leading up to the fire—her thoughts, her energy, her daydreams centered around virtually one thing and one thing only.

Jeff.

What an idiot she'd been.

Jeff had ceased being her problem the moment she found him in the coat closet with Julia. Why she'd let his presence in Sweet Briar ruffle her feathers so much that she could have missed someone in her office was nothing short of shameful.

"Chief Dallas is going to have to figure this one out on his own," she mumbled.

"Oh no, the arson investigator, Chief Granderson—they're *all* going to be involved in finding out who did this."

Tori raked a hand through her shoulder-length brown hair and exhaled loudly. "I don't mean the fire. I mean Jeff's murder."

Margaret Louise gasped. "So it's true? That cheatin' lyin' ex of yours was murdered?"

She shrugged. "According to Chief Dallas it's certainly a consideration."

"What does that have to do with you?" Georgina asked.

"I guess the chief feels my history with Jeff might be useful in figuring out the who and why." She raised her arms above her head as if pushing at an invisible weight that threatened to blanket her very being. "But it isn't. I haven't known Jeff for over two years. Who he hurt, who he wronged since then can't and isn't my concern any longer. My focus, my attention has to be on the library."

"Amen." Margaret Louise linked her left arm through Tori's and reached for Georgina with her right. "Now nothin' is gonna be figured out standin' here. Let's go inside, work on some of those comfort pillows Rose wants us makin' and get everyone caught up. I know that I, for one, am nearly burstin' at the seams waitin' to hear how the children's room fared."

"It fared amazingly well." Arson or not, that, at least, was a fact. A fact she found herself anxious to say aloud—as if sharing it would restore the hope that had been ripped from her chest the second she learned the fire had been deliberate.

"The dress-up clothes? The stage? The murals? It's all okay?"

"Nothing some dryers and a few power fans can't fix." Georgina fell into step beside Margaret Louise, her no-nonsense demeanor back where it belonged. "Other than Victoria's office, the library itself suffered very little damage."

"That's good news. Tremendous, actually," Margaret Louise said, casting a sideways glance in Tori's direction. "Though hearin' that almost makes you wonder whether the person responsible was truly after the *library* or just *Victoria,* don't it?"

Chapter 19

Relaxation was Tori's for the taking. All she had to do was jump in on any number of conversations that were alive and well around the room. She could talk recipes with Margaret Louise and Debbie, or the latest children's titles making the rounds of the elementary school set with Beatrice and Melissa. She could debate the town council's decision to add yet another festival to the calendar with Georgina and Dixie, or help Leona hash out a suitable diet for Paris. And, if none of those struck her fancy, she could get to the bottom of all the worried looks Rose kept casting in her direction.

But try as she might, she couldn't get Margaret Louise's comment out of her thoughts. Because, quite frankly, there was a ring of truth to the woman's musing that had taken hold of her stomach and twisted it into knots.

If someone had been intent on setting the library on fire, why wouldn't they have put their little outlet-shorting device into the main room? She supposed it could be a simple matter of opportunity—more people translated to more watchful eyes—but slipping into a personal office during work hours seemed just as risky. Maybe even more so.

She glanced up from the case she was making for her comfort pillow and took in Dixie's reformed demeanor. Gone was the woe-is-me attitude she'd worn like a badge of honor in the car ride. Gone were the additional lines around her eyes that had been so prevalent the night before. In their place was a woman who was not only animated in her discussion with Georgina, but also happy.

There were so many questions she wanted to fire her predecessor's way, questions that might yield helpful answers.

Had Dixie given anyone permission to use the phone in Tori's office recently?

Did she remember seeing anything unusual?

Did she know of anyone who might hold a measure of animosity toward the library or the board . . . besides herself, of course?

She sucked in her breath.

Was it possible? Could Dixie have finally exacted revenge on the board for ousting her from her beloved job two years ago?

She certainly had access with Nina on bed rest.

Tori shook the thought from her head as quickly as it surfaced. No. Dixie loved the library. Any anger the elderly woman still carried about her forced retirement was aimed at the board.

And, perhaps, still Tori to some degree—

"*. . . almost makes you wonder whether the person responsible was truly after the library or just Victoria, don't it?*"

She felt her mouth go dry.

"Victoria?" Leona's voice emerged from behind her travel magazine. "Are you okay?"

"Huh? What?"

The woman's cluck of disgust made her sit up tall.

"Must you talk like such a—such a commoner, dear?" Leona set her magazine to the side, then leaned forward and wrapped her arms around a sleeping Paris. "A simple yes or no would have been fine."

"Huh?"

Leona glared at Tori over the top of her glasses. "Your Chicago is showing."

"And you've never been distracted, Leona?" Rose mumbled from her spot behind one of the portable sewing machines that had made the trip from Sweet Briar for the weekend.

"What could I possibly have to be distracted by?"

One by one, Rose began ticking away at the fingers on her left hand. "A designer suit in a store window, a travel deal to Paris or London or wherever you're salivating to go, whatever young man happens to walk by in a uniform at any given moment for starters."

Leona took pause over the last item then merely shook it off. "Distraction is for old goats like you, Rose."

Rose's eyes narrowed.

Leona's chin lifted.

The battle lines were drawn and Tori was smack-dab in the middle. "Hold on you two. Let's not start, okay? Yes, I'm a little distracted. No, I didn't use proper grammar when I answered you, Leona, and for that I'm sorry. I guess I just have a lot on my mind."

Rose pulled her focus from Leona and fixed it, instead, on Tori. "The library will be fine, Victoria. There's not a person in this town who won't move heaven and earth to make sure that building is good as new in no time."

Leona nodded. "I've been after you to make that office of yours more romantic since day one. Perhaps this turn of events will provide the fire to make it happen."

"No pun intended, of course," Rose countered.

"Pun?" Leona closed her eyes, bobbed her head, and then opened them again, a slight smile lifting the corners of her mouth upward. "Ahhh. I am rather clever, aren't I?"

"That's not a word I'd use to describe you, Leona." Rose wiggled out from behind the sewing machine. "I'd choose something more fitting—something like shallow, or egotistical, or desperate, or—"

"Desperate?" Leona gasped. "Desperate?"

"That's what they call women who feel the need to have a man by their side twenty-four/seven, isn't it?" A hush fell over the room as Rose continued. "Because they're desperate for attention, desperate for validation, desperate for love."

Leona sprang to her feet, Paris's ears in full sensory mode. "I am not, nor will I *ever* be, desperate for a man."

"Oh no?" Rose snapped. "What about in the past? Were you ever desperate for a man in your past?"

Beatrice's shoulders slumped behind her machine as the tension mounted in the room.

Melissa cast a nervous glance over the edge of Molly Sue's travel crib.

Margaret Louise moved to rest a gentle hand on her sister's shoulder and whisper something in her ear.

Leona jerked away. "Paris and I are going to bed. Victoria, you know where my room is should you want to talk." One by one, Leona looked at everyone in the room except Rose. "Good night, everyone. Or should I say, *almost* everyone."

Rose snorted.

"Rose!" Debbie reprimanded. "Must you poke at Leona all the time?"

"Yes."

Conversation volleyed around the room as Tori

mentally replayed the heated exchange. There was more to Leona and her behavior, of that she was certain. The trick, though, was smoking it out of a woman who had a lot to say about others yet very little to say about herself.

Sure, there was a part of her that thought it best to let Leona keep whatever hurt she'd experienced to herself. It was Leona's right and, obviously, her preference.

But the part of Tori that had come to love and treasure Leona as a friend wanted to help. Even if that help could only be a pair of ears. Lord knew Leona had been that and then some for Tori on many occasions.

She glanced up to find Margaret Louise staring at her. "What?"

"You should go talk to her."

"To Leona? Me? Why? She's not going to talk to me." But even as the words left her mouth, she knew Margaret Louise was right. The woman was always right.

She rose to her feet and moved in beside Leona's twin sister. "We've been friends for two years now and I had no idea she'd been hurt by love until just the other day. And even then it was because I put it together, not because she told me."

"The wound is deep."

Her heart broke for Leona. "But how do I get her to tell me?"

Margaret Louise shrugged. "I'm not sure she will. But that whole thing with Rose just now happened because she was in a worried snit 'bout you."

She felt her own shoulders slump. "I can't control what Rose says."

"Of course you can't. None of us can. And that sister of mine is hardly an innocent party where their constant feudin' is concerned. I know that. You know that. Everyone knows that. But you bring out a nurturin' side in my sister I haven't seen in years. So let her nurture. Maybe it'll bring those walls she's fancied 'round her heart tumblin' down once and for all."

Reaching out, Tori gave her friend's arm a gentle squeeze. "I'll see what I can do."

She slipped from the room, her departure virtually unnoticed as the members of the Sweet Briar Ladies Society Sewing Circle did what they did best—sew, gossip, and eat. Though, if she were a betting woman, she'd plunk down a few extra bucks on Rose being aware of both her exit and her destination.

The wood-paneled hallway that branched off the main room splintered off in two more directions as she approached the midway point. The right would take her to the room where she was bunking with Rose as well as the rooms shared by Debbie and Melissa, and Georgina, Beatrice, and now Dixie. She took the hallway to the left, stopping at the closed door that served as a gatekeeper for the woman inside.

Tori knocked softly. "Leona? It's Tori. Can we talk?"

"Are you alone?"

"Yes."

"That hateful old woman isn't with you?"

She stifled the urge to laugh. "No. It's just me. Victoria."

"Come in."

With a quick flick of her wrist, she pushed the door open and stepped inside, the only light in the room coming from a series of votive candles flickering on a side table. Beside them, sat Leona, rocking, a far-off look in her eyes.

Tori crossed to the bed and sat on the edge closest to Leona. "Are you okay?"

Leona's false eyelashes fluttered and then closed. "I'm worried about Paris."

Her gaze jumped to the wide-eyed bunny in the cushioned dog bed nestled beside the rocking chair. "He looks okay. Just not very tired."

Leona opened her eyes and pointed at the bunny. "Watch his sides. He seems to be having difficulty breathing."

Lowering herself from the bed, Tori looked closely at Paris. Leona was right. "Has he been doing this all day?"

"No." Leona's mouth twisted in grief. "Just since I brought him in here."

"Maybe he's just reacting to the smell of the candles."

The woman shook her head. "I brought them from home. It's his normal bedtime scent."

She looked up at Leona. "Bedtime scent?"

"It soothes him."

Crinkling her nose, she inhaled sharply, a familiar smell bringing her up short. "What is that?"

Leona pointed a bejeweled finger at the first of four candles. "This one is Ocean Wave, this one is Warm Leather, and—"

"Ocean Wave?" She could hear the laugh waiting behind her words but she did her best to stamp it down. "Warm Leather?"

Leona arched an eyebrow at Tori. "Is there a problem?"

"No, no problem." She looked back at Paris as the inventory of scented candles continued. The bunny's nose began twitching at a rapid pace.

"This one is Sugar Cookie and the last one— which is his favorite—is Carrot Cake."

Carrot cake . . .

"What has he eaten today, Leona?"

"His usual organic carrot."

"And . . . ?"

"That's it."

She glanced up at Leona. "Are you sure? Because just since I got here I've seen him eating a piece of cracker and a shred or two of lettuce."

223

Leona waved her hand in the air. "He has a way of making everyone give him scraps. It's his charm."

"Well, his charm has, apparently, earned him an upset tummy." She reached out, stroked the back of Paris's head. "He'll probably feel better by morning."

Leona reached over the side of the rocker and patted the bunny's back. "Do you really think so?"

She couldn't help but grin at the worry in her friend's voice. She may have helped bring out a nurturing side in Leona Elkin but Paris had taken the ball and run with it. "I really think so. Though you might want to consider extinguishing Sugar Cookie and Carrot Cake. If his tummy is as full as I think, the reminders might be making things worse."

And, just like that, two of the four candles went dark.

"Thank you, Victoria."

Rocking back on her bottom, Tori opted to stay on the floor beside Paris, his soft fur begging to be stroked. "I'm sorry that Rose upset you out there."

Leona's body tensed.

"I don't think she means any harm."

"Maybe. Maybe not. But she crossed the line tonight." Leona rested her head against the back of the rocker. "I enjoy the company of men, I always have. And I suppose I enjoy the company of younger men because of my own youthful ways."

She resisted the urge to comment a la Rose Winters, choosing, instead, to simply nod. That's why she was there, wasn't it? To listen?

"But I will never, *ever* allow a man to become so important to me that I lose sight of myself."

She tried Leona's words on for size, realized they didn't completely fit. "What do you call what you did to me during the Tiffany Ann Gilbert debacle? When you had your sights set on Investigator McGuire from Tom's Creek?"

The low lighting didn't mask the crimson that rose in Leona's cheeks at the reminder. "I call that distraction."

"I thought you told Rose you don't get distracted."

Leona rolled her eyes skyward. "Of course I get distracted. *Everyone* gets distracted. But I don't have to admit that to Rose."

"In other words you enjoy yanking her chain just to yank it, yes?" It was a rhetorical question, really.

"Of course I do. It's fun."

She felt Paris flinch beneath her hand and wished she could help ease his discomfort. "So your distraction with the investigator wasn't a case of you losing sight of things because of a man?"

"I might have lost sight of my growing friendship with you at that time—and for that I'm sorry. But I never lost sight of myself. No man is worth doing that ever again."

Ever again . . .

She looked closely at her friend, saw the familiar lines of hurt and regret—lines she'd seen in her own face for months following Jeff's betrayal, lines she still saw when she allowed her mind to revisit that painful time.

Margaret Louise was right once again. Leona's wound was deep.

It was, perhaps, the one and only reason Leona had never married, never stayed in any relationship for longer than a few weeks.

"What was his name?"

Judging by the way her own mouth dropped open the second she uttered the words aloud, the question surprised her every bit as much as it did Leona.

"Who?" Leona finally asked.

"The one who broke your heart."

For several long moments, the only sound in the room came from Paris as the rabbit shifted position in a futile attempt to get comfortable. Yet, just as she began to realize she'd overstepped her bounds by pinning Leona down for information, the woman spoke, her eyes glazed over with a pain so raw Tori's heart ached for her friend. "Emmett."

"Emmett," Tori repeated, the name on her tongue causing a reactionary fisting of her hands. "I'm sorry, Leona."

"So am I."

"Wh-what happened?"

"I loved him. He didn't love me."

She considered her friend's statement. "How so?"

Leona pushed off her chair and wandered around the room, her soft pink slippers making a tap-tap against the hardwood floor. "I had a talent for drawing when I was a young girl, did you know that?"

She shook her head as she followed Leona around the room with her eyes. "What kind of drawing?"

"Homes, buildings, that sort of thing."

"Architecture?"

Leona shrugged. "I guess. Though it wasn't a field for women at that time."

"Why didn't you pursue it?"

Leona spun around. "I did. It's why my best friend Ginny and I moved to Chicago and—"

"Chicago?" she repeated, dumbfounded.

As if Tori hadn't said a word, Leona continued, her voice taking on an almost robotic quality. "I took classes, I planted myself outside a prestigious architectural firm in the city and made a pest of myself until they gave me a shot. I followed the head of the firm everywhere, watching everything he did. And then, one day, a client came through the door wanting them to design a home for his son. Something refined while pushing boundaries, innovative yet traditional."

She couldn't help but notice the way a spark ignited in Leona's eyes as the story continued to unfold. "So I started drawing. On my own time. I sketched during breaks, I sketched during lunch, I sketched after all of the associates left each day, I sketched during the weekends instead of going out with my best friend, Ginny."

"And?" she prodded when Leona stopped to look out the window. "What happened next?"

"I left my sketch on a table in the break room one day. I'd up and left it sitting there along with my case of pencils. And the head of the firm saw it sitting there."

She sucked in her breath. "Did he steal it?"

Leona turned from the window. "No. Good heavens, no. Russ Smithton was an honest man through and through. No, he saw it and called me to his office. He loved what I had done, said it surpassed what he, himself, had come up with."

"Oh, Leona, that's wonderful!"

Leona's eyes became hooded. "It was until I met the client's son, the one whose house I'd drawn."

She stared up at Leona. "Emmett?"

"Emmett," Leona confirmed. "The second I

saw him, I fell in love. He was smart, he was funny, he had charm and mystique, and he told me I had talent. The kind of talent he said could move mountains."

Her stomach churned as her mind began to race ahead to the details she'd yet to hear, yet had a sneaking suspicion she knew. "And he offered to help move those mountains?"

Leona nodded. "He had the means to set me up with my own firm, to track down connections and send business my way. It was a dream come true. A dream come true on top of one I wanted even more."

"Emmett?" she repeated.

"We got engaged. The business was virtually set to launch. We'd moved into the home I'd designed, the one that brought us into each other's lives. Everything was perfect. Or so I thought."

She sat perfectly still as Leona continued, a faint rustling in the hallway doing little to distract her. "One day, after a meeting with my first potential client, I came home early, bursting at the seams to tell him everything that had happened, to share my excitement with the one person who believed in me more than anyone ever had. Only, when I got there, he wasn't alone."

The room began to spin, words her friend had said suddenly coming together to form the picture that had been Leona's reality—a reality that had forever altered the course of her life from that one fateful day, forward.

"He was with Ginny, wasn't he?"

"Yes," Leona whispered.

"That little *hussy*," Rose hissed as she pushed her way into the room. "I hope you kicked her clear to the curb, Leona Elkin!"

Tori swallowed as Leona's face drained of all discernable color. "Rose Winters, you had no business standing outside my door, eavesdropping on my private—"

A funny noise from Paris's bed made them all turn just in time to watch Leona become a grandmother for the very first time.

Chapter 20

Chaos.

It was the only word she could think of to describe the moment Paris revealed himself to be a female. A rapidly multiplying female, to boot.

"What is he doing?" Leona screamed.

Rose snorted. "He's having a baby—I mean, *babies*."

"But how? He's a *he!*"

Tori scooted back as a fourth and fifth baby made its appearance on the cushion. "Um, I think it's safe to say Paris is a girl."

Leona's hand trembled as she brought it to her mouth. "But I bought him a bow tie . . ."

"I guess she thought it was a choker." Rose shuffled closer to the dimly lit corner.

"I spoke with him about the proper way to treat a lady . . ."

Rose shrugged. "Maybe that helped her find a better mate."

"But to have babies, he—I mean, she—would have had to have a mate. Paris never left my side."

Tori felt her cheeks lift. "Never?"

Leona crossed her arms. "Never."

"Land sakes what is goin' on in this room?"

Margaret Louise strode into the room, her heavy footsteps echoed by several lighter pairs. "We could hear all your hootin' and hollerin' clear into the other room." She stopped inches from the birthing cushion and looked down, her mouth gaping open, then shut, then open again. "What on earth?"

"Paris is a girl," Rose offered.

"And she just had six—no wait—seven babies." Tori grinned. "Seven teeny tiny baby bunnies."

Leona swooned into the rocker and fanned her face with her hand.

"Well I'll be darned." Margaret Louise clapped her hands together then poked Melissa in the side. "Paris must have found herself a Jake, too."

Melissa's face reddened. "Paris only has seven."

"And so do you."

Melissa looked from her mother-in-law to the bunnies and back again, the color her cheeks sported deepening all the more. "Talk to me again in about six months. I'll have him, I mean *her,* beat then."

A chorus of gasps sprang up around the room while Margaret Louise shook her head. "And when were you goin' to tell me this?"

"When the opportunity presented itself?" Melissa teased before turning to Leona and verbalizing the reality that had so far gone unspoken. "Congratulations to you, too, Aunt Leona. I guess we can call you Grandma now, too."

Leona's chin rose into the air. "I am much too young to be called such a thing."

Rose grabbed hold of the rocker's arm with one hand and Tori's shoulder with the other and slowly lowered herself to her knees, her gaze firmly fixed on Paris and her babies. "How about Nana?"

"Hmmm," Leona pondered. "Nana? Nana. Yes, I like that."

"What are you going to call them, Nana?"

Leona waved her hand in the air. "Call them? I'm not even sure how they got here."

Margaret Louise's laugh thundered around the room. "You're not sure how they got here?"

"Oh stop it, Twin. Of course I know *how* they got here, I just don't know how it happened. Paris is with me at all times."

"Not all times."

Leona stared at her sister. "What are you talking about?"

"I'm talkin' 'bout that time Paris got out. Took Lulu to track him down, remember?"

"It couldn't have happened then," Leona protested. "He—I mean, she—was only out for thirty minutes. Tops."

"That was twenty-nine more 'n she needed, I imagine," Margaret Louise mused.

Leona sucked in her breath then peered down at Paris. "Did I not teach you to play hard to get a little better than that?"

Tori couldn't help but laugh. "Maybe that's what she used the first twenty-nine minutes for."

Leona shot a glare in her direction. "This is not funny, Victoria."

"No, it's sweet." Rose reached out, gently stroked the top of Paris's head. "Happy Mother's Day, Paris. You did a wonderful job."

And just like that, Leona's face and stance softened as she, too, left the comfort of her chair to kneel beside Rose and congratulate her precious Paris.

One by one, the latecomers left, tiptoeing from the room to resume their various sewing tasks, Melissa's news and a gender-changing bunny no doubt landing the top spot on the group's list of topics to dissect and discuss over the whir of the portable machines.

When they were gone, Tori released a sigh that made the new mother's ears twitch. "Oh, I'm sorry, Paris," she whispered. "I didn't mean to upset you."

"You don't need a two-timer like that Emmett fellow to enjoy life, Leona. And you certainly don't need the kind of friend that would treat you the way that . . . that *Ginny* treated you." Rose cleared her throat and continued, her voice hushed yet firm. "If you'd married that clown, you wouldn't be here now."

Tori cast a sideways glance in Leona's direction, saw that Rose's words were striking a chord.

"True friendship is a beautiful gift, Leona. It's why it doesn't come along every day. And I, for one, am glad you eventually found your way here."

Leona's swallow was audible. "You are?"

"What are you? Deaf?" Rose snapped. "I said it, didn't I?"

Tori teed her hands in the air. "No fighting around the babies, you two."

Leona turned to Rose, her mouth lifting in a smile. "You're not so bad for an old goat, you know that?"

"Don't tell anyone, Nana." Rose's head bobbed from side to side. "I'm not quite sure what I was thinking when I got down here but one thing is for sure, I wasn't thinking about how to get back up again."

Tori jumped to her feet then bent forward to hoist Rose upward. "Whoa. There you go. Why don't you sit here in the rocker."

Rose did as she was told, her gaze still riveted on Paris and her seven babies. "Nothing like Paris playing us all for a fool."

Leona laughed. "Here I was thinking he was a male, telling him about women and dressing him up in bow ties. And all the while he was a girl. Perhaps I need new glasses."

"Nah," Rose countered. "It's just life. It's when people—or in this case, bunnies—stop surprising us that you start to worry."

"Do you think Dixie could have purposefully started the fire in my office?" The second the words were out, Tori wished she could recall them. It was a notion she'd entertained yet hadn't meant to share aloud. Not to this crew, anyway.

But it was too late. The statement had already drawn a gasp from Leona and a glare from Rose.

"What did you say, Victoria?" Rose spat through teeth that were suddenly clenched.

"I—I . . ."

"She asked if Dixie could have started the fire." Leona raised her body up with her hands then shifted her feet to the side before settling back down on the floor beside Paris. "Isn't that right, dear?"

"I—I . . ."

"How could you think such a thing?" Rose demanded.

How indeed.

She held up her hands in surrender. "Can we just pretend I didn't say that? Chalk it up as post-traumatic stress or something? I mean, I just watched Paris become a girl and a mother in a matter of seconds."

Leona shrugged. "It's okay with me."

"Well it's not okay with me." Rose toed the floor, finding the pace with which she wanted to rock. "Dixie may be grouchy and set in her ways, and she may be a bit of a grudge holder but—"

"A bit?" Leona repeated.

"She would never do something so destructive as set a fire and she most certainly wouldn't do it to the library." Rose rested her head against the back of the chair, her gaze never leaving Tori's face. "I would have thought you'd know that by now."

Tori sat on the edge of the bed and twisted her hands in her lap. "I did. And I do. I guess I just let the events of the past week get to me . . . get to my good sense."

"Then let me help you get it back." Rose stopped rocking long enough to look over the side of her chair at the bunnies, the glare in her eyes softening instantly. "First, there's the matter of the fire. From what you and Georgina said when you got here this afternoon, it was deliberate. The library is a very public place. Someone saw something. So start asking.

"Second, there's the matter of that tomcat who was murdered in the middle of the street."

"We don't know he was murdered," Tori mumbled.

"Yes we do."

She jerked her head up and stared at Rose. "We do? How?"

"Lynn called just after you left the room to talk to Leona. She said the preliminary autopsy has indicated his death wasn't from natural causes."

She heard the sharp intake of air through her mouth, felt the way her stomach clenched and her hands moistened at the news.

Leona looked up, too. "Was that why you were outside the door?"

Rose nodded at Leona then turned to Tori once again. "The toxicology report has been fast-tracked but his death is now classified as a murder."

"A murder," she whispered in echo.

"Which brings me to the next item in front of you," Rose said. "Figuring out who killed him and why."

Leona's hand flew into the air. "I don't see how or why that's Victoria's concern."

Rose nodded again. "True. It's not. But this is Victoria we're talking about, yes?"

Leona's ensuing silence said all that needed to be said. They knew her better than she knew herself.

"But how am I going to figure out who killed him when I don't know anything about his life these past two years?"

"Look at what you know most recently."

She considered Rose's statement even as Leona asked the obvious why.

"Because it was *here* that he was killed," Rose explained.

It made sense. It really did. But still . . .

"I don't know anything about him here, either."

"Yes you do." Rose shifted her legs outward, a grimace masking her facial features as she did. "You know he tried to get you back and failed. And you know that he came into a large sum of money."

"What does trying to get me back have to do with anything?" she asked.

"Perhaps a lot," Rose mumbled as her eyes grew heavy. "Or, perhaps nothing at all. That's what you're going to have to figure out if you get involved in this."

"Rose?" Leona's hand shifted from the rabbit to Rose's knee. "Are you okay?"

"I'm old, Leona. That means I need bifocals to see, people to scream, medication to walk without pain, and the television set to be on so I don't get lonely." Rose's hand closed over the top of Leona's. "Besides that, I'm simply wonderful."

Silence fell over the room as each of them retreated into their own thoughts, their own worries. In the end, though, it was Leona who finally spoke.

"You get lonely, Rose?"

"That's what I said, isn't it?"

Leona looked from Rose to the bunnies and

back again, a sparkle in her eyes making Tori suck in her breath in anticipation. Sure enough, Leona did not disappoint.

"How would you like to be a mother?"

Rose's eyes sprang open. "What are you talking about, woman?"

Leona gestured toward the makeshift delivery room at her feet. "You can have the first pick."

"I couldn't keep a bunny."

"Why not?"

"Leona is right, Rose, why not? It would be fun."

"The first pick?" Rose whispered.

"The first pick," Leona confirmed.

A quick burst of emotion splashed across Rose's weathered face, prompting the woman to swipe a trembling hand across her eyes. "The gray one with the little white spot between his ears reminds me of a cat I had as a young girl."

Tori placed her hand on top of Rose and Leona's. "What was its name?"

"Patches."

"Patches it is." Leona leaned forward, her mouth nearly touching the new mother's ear. "When you're ready, my sweet Paris, your baby just found a wonderful home."

Chapter 21

As a devout reader, Tori had always considered setting to be important in literature. It set mood and tone in a very sensory way. But she'd never stopped to think of setting's role in real life until just that moment.

Twenty-four hours earlier, she was relatively relaxed in Margaret Louise's rented mountain cabin—the isolated location and rustic feel lending itself to an aura of safety. As if nothing bad could find her in the middle of the woods, surrounded by her closest friends.

Yet now that she was back among civilization, standing in the main room of the library, she didn't feel quite so safe and it bothered her. From the moment she'd moved to Sweet Briar, the library had been her safe haven, the place where she could think her way through just about anything while feeling relatively calm and content.

Knowing that someone had deliberately set her office on fire two nights earlier changed all of that.

She said as much to Fred Granderson.

"We'll figure out who did this, Victoria. Too

many people are in and out of this building in the course of a day, people who cherish this library and cherish you. Once word gets out that this was deliberate, people will start searching their memory banks for anything they may have seen." Fred crossed to the center of the room and shot his arms out. "The structure is sound. This room is fine. That's why you have the green light to open as early as tomorrow if you want. But the children's room needs a good cleaning. Might want to hold off on opening that up until the end of the week."

She nodded in lieu of trying to speak around the lump in her throat. It wasn't that she wasn't grateful for the lack of damage, because she was. Things could have been a million times worse. Still, the notion that someone had set out to hurt the library was upsetting at best.

"Your office, though, is another story. That will take weeks, maybe months before it's back to normal." Fred pulled his arms in and fiddled with the master key ring the department held for the various public buildings in town. "You do realize that everyone is going to chip in and do what they can to get you and Ms. Morgan back in there as soon as possible, right?"

Nina.

She closed her eyes against the image of her intensely shy yet loyal assistant who was at home, feet up, awaiting the birth of her first child. The woman had been Tori's right-hand man since day one, helping her acclimate to the library and its patrons in much the way her late grandmother had taught her how to sew.

Oh, how she missed Nina's contagious calm. Especially now.

"I know that, Fred. The people in this town are beyond generous when it comes to this library. But . . ." Her words trailed off as she soaked in the room—the books, the computer bank, the information desk, the reading chairs. "I guess I just feel, oh, I don't know. I'm rambling like an idiot."

Fred's large hand closed over her forearm. "Are you worried someone will try to finish the job?"

"I suppose." Though, in all honesty, that thought hadn't crossed her mind. Yet.

"It's not gonna happen, Victoria. Everyone is on high alert."

"Don't you think that for someone to take an outlet cover off the wall and install a device that's designed to set a fire they have to be pretty motivated?"

"That's one word to describe it." Fred loosened his grip on Tori's arm and stepped backward. "Though, if you ask me, I'd say angry."

"Angry?"

He shrugged. "Not the kind of angry that makes a person snap and pour gasoline all over, but the kind that makes a person plot."

She released a pent-up sigh. "Seems as if this town has had a lot of angry people doing angry things this past week."

"How so?" he asked, cocking his head to the side.

It was her turn to shrug as she struggled to put into words the thoughts that had been teasing at her subconscious all day long. "Do you know about that man who died while running?"

"Sure I do."

"The coroner apparently suspects foul play. Which means yet another person was angry enough to cause harm." She stepped behind the information desk and sat down on the stool. "But who does these things? And why?"

Fred turned around and leaned forward on the counter, his triceps bulging from the pressure on his forearms. "I'm not a cop but I read. And all those thriller novels can't be wrong, can they?"

"I don't follow."

"What drives people to kill in all those books? Revenge, greed, jealousy, betrayal, right? I imagine those same things can apply to someone who would want to set a fire, too."

"It's a good thing I wasn't the killer type two years ago," Tori quipped, the words flowing from her mouth without any sort of filter. When her brain caught up, she swallowed. Hard. "Oh, wait, that didn't sound right."

A smile spread across Fred's face. "Oh no. You

don't get to say something like that and then get all prissy."

"Prissy?" she echoed.

"C'mon, spill it, Miss Victoria. Who would you have killed two years ago?"

She shot both hands up. "I wouldn't have killed anyone. I don't have it in me."

He made a face. "Like I needed you to clarify that. C'mon. Who would you have killed if you had it in you?"

She gave in. "Well, based on your list, I would have beat whoever killed Jeff to the punch. I did, after all, have betrayal and revenge as motive."

"Whoever killed Jeff? Who's Jeff?"

"The guy who dropped dead in the middle of Sweet Briar last week."

Fred's mouth hung open.

"I knew him. From Chicago. We were engaged at one time."

His mouth slammed shut.

"He cheated on me with a mutual friend and I called off the engagement."

A long, low whistle escaped through Fred's lips. "Wow-ee, I had no idea."

"It's not exactly the kind of information you share when you're new in town."

He laughed. "Well, that certainly narrows the field for who might have done him in."

"How so?"

"If he betrayed you, you can bet he betrayed

some other unsuspecting female. Clowns like that have a pattern of hurting women. Makes them feel powerful, I guess."

She considered the fire chief's words, compared them with the things she already knew about the Jeff of today, or, rather, the Jeff of last week. Had he done the same thing to Julia that he'd done to her? And what about Kelly? She certainly seemed to think the world of Jeff at the funeral home, yet Jeff had been nothing short of rude to her in return. Ditto to how he'd talked to her on the phone while standing on Tori's front—

"Oh. Oh my," she mumbled. "I may have just come up with a"—she looked up, felt her face warm under Fred's scrutiny—"never mind. I'm rambling again."

"Sounds to me like something just rang a bell of truth in that pretty little head of yours."

Had it? Or was she grasping at straws?

"Maybe." She reached her arms above her head and stretched them toward the ceiling. "People are hard to figure out sometimes, aren't they?"

Fred pushed off the counter and tipped his ball hat to Tori. "Only if you try, Victoria. Only if you try." He repositioned his hat atop his hair and studied her closely. "Can I walk you out to your car?"

"I don't have my car. Margaret Louise dropped me off on our way back from the mountains."

"Then can I drive you home?"

For a moment, she considered it, the pull of her bed and the safety of her little cottage beckoning like a lighthouse in a storm. But, in the end, a stronger, more comforting force won out.

She glanced at the clock on the wall then turned back to Fred.

"Actually, it's still plenty light out. I think I'm going to head over to Debbie's and get a little treat before calling it quits for the night. Sugar helps me think."

His hearty laugh boomed around the room. "Sugar helps you think? Hmmm, that's not one I've heard before."

"You're not a woman."

"True." He wandered over to the door, stopping to look at her one last time. "You need anything, give me a call, okay? And quit worrying about who rigged your office. We'll take care of that. You just concentrate on getting that kids' room back up to speed."

She smiled her first real smile all day. "You've got yourself a deal."

A deal she knew she'd break even as he walked out the door. Worrying was in her nature. Especially when it involved the library or people she cared about.

Taking in the clock one more time, she pulled her cell phone from her pocket and dialed the familiar number.

It was answered on the second ring.

"Meet you at Debbie's?"

"I'll meet you there," she repeated as the calm that had been eluding her all day finally settled over her heart. Margaret Louise's unwavering sense of loyalty had a way of doing that for her, as did the woman's fifth grandchild.

Lulu . . .

From the moment she'd first laid eyes on Lulu while reading to the child's class nearly two years earlier, she'd felt a connection with the little girl. A connection that went far beyond their shared love of Little House books. She'd tried to smoke it out, to put her finger on the exact reason the two had bonded, but she'd been unsuccessful beyond the obvious. Lulu Davis was simply a sweet little girl who brought sunshine and hope wherever she went.

"Any chance you could bring along a certain somebody? I could use a few of her hugs right about now."

"Done."

"Done?" Tori repeated, dumbfounded. "But how? I just asked."

"Anticipation is my strong suit."

She laughed. "One of many, Margaret Louise. One of many."

"Want us to swing by and pick you up?"

The offer, while enticing, was one she turned down in favor of a little exercise and some fresh air. The walk would do her good. Besides, it would give her an opportunity to shake off any residual glumness before she came face-to-face with Lulu.

Part of the child's charm was the way in which she embraced her childhood—the innocence, the fun, the joy. The last thing Tori wanted to do was mar that in any way.

"I think I'll walk. It's a beautiful evening." She stepped off the stool and pushed it against the counter. "Can you meet there in about ten minutes?"

"We'll be waiting."

Closing the phone in her hand, Tori walked across the room, pausing at the hallway that led to her office. Was there a clue somewhere Fred may have missed? Something to indicate the who behind the act?

It's not your job . . .

Inhaling sharply, she forced her feet to bypass the hallway and head toward the front door. Once there, she shut off the lights, stepped outside, and locked the door, stopping to double- and triple-check her efforts.

She knew Chief Dallas would be patrolling the grounds, knew that every person who drove by the library would be on alert for anything amiss, but still, she hesitated. Someone had tried to do the building harm once. Who was to stop them from coming back again and finishing the job?

Slowly, she descended the steps, the heat of the

day finally settling into a more tolerable evening. She moved slowly across the grounds, the hundred-year-old moss trees providing a canopied walkway from the front door to the sidewalk. When she reached Main Street, she turned left, the pull of seeing Lulu guiding her steps the rest of the way until she found herself at Debbie's Bakery.

The bakery itself was the fulfillment of a lifelong dream for fellow circle member, Debbie Calhoun. The fact that it was thriving beyond the mother of two's wildest dreams was a testament to just how hard she'd worked for that dream.

Tori pushed the glass door open and stopped, breathing in the potpourri of aromas that pulled her stomach in so many different directions.

"Miss Sinclair! Miss Sinclair! You're here!" Lulu jumped off the lattice-back chair she'd claimed to the right of the door and ran toward Tori, her long black braids flapping against her back.

Tori leaned down and wrapped her arms around the little girl. "Hi, Lulu! How are you, sweetie? Did you have a nice weekend with your dad?"

Lulu hugged Tori even harder, her head bobbing up and down against Tori's cheek. "We camped in the middle of the family room and it was so much fun!" The little girl stepped back and peered up at Tori. "But I missed Mommy and Molly Sue. Mee-Maw, too."

She ran a hand across the top of Lulu's head, reveling in the feel of the child's soft hair. "They missed you, too. But now you all have lots of stories to tell each other, don't you?"

Lulu grinned. "I made a story about our weekend so I could read it to Molly Sue. I even made pictures to go with each page. Though my pictures aren't as good as the ones that lady takes."

She followed the path of Lulu's finger, her smile widening at the sight of Margaret Louise and a bandana-wearing Lynn Calder bent over a package of photos. "I bet your pictures are even more special."

"But hers are real."

Reaching out, she tugged Lulu's left braid. "So are yours. The difference is, you used your own imagination on your pictures. Mrs. Calder's camera simply recorded what it saw. Now, can I get you a treat?"

"Nah, Mee-Maw got me a brownie. She got one for you, too. They're the same kind Mr. Wentworth got me last week."

Just the mere mention of Milo's name brought a longing deep in her soul. Oh, how she couldn't wait for his summer program to be over.

"He got it for me 'cause I helped him with his homework just like he used to help me with mine." Lulu bent forward, her breath warm against Tori's ear. "They're really, really chocolaty and gooey."

Her stomach growled. "Chocolaty and gooey, huh?"

Lulu's eyes sparkled. "C'mon. Follow me."

When they reached the four-top table Margaret Louise had secured, Lulu climbed into her chair and patted the one next to her. "I saved this seat special for you, Miss Sinclair."

"Thank you, Lulu." She turned to the pair looking at pictures. "It's good to see you again, Lynn. How are you?"

A slow smile broke out across the woman's tired face. "I'm doing okay. Spent the afternoon with Rose working in her garden."

Margaret Louise handed the stack of photos to Tori. "You should see Lynn's garden. Looks like somethin' out of some fancy magazine."

Lynn blushed.

"Can I see?" Lulu asked.

"Of course." Tori slid onto her chair and pulled Lulu closer, the top picture on the stack nearly taking her breath away. "Oh, these are so pretty. What are they?"

"Those are crepe myrtles," Lynn explained. "It's a flowering shrub with clusters of white, pink, and lavender blooms. They're one of my favorite."

"I can see why," she whispered as she shifted

the picture to the bottom of the pile and studied the next one in the stack.

"I like those ones! They're real tiny," Lulu said.

Lynn nodded her agreement. "Those are Osmantheis and they're a very fragrant flower."

She nodded, taking in the information as Lulu moved the picture to the bottom, both of them releasing an "oohh" at the sight of the purple bell-shaped flower now on top.

"That's the common foxglove plant."

"It's beautiful."

Lulu slid the picture off the top and tucked it underneath the rest, her body suddenly bouncing next to Tori. "I remember that lady!"

Tori stared down at the fair-skinned blonde with the long tresses. "That's Kelly. Jeff's girlfriend." She looked up at Lynn. "How's she doing?"

Lynn shrugged. "Hard to tell. She's not exactly what you'd call open, or even friendly. She hightailed it out of here about four days ago. Haven't heard from her since, though, now that his death's been classified as a—"

Margaret Louise coughed. Loudly. Then jerked her head in Lulu's direction.

Tori's heart sank. They'd come much too close to speaking of things Lulu had no need to hear.

"She gave me a lollipop when I saw her. A great big red one!"

Lulu's words broke through her wool-gathering. "Who gave you a lollipop?"

"That lady," Lulu said, pointing at the picture of Kelly. "She gave it to me that day we were at the library, Mee-Maw. Remember?"

Margaret Louise cocked her head to the right and pondered her granddaughter's words. "Yes. Yes, I remember. We had to leave the children's room because Sally was in a snit 'bout not gettin' a lollipop, too."

"Where was I?" Tori inquired.

"Dixie was covering while you checked in on Nina."

"Oh." She stared down at the photograph, noting the many features that probably attracted Jeff in the first place. The toned body, the voluptuous curves, and the pretty face. Though, falling for a reader was a bit of a surprise.

"She only had one lollipop. Her other hand had one of those turny things Daddy uses."

"Turny things?" Tori asked, shaking her focus from the picture to the little girl beside her. "What turny things?"

"That thing Daddy uses when he has to put a battery in one of our toys."

She looked a question at Margaret Louise. "Turny thing?"

"A screwdriver." Margaret Louise furrowed her brow at Lulu. "Land sakes, child, why would that woman have a screwdriver in the children's room?"

Lulu shook her head emphatically. "She wasn't in the children's room, Mee-Maw. She was in Miss Sinclair's office."

"My office?" she echoed with a voice that was suddenly shrill. "Why was she in my . . ." The words slipped from her mouth as a roar filled her ears, a near-deafening sound broken only by the sound of Margaret Louise's gasp.

Chapter 22

There was something about sitting in Margaret Louise's kitchen that calmed Tori, made her feel as if everything was going to be okay, one way or the other. She supposed some of that was the cheerful artwork and magnetic alphabet letters that covered nearly every square inch of the grandmother's refrigerator, creating an atmosphere of warmth and love and innocence. The rest, though, came from the woman who lived there—a woman who exuded a steady hand, a cool head, and an uncanny ability to reach into the haystack and pull out the lone needle.

"Do you think Lulu knew something was up?" Tori wrapped her hand around the water glass and peered inside, the rapidly disappearing ice cube Margaret Louise had added at the last minute a testament to the day's heat and its disregard for the late hour. "I tried not to react to what she said, I really did."

Margaret Louise lowered herself onto the chair across from Tori. "That child was too tickled by the peanut butter cup she found in the middle of her brownie 'bout the same time we put two and two together."

She hoped Margaret Louise was right.

"Two and two looks pretty damning, wouldn't you say? Especially when you take into account the fact that Jeff met this woman when she came to help her father do some electrical work at the gym where he worked."

"I'd say." Margaret Louise stretched her short pudgy legs beneath the table and leaned back, a smile still playing on her lips despite the creasing between her brows. "Guess what I said the other day was more on the mark than I realized."

"What are you talking about?" Tori asked as she studied her friend. Despite their twin status, Margaret Louise and Leona were as different as night and day, putting a capital *F* on *fraternal* in a way she'd never seen before. Where Leona was thin and stylish, Margaret Louise was plump and casual. Where Leona was a stickler for rules, Margaret Louise was more carefree. Where Leona tended to exercise skepticism, Margaret Louise was willing to give it a shot and see what happened.

"You know, what I said when you got back to the cabin yesterday afternoon. 'Bout the fire in your office bein' more 'bout you than the library."

"But why would Kelly be after me?" It was a rhetorical question, really, especially since the answer popped in her head before she'd even finished the sentence. "Wait. Don't answer that.

She saw me as a threat to her relationship with Jeff."

"Sounds 'bout right to me. Though I'm thinkin' she should have been bringin' you presents for that instead of tryin' to set your things on fire." Extending her index finger outward, Margaret Louise chased a drop of condensation down the outside of her own glass.

Tori lifted her glass to her mouth, pausing it mere inches from her lips. "Presents?"

"From what I saw with my own two eyes while he was in town, she'd have been better off without him." Margaret Louise inspected her finger and then popped it in her mouth. "Now she's probably goin' to be sittin' in jail on charges of arson and murder."

Tori choked on her water. "M-murder? What are you talking about?"

"That's the two and two I put together while droppin' Lulu off at her Mamma and Daddy's just now."

She stared at her friend. "You think she killed Jeff?"

"Of course. If green eyes could make her rig a room, then anger could certainly make her kill."

Anything was possible. Tori, of all people, knew that. But still, it was hard to imagine the fair-skinned blonde she'd seen at the funeral home setting fires and—

"We still don't know how Jeff died, do we?"

Margaret Louise shook her head. "Not that I've heard. Seems his family would hear somethin' first."

Pushing back her chair, she stood, her feet moving across the room almost of their own volition. It was as if they knew their movement helped her think, plan. "Will you go with me to talk to Fred Granderson tomorrow morning? I imagine he'll want to talk to you and to Lulu, too."

"Of course. Though I"—Margaret Louise rested her chin atop her hands—"can't help but feel a little sorry for this girl. Can you imagine bein' so caught up on someone that you take leave of all common sense? I mean, where is her *mama?*"

She stopped in front of the window that overlooked the side yard, a cornucopia of toys strewn across the grass. "Striking a match might be considered a rash act. But to unscrew a wall plate, rig a device to the inside, put the plate back on, and then wait for someone to use it? In a public building? That took thought." Hearing the heightened pitch to her voice, she turned to face the table. "Margaret Louise, I'm sorry, I'm not angry with you. I'm just . . . I don't know. Sad, frustrated, disgusted. And if she really killed Jeff, she deserves to be locked up."

"You still have feelin's for that man?"

Her mouth gaped open. "Feelings? For Jeff?

259

No! I just don't think he deserved to be murdered." She ran a hand through her hair. "Was he a jerk at times? Absolutely. The worst kind of jerk, quite frankly. But that didn't mean he should have his life taken from him."

Margaret Louise dropped her hands to her side and shrugged. "I know you're right, Victoria. I guess I'm just havin' a hard time rustlin' up any sympathy for a man who hurt someone as special as you. And I'm not the only one. Leona feels exactly the same way as I do. So does Rose. Milo, too."

"You've talked to Milo?"

"Just last week. He needed a little help from Lulu with a project—"

"Last week? Last week, when?" She thought back through the weekend. "You mean Friday night?"

"No. I was at the cabin Friday night. This was Tuesday morning. I remember because we met Milo right after Sally's swim class. It wasn't quite noon, but I let him buy the girls brownies anyway."

"He was here Tuesday? Why didn't he tell me?"

Margaret Louise drained the last of her water glass and then wiped the back of her hand across her mouth. "He said it had to be a quick stop and he didn't want to upset you by breezin' in and out so fast."

She reclaimed her chair at the table. "Let me get this straight. He drove all the way to Sweet Briar to work with Lulu and then drove all the way back to his hotel that same day? Without telling me?"

"He drove here and back all in that same *mornin'*, actually. But don't you fret none, Victoria. He wanted to see you, I can attest to that. He just didn't want to upset you, is all."

"Upset me? Why?" But even as the question left her lips, she knew the answer. Milo had offered to come back when they'd spoken on the phone Monday night, yet she'd begged him not to, reassuring him again and again that she was fine despite the conversation he'd overheard between her and Jeff.

"It's a good thing he *didn't* stop by the library after those brownies, 'cause you'd have been too preoccupied to pay him any attention, anyway."

"Preoccupied?" She stared at her friend, her thoughts running in one unending loop of confusion. "What are you talking about?"

"He was here *Tuesday,* Victoria. The same day that ex-fiancé of yours was murdered." Margaret Louise reached across the table and patted Tori's hand. "That man is crazy 'bout you, Victoria. Seein' you shed so much as a tear over Jeff might have crushed him. Remember how you were last spring when his old college girlfriend blew into town?"

Her shoulders slumped. "I guess you're right."

"What matters is the fact that he'll be home for good tomorrow evenin', just in time for all this nonsense to be wrapped up."

She met her friend's gaze head-on. "You really think Kelly is the answer to all of this? The library, Jeff's death?"

"I'd have to have my head examined if I didn't."

Margaret Louise was right. The pieces fit perfectly.

Rising from the table once again, Tori carried her water glass to the sink and set it inside. "It's getting late, I better go."

"What time should Lulu and I meet you to talk to Fred Granderson?"

"About nine, maybe?"

"We'll be there." Margaret Louise stood and followed Tori to the door, only to stop midway and double back. "I realized, in all the commotion, that Lynn's pictures ended up in my purse. Any chance you could run them by her house on your way home? It's a little out of your way but I feel bad havin' them. Those flowers seem to give her such joy."

The idea of driving on the country roads that separated Sweet Briar from Lee Station sounded perfect at the moment. The time alone would give her a chance to think, process.

"I'd be happy to run them out to her house. But

let's hold on to the picture that had Kelly in it. Fred Granderson might want to see it for himself."

"Good thinkin'." Margaret Louise pulled the sleeve of pictures from her oversized purse and opened them, sifting through the contents for Kelly's image. "You want to hold on to this one or should I?"

She waved aside the photograph and reached, instead, for the remaining pictures. "Why don't you keep it? I've seen enough." Tori brushed a kiss across Margaret Louise's rounded cheek. "Thank you. For everything. I don't know what I'd do without you."

"The feelin' is mutual."

Tori paused with her hand at the door and inhaled deeply, second thoughts flooding her mind in rapid succession. What on earth had she been thinking when she agreed to bring the pictures out to Lynn? Surely she could have turned up the radio in her living room and belted out the lyrics just as loudly from the comfort of her armchair as she had in the car.

And if she had, she wouldn't be standing on Garrett Calder's front porch, trying to figure out what, exactly, one should say to a man about the death of a pseudo relative he wasn't particularly crazy about in the first place. Especially when she had a history with said relative.

"Ugh, ugh, ugh," she mumbled as she looked from the packet of pictures to the door and back again. "Nothing like walking into a hornet's nest."

Then again, Garrett had a mistress. So maybe, just maybe, he wasn't even home.

She lifted her finger and pushed the doorbell, the sound wafting through the screen.

A chair squeaked somewhere inside, followed by the sound of footsteps and Lynn's voice. "Who's there?"

Her shoulders sagged with relief as the woman she barely knew came into view. Even if Garrett were home, she might be able to do the handoff and be gone before he even had a clue.

"Hi, Lynn." She held the package of pictures up to the screen and smiled. "Margaret Louise asked me to bring these to you. I guess they got mixed up with her things at the bakery earlier this evening."

"I think it's more likely I forgot. Seem to be doing a lot of that lately." Lynn pushed the screen door open. "Don't know if it's the stress of the last week or so that's getting to me or not, but I just haven't been feeling like myself these last few days."

The instinct to decline the invitation disappeared as she studied the woman closely. Whatever strength she'd seen in Lynn's eyes during treatment seemed muted at best, the woman's hand self-consciously tugging at the bandana her chemo necessitated.

"Are you okay?" she asked as she stepped inside. "Is there anything I can do?"

"Not really. I'm just having a down-on-myself kind of day." Lynn led the way toward a small parlor off the hallway. "I have those sometimes. Comes with looking like this."

Her heart ached for the woman who fought the kind of daily battle she could only imagine. "Do you know what I see when I look at you?"

"A bald woman who looks like she's in her late fifties instead of her mid-forties?"

Tori shook her head. "I see a woman with spunk and tenacity, a woman who has been thrown the kind of curveballs that would make anyone stop and scream. Yet you keep standing. And fighting."

A hint of crimson rose in Lynn's face just before her gaze dropped to the ground. "I—I don't know what to say."

"Then don't." Tori swept her hand toward the couch, setting her purse at the base. "I have a few minutes if you'd like to visit. Are you alone?"

Discomfort morphed into amusement as Lynn lowered herself to the sofa. "Who else would be here? My faithless husband?"

She couldn't help but pity the woman beside her, pity the loneliness and despair that surely came from navigating one's way around life's potholes alone. "Why do you stay?" she finally asked.

Lynn reached up, pulled the bandana from her head, and pointed at the peach fuzz that covered her otherwise bald scalp. "Staying is my only chance of survival."

"Don't you have family? People that could help keep a roof over your head while you fight this?"

"It's not the roof I need. It's the insurance."

She stared at Lynn. "Can't you get some sort of insurance when you first leave?"

"For three years, sure. If I'm dead inside that time, it works. But if I'm not, then what? No insurance company is going to want to touch me with a ten-foot pole. Not without charging me premiums only the wealthy can afford." Lynn leaned her head against the back of the sofa and released a weary sigh. "And I am not a wealthy person."

Anxious to find something, anything to lessen the charge she felt in the room, Tori inventoried their surroundings, her gaze moving across shelves of books and knickknack strewn tables before coming to rest on the framed photographs that graced the wooden mantel. Most of the faces she recognized as ones she'd seen in Jeff's albums—a youthful Vera at the beach, an older Vera on the day she married Garrett's father, and Jeff as he crossed the finish line of his very first marathon nearly a decade earlier. In the opposite corner was a smaller framed photograph of a much younger, healthier Lynn on her wedding day, surrounded by her bridesmaids.

They were the kind of pictures you expected to see in a person's house with one exception. Not a single, solitary shot of Garrett could be found anywhere.

"I'm surprised there's a picture of Jeff on your mantel," Tori said aloud, her mouth putting words to her thoughts. "I never thought he and Garrett were terribly close."

"If it was our mantel, it wouldn't be there."

She pulled her attention from the photographs and fixed it on Lynn. "What are you saying?"

Lynn tossed her bandana onto the coffee table in front of them. "This was Vera's house."

"Vera's house?" she echoed. "But why? I thought Vera and Garrett locked horns all the time."

Bitterness replaced fatigue in Lynn's voice. "They do—I mean, did. But when you take your paycheck to the horse track each week and have a girlfriend to wine and dine, a home mortgage can be rather draining."

She swallowed back the desire to scream. "So you stay here and put up with this man because why?"

"So I can live."

Reaching across the cushion that separated

them, Tori patted Lynn's knee. "I'm so sorry. I truly am."

Lynn shrugged. "It wasn't so bad. Vera was actually pretty good to me most of the time."

"So what happens now that Vera is gone? Do you get to stay here?"

Relief swept across the woman's lined face. "I do. She left the house to me."

"You mean to Garrett?"

"No. To me."

She laughed. "Wow. That must have made him mad."

A smile played at the corners of Lynn's lips. "I imagine it did, though that's not what had his undies in a bunch when Vera's attorney stopped by after her funeral."

"What then?"

"She left her money to Jeff, not Garrett. He was only named as a secondary to appease her late husband."

Ah yes, the inheritance that had emboldened an already bold man to show up on Tori's doorstep and ask for a second chance.

"Well, it's that move that probably cost Jeff his life," she mumbled.

"I couldn't agree more." Lynn pushed off the couch and walked to the center of the room. "Can I get you something to drink? Eat? I have some freshly made lemonade in the refrigerator."

She glanced at her watch and noted the late

hour. If she didn't get going soon, she wouldn't be able to call Milo before bed. "I'd love to, Lynn, I really would. But I have to get home and get some sleep. I have a big day ahead of me. I've got to get a cleaning company into the library to see what they can do about the smoke smell."

Lynn wandered over to the mantel and swiped her hand across the dust-covered surface. "I heard about the fire. I'm sorry."

"So am I. Though, now, thanks to your pictures, we know who did it."

"I was wondering what all those looks between you and Margaret Louise were this evening. I wanted to ask but I got the impression you didn't want to talk about it in front of the granddaughter."

"Thank you for that," she said, flashing a smile at Lynn. "Seems Jeff's latest girlfriend had an ax to grind with me—an ax she opted to grind after Jeff got his money and came knocking at my door."

The woman's brows furrowed. "Kelly?"

Tori nodded. "The best I can figure is she was jealous about Jeff trying to get me back and decided to seek a little revenge."

"Kelly started the fire?"

"Looks like it." Tori hoisted her purse onto the couch and rooted around inside it for her keys. When she located them, she rose to her feet and headed toward the front door. "And you know what? If I was a gambler like Garrett, I'd put my money on Kelly as a suspect in Jeff's murder as well."

A low mirthless laugh followed her out onto the porch as Lynn let the screen door shut between them. "If you did, you'd be living under someone else's roof, too."

Chapter 23

By the time she got home and finished her call to Milo, she was exhausted. Absolutely, positively exhausted.

Yet, if she was honest with herself, it was the kind of exhaustion that had nothing whatsoever to do with her hellishly long day and everything to do with the hopelessness that had gripped her heart the moment she stepped off Lynn's porch.

Try as she might, she simply couldn't shake the image of the woman standing in the door as Tori pulled away, the mixture of concern and sadness she saw in her face drowning out everything else.

Favorite songs hadn't erased the image.

The thrill of a few hairpin turns hadn't erased the image.

The warmth of Milo's voice in her ear hadn't erased the image, either.

And she knew why.

Lynn was in pain. The kind of pain that gripped your heart and made you doubt everything about the world as well as yourself. Tori knew that pain, remembered that pain, and it was enough to make her ache for this woman she barely knew. Toss in the fact Lynn was sick, too, and, well, it was the kind of reality that made Tori restless to do something.

The problem, though, was figuring out what that something was or could be.

Having Jeff humiliate her in front of her friends and family two years earlier had been devastating but she'd been able to move on, to pick herself up and brush herself off. Lynn couldn't do that. The woman's health situation made it impossible for her to move on, forcing her, instead, to live with the humiliation that came from Garrett's behavior day in and day out.

She flopped onto her bed and stared up at the ceiling, her hand blindly reaching for the neck pillow she preferred to hug while deep in thought. It was incomprehensible to her how Lynn could look the other way at Vera's wake as Garrett so boldly positioned his mistress beside him in the receiving line.

It took guts and class to handle such a hideous act of betrayal in the way in which Lynn had that day. The kind of guts and class Tori wasn't sure she could have possessed under the same circumstances.

Yet *Lynn* was the one struck by a life-threatening disease?

It was the kind of life question for which there was no answer, the kind of cruel irony that propelled her to search out ways to make things better. But, short of standing Garrett in the middle of the Sweet Briar town square and handing rocks to every woman she knew, she was at a loss on how.

And while the stoning image was appealing, it wouldn't make things better. In fact, it would probably make things worse for a woman who counted on the louse for the very life he was crushing with his behavior.

"At least she has the house," she whispered into the darkness, the statement bringing little comfort in return.

If Lynn was healthy, she could leave, start a new life far away from Garrett Calder. But she wasn't.

One by one she considered and discarded various ways she could help . . .

She could hold a fundraiser.

She could draft her friends to make dinners.

She could meet with Garrett and beg him to be a man.

But none of them would be enough for the long haul or someone battling the kind of breast cancer Lynn had. *That* would take a miracle. The kind of miracle Tori was incapable of setting in motion.

Hence the feeling of hopelessness that had not only made the drive home with her but also seemed poised and ready to spend the night.

In three days Milo would be home. There would be time enough to ask him the nagging questions that had surfaced at the bakery, and time enough to bounce her concerns for Lynn off his always understanding ears.

For now, though, she had to find a way to push the things she couldn't change to the background in favor of the things she could.

Top on the list? Kelly's probable hand in the library fire and her equally likely involvement in Jeff's death.

While the former was a subject she looked forward to addressing, the latter was sure to rustle up feelings she longed to bury once and for all.

Baby steps.

She rolled onto her side and stared at the digital clock on her nightstand.

10:30

Oh, how she longed to call Leona, to work through some of the emotions tugging her heart in too many directions at one time. But she couldn't. It was simply too late.

Or was it?

Nibbling her lower lip inward, she ran through the pros and cons of calling her friend at such a late hour, the empty pro column winning out in the end.

If she thought she was a sight, standing there on Leona's front porch, pink fuzzy slippers in hand and an overnight bag slung over her arm, she hadn't properly imagined Leona.

The Leona she knew wore fitted suits and stylish heels, sported a flawlessly made-up face, and always touted whatever purse was all the rage at the moment. The Leona standing in front of her now was, well, different.

As in, night and day different.

She tried not to gawk, she really did, but, if the exasperated glint in Leona's eyes was any indication, she was hugely unsuccessful.

"Is there a problem, dear?" Leona said as her unpolished fingers settled on her fuzzy pink hips. "I mean, beyond the fact that you woke me from a peaceful slumber and hoodwinked me into inviting you over?"

Her mouth gaped open. "Hoodwinked?"

"Would you prefer coerced? Or, perhaps, strong-armed?"

"Leona, I just called to talk. If you'd told me you were tired, I'd have simply called back tomorrow."

"And what kind of friend would that have made me? I've already been unfairly branded in that regard." Leona jutted her chin into the air and then spun around. "Follow me, I've moved Paris and her babies into my room and made the guest bed up for you. Do you like cookies and milk before bed or do you prefer tea?"

She closed her mouth only to let it flap back open. "Y-you made cookies?"

Leona rolled her eyes. "Good heavens,

Victoria, no. I bought them this afternoon. Paris likes a nibble before bed and I wanted to make sure she had nothing but the best after her very busy weekend."

Shaking her head free of any lingering shock, Tori forced herself to get it together. "How is our little Ms. Paris doing this evening?"

"Well, thank you. Although I imagine having all those babies hanging all over her would be draining."

No pun intended.

To Leona she simply nodded. "And the babies? How are they?"

The left corner of Leona's mouth twitched ever so slightly. "They're marvelous. So very, very sweet."

She followed Leona into the master bedroom and peeked into the cushioned box that had been created for the new family. "Oh, Leona, they're even cuter now than they were at the cabin."

Leona beamed. "Would you really expect anything less from my little Paris?"

She couldn't help but laugh. "Now that we know Paris is a girl, no."

Leona kneeled beside the box and reached her hand inside, her fingers taking a moment to stroke the head of each and every baby before lingering on Paris. "I've been on the computer all evening learning everything I can about baby bunnies. Did you know that they can start eating carrots when they're just eight days old? And they can be weaned from Paris by the time they're just two weeks old?"

It was a charge to watch Leona taking such an interest in the care and nurture of these unexpected additions to her family and Tori said as much out loud.

"What do you expect me to do?" Leona accused. "Cower in the corner with my hands over my ears begging for someone to ride to my rescue?"

Cower wouldn't necessarily have been Tori's choice of words, a fact she opted to keep to herself. Instead, she squatted down beside her friend and lifted the white and gray spotted baby from the box, instinctively drawing it to her chest for extra warmth. "I think your offer to let Rose have this one was very special. It meant a lot to her."

Leona waved her words aside. "I have my moments, I suppose."

She met her friend's gaze and held it for a beat. "You have many, Leona. You really do. It's why I'm here, I guess."

Reaching across the box, Leona extracted Patches from Tori's arms and set her beside a nose-twitching Paris. "What has you so upset, dear?"

And, just like that, the reality of her evening yanked her back to a place that was a little less warm, a little less sweet. "Can we talk in another room? I don't want to keep Paris up."

Leona nodded and stood, blowing a kiss at the rabbits as she did. "I think that's a good idea. Childbirth can be fatiguing."

Tori bit back the urge to make a joke, a joke she'd have thought nothing of making before learning of Leona's painful past. Instead, she followed her friend out into the kitchen and claimed a spot with her back to the plateglass window that overlooked Leona's French patio.

"Have you talked to your sister this evening?" She leaned back in her chair and allowed Leona to plunk down a plate of Debbie's chocolate chip cookies and a lone glass of milk. "Are you going to have some?"

Leona pivoted on her footy pajamas and reached into the cabinet above the sink, extracting a wine goblet. "I need something more soothing. Becoming a grandmother has a way of unsettling your nerves."

She laughed. "I can only imagine."

With quiet consideration, Leona selected her wine and poured it into her glass before taking a seat across the table from Tori. "So tell me, what brings you by at"—the woman peered up at the clock anchored just above the sink—"such an undignified hour?"

Gripping her glass to her chest, she met

Leona's questioning eyes. "Thanks to your great-niece, I think I know who started the fire in my office."

"My great-niece?"

"Lulu."

Leona rolled her eyes. "Victoria, dear, I know you think the world of that little girl and it's sweet, really. But to credit her for solving crimes? Isn't that a bit over the top?"

"No." She released her glass and reached for the plate of cookies. "She identified the suspect in a picture and was able to describe the kind of actions that make it virtually certain."

Tipping her head downward, Leona stared at her over the top of her glasses. "Suspect? Suspect? Have I not tried to teach you to act more ladylike? To leave the cops and robbers routine to the proper authorities?"

It was Tori's turn to roll her eyes. "In the past two years, anytime I've gotten involved is when those proper authorities of which you speak weren't doing their job in the way that they should. I found my efforts a better choice than sitting back, watching people I care about getting railroaded for things they didn't do."

Leona lifted her wineglass to her lips and took a sip. "And now, dear?"

"The fire just happened. The investigation is brand-new. But when someone sits right next to you and points a reliable finger toward the answer we're seeking, it's hard to turn and look the other way."

"A reliable finger? Isn't that overstating things just a little? Lulu is only, what? Ten?"

She paused, a larger piece of cookie just outside her lips. "She pointed at a picture of Kelly."

"And Robert is supposed to just throw this woman in jail on account of a ten-year-old?" Leona took another sip of her wine, closing her eyes as it slid down her throat. "My condolences to Kelly." Opening her eyes, Leona sat up tall. "Did you say, Kelly? As in the Kelly who was dating that weasel of a man you were once engaged to?"

She lifted a cookie from the plate and toasted it against the side of Leona's wineglass. "One and the same."

Leona's brows furrowed. "A fire. Hmmm. I wonder why that never crossed my mind with Emmett."

"Hey! That's not funny." Tori set the cookie on the table in front of her and stared down at it. "First of all, I wasn't going after her boyfriend. Second of all, she could have *killed* someone."

"You may not have been going after her boyfriend but her boyfriend was certainly going after you." Leona pushed her wineglass into the center of the table and helped herself to the smallest cookie on the plate. Staring at it as if it were a foreign object rather than a staple in many homes, she shrugged. "Jealousy is certainly a powerful motive."

"Exactly."

Leona cocked her head to the side and studied Tori closely. "Where is this woman now?"

"I don't know. Chicago, I imagine. I don't think she expected Jeff's body to be detained the way it has."

"Did you know that *betrayal* is a popular motive for committing a crime as well?"

She nibbled back the urge to laugh. "You better be careful, Leona Elkin, you just might start saying a word like *suspect* all on your own."

"The only reason I know about motive is from that detective show on the Uniform Network," Leona explained.

"*Uniform* Network?"

Leona grinned. "Men in uniforms twenty-four/seven."

It felt good to laugh, to release some of the tension that had been weighing her down in waves for weeks now. "I didn't betray anyone."

"You might not have, dear, but Jeff certainly did."

She wished she could object, but she couldn't. Leona's comment simply shored up a possibility that had been nagging at her heart since Lulu was able to put Kelly at the scene of the fire. "I can sort of see why she may have been jealous about Jeff seeking me out when they were supposed to be involved. I can even see why she might do something stupid like lash out at me. But to kill Jeff? Wouldn't that kind of defeat the purpose?"

"Only if they were still dating, dear. Which, after the way that man spoke to her while standing on your front porch, is highly doubtful."

Leona's comment brought her up short. Had Kelly given Jeff the old heave-ho? Or had Jeff done the deed, prompting her to lash out in tragic fashion?

It could certainly fit.

Plus it would eliminate that irrational fear that kept bobbing up and down in her psyche. A fear that stemmed from knowing Milo had been in town the day Jeff died.

"What is that look about, dear?"

She shifted in her seat. "Look? What look?"

Leona made a face. "Don't be coy, dear. I'm a master at the ploy."

She laughed. "A master, huh?"

"What else is bothering you?"

Should she tell? Admit to having some reservations where Milo was concerned?

No. Not yet. Not until things with Kelly were more clear. To say anything sooner would only invite questions Tori didn't know how to answer.

She searched for something else to say,

something to explain away the worry she knew Leona had detected. "I'm worried about Lynn. Her life is so sad."

"Who on earth is—oh, yes, Rose's friend from the hospital."

Tori rushed to offer further clarification. "The woman married to Jeff's stepcousin."

"Doesn't her husband have that cliché mistress we saw sashaying around the funeral home?"

"One and the same," she confirmed.

"Perhaps Lynn might do well to solicit tips from Kelly."

Indeed.

"She can't leave him the way you and I did. Because, if she does, she won't be able to treat her cancer."

Something resembling anger flashed in Leona's eyes. "What can we do to help? Offer to string him up by his various parts?"

"Actually, a stoning went through my head," Tori admitted.

Leona shook her head. "Too good for him. He needs to suffer more."

"While that notion is more than a little appealing, I think our efforts would be better served helping Lynn. I just don't know how."

"Perhaps a bunny would help?"

She smiled. "Maybe. But let's give it a little more thought, okay?"

Leona nodded, then reached across the table

and patted Tori's arm. "Can I tell you something?"

"Of course."

"I made a choice all those years ago to never put my heart on the line the way I did with Emmett ever again. Looking back, I wonder sometimes if I made a mistake."

She covered Leona's hand with her own and waited, the woman's naked honesty catching her by surprise.

"Not because I didn't get married, mind you. But because I never had the chance to be a mother."

Her mouth gaped open. Who was this woman sitting across the table—this woman who avoided children like the plague and doused herself in antibacterial sanitizer every time she came in contact with her great-nieces and -nephews?

"Close your mouth, dear, it's a most unflattering pose," Leona reprimanded.

She closed her mouth.

"And don't stare, it's rude."

She averted her gaze to the nearly empty cookie plate in the center of the table only to look back at Leona seconds later. Wide-eyed.

Leona rolled her eyes skyward. "Oh trust me, I have no bizarre longing for stretch marks and photographs of me posing with a stomach the size of Texas, because I don't. But . . ." Leona's voice trailed off as she wriggled her hand out from under Tori's. "I do believe my interrupted beauty sleep has caused me to babble."

Wrapping her hands around both of their glasses, Leona stood and carried them to the sink. "There are fresh sheets on your bed and fresh towels on the chest in the corner of your room."

Tori stood, too, the rapid change in conversation leaving her more than a little confused. But if she'd learned one thing about Leona Elkin over the past two years, it was the woman's tendency to retreat behind a prickly shell when pushed.

Whatever it was Leona had been ready to say would have to wait for another day.

Leona looked back over her shoulder as she reached the doorway leading to the bedroom hallway. "Oh, and dear? If you tell anyone about my pajamas, I will tell them you snore like a lumberjack."

Chapter 24

The morning was a blur as insurance adjusters, carpet cleaners, and various volunteers went about the business of getting the library's main room open once again. Even the children's room began to show progress as Debbie and Melissa moved in, noting what needed to be done and then dispatching their expertly assembled army of moms to make it happen.

By midday, the notion of opening the next day was looking more likely than not and Tori was beyond pleased. Still, though, she found herself looking at the wall clock or her cell phone again and again, anxious for her meeting with Fred Granderson.

She'd checked a half dozen times to make sure Margaret Louise was, in fact, coming and that the woman still had the photograph Lulu had identified. It wasn't that she couldn't relay everything Lulu had said about the woman without the picture, because she could. But she couldn't shake the feeling that two witnesses and a photograph were better than one and nothing.

"We're here, we're here," Margaret Louise bellowed as she walked through the propped open front door, a wide-eyed Lulu in tow. "Melissa got home just as the youngins were gettin' off the bus. I handed Molly Sue off to her mamma and got in the car. Next thing I knew, Lulu was clamorin' to come. Figured it couldn't hurt since she's the one who saw everything."

Tori opened her mouth to speak but clamped it shut as the woman continued. "Woo-wee ya'll did a great job in here today. Almost can't tell anything happened, can you, Lulu?"

Lulu nodded but said nothing.

"Why, if it weren't for the door bein' wide open and the yellow tape 'round the outer wall of your office, I'd think this whole business was nothin' more than a dream."

"If only that were the case," Tori mumbled, her gaze locked on an eerily quiet Lulu. "You okay, sweetie?"

Lulu looked up at Tori, swallowed, then averted her focus back to the floor.

"Lulu?" Tori bent at the waist and nudged the little girl's chin upward with her finger. "What's wrong? Are you feeling sick?"

"What happens if I'm wrong?" Lulu finally blurted. "I don't want to get that lady mad at me."

Tori's heart sank. "Do you think you're wrong?"

The child's shoulders rose and fell. "I don't know."

She looked up at Margaret Louise only to see a second, more pronounced shrug. "So you're not sure if you saw her in my office?"

Lulu shook her head. "I saw her."

"Then you're not sure if she was holding a tool like your daddy's in her hand?"

Again, the child shook her head. "I saw that, too."

She straightened up and guided Lulu into her arms, relief coursing through her body as she did. "Then you're not wrong. You simply tell the fire chief what you told your Mee-Maw and me at the bakery last night. That's all."

"Same thing I told you, ain't it, Silly Bug?"

Lulu nibbled back a grin. "Yes, Mee-Maw."

Lifting her nose into the air, Margaret Louise inhaled. "The smell ain't so bad, either. What'd you use?"

It was Tori's turn to shrug. "The carpet guys came in with a deodorizer for the carpet and another for the air and, voila."

"Hold on to their name, will you? Now that there's another grandbaby on the way, the stomach flu is goin' to be a monthlong event in Melissa and Jake's house." Despite the words, Margaret Louise couldn't be happier. One more grandbaby simply meant one more child to love.

Heavy footsteps behind them made them all turn, the backlight from the sun making it nearly impossible to see. She bobbed her head left, then right, squinting against the blinding afternoon rays.

A burly body stepped left, successfully blocking the sun from her eyes. She dropped her hand to her side and blinked once, twice.

Fred Granderson.

"Things look good around here, Victoria." Fred stepped farther into the room then gestured over his shoulder as a second figure strode into the room. "Chief Dallas is here, too."

Her stomach churned.

"Makes sense," Margaret Louise mumbled next to Tori's ear.

And it did. She just couldn't shake the near Pavlovian response the Sweet Briar police chief had instilled in her soul.

Had Tiffany Ann Gilbert not shown up dead in the library parking lot shortly after Tori moved to Sweet Briar, she'd probably regard the man like everyone else in town. But the town sweetheart had, and so Tori didn't.

Still, she tried, even forging a tenuous connection with the police chief over a homemade chocolate mousse pie following the death of Rose's next-door neighbor. And, for a while, things were okay, bordering on friendly, even. But all of that was undone when she was later questioned in the death of a local mom tied to Melissa and Beatrice, and then again in a smaller way on Friday night in regards to Jeff.

She gulped.

The chief tipped his hat. "Miss Sinclair."

"Chief."

Fred looked from the chief to Victoria and back again before rocking back on his heels and releasing a low whistle. "Hmmm . . ." He looked to Margaret Louise for help. "I hear you ladies have found a possible suspect in the fire?"

Margaret Louise pointed at Lulu. "This one is sharp as they come. Nothin' gets by my Lulu."

Fred softened his pose and smiled at Lulu. "So you saw something you think can help us?"

Tori felt Lulu's hand inside hers, forcing her to refocus, to put her issues with Chief Dallas aside. She squeezed the little girl's hand three times. "You know what you saw, Lulu. That's all you have to tell Chief Granderson. Anything that does or doesn't come from it will be up to him, not you."

Lulu looked at the floor and returned three squeezes of her own. "I saw a lady in Miss Sinclair's office when I went to the bathroom."

She saw the exchange of looks between the two men.

"Was she one of Miss Sinclair's friends?" Chief Dallas asked.

Tori clenched her teeth.

"I didn't know her."

Fred marched past them, retrieving the stool from behind the information desk and pulling it into the open room. He patted the seat. "Why don't you sit, Lulu, and tell us what you remember."

Lulu climbed onto the stool at Tori's nod and crossed her dangling sneaker-clad feet at the ankles. "She had a turny thing in her hand and she was over by that table Miss Sinclair has, the one where she keeps her snacks."

"What kind of a turny thing?" Fred asked as he crouched beside the stool. "Can you describe it?"

Margaret Louise moved in behind her granddaughter. "Describe it just the way you did to Miss Sinclair and me at the bakery."

Lulu sucked in her lower lip then released it slowly. "She had one of those things my daddy uses when he changes the battery in one of our toys. Only hers had a red handle and my daddy's has a black handle."

Fred's eyes brightened. "Wait right here, I think I have one out in my truck."

They waited as he disappeared through the front door in search of a visual aid.

Chief Dallas stepped forward. "Can you describe this lady you saw, Lulu?"

Margaret Louise held up her hand. "We can do better than that. We have a—"

Fred jogged into the room with a screwdriver in his left hand and a hammer in his right hand. He held them up in front of Lulu. "Are you talking about one of these?"

Lulu reached out and touched the tool in Fred's left hand.

Tori saw a second and more telling exchange of looks between the men.

"Did she say anything to you?" Chief Dallas asked.

Lulu nodded. "She asked if I'd like a lollipop."

Fred shook his head and jammed the tools into his pocket. "Then what?"

"I took the lollipop and went to the bathroom."

Chief Dallas hushed his voice despite the rapt interest Tori knew was there. "Was she still there when you went back to wherever it was you were going?"

"She'd been in the children's room with me, readin' stories with her little sister," Margaret Louise offered as she, along with Tori, waited for the answer to a question they hadn't thought to ask her the night before.

Lulu nodded. "I think she dropped something under the table."

Tori's mouth went dry as she looked to Fred and Margaret Louise for confirmation of what she was hearing.

"Why do you say that?" Fred prompted.

"Because she was kneeling on the floor and her head was under the table."

Fred clapped his hands together. "Can you describe this woman to us, Lulu?"

Chief Dallas crossed his arms. "I already asked her that."

"Can you, Lulu?" Fred asked again.

"I saw her in that lady's picture last night."

Fred's brows furrowed. "What lady?"

"Lynn Calder," Tori explained. "She's a friend of Rose Winters."

"This woman had a picture of the arsonist?"

Plucking the photograph from an inside zippered compartment of her tote bag, Margaret Louise held it out to Fred as Tori spoke. "Margaret Louise and Lulu ran into Lynn at Debbie's Bakery last night just before I arrived. She was showing a packet of pictures to Margaret Louise when I got there. When they were done, Lulu and I started looking through them together, too. That's when we came across this one."

Fred took the picture, made a face, then pried a second photograph from the bottom. He looked at both then handed one back to Tori. "I'm guessing this isn't the one you want us to see."

She glanced down quickly, recognized the bell-shaped flowers from Lynn's packet of pictures, and stuffed it onto a shelf behind the information desk. "Sorry about that."

Fred waved away her apology and looked at the photo in his hand, handing it to Chief Dallas when he was done. "So what happened? Why is this picture so special?"

Lulu climbed off the stool and walked over to Chief Dallas. Extending her index finger, the little girl pointed at Kelly. "That's the lady I saw in Miss Sinclair's office."

Chief Dallas narrowed his eyes. "Are you sure?"

Lulu nodded.

"Do we have any idea who this woman is?" Fred asked as he took in the photograph once again.

"Her name is Kelly. I don't know her last name. But—"

"She's the girlfriend of that out-of-towner who was murdered last week."

Tori tightened her grip on her purse, the shock of the police chief's words hitting her with a one-two punch. Somehow, someway, despite knowing it was true, hearing Jeff's name in conjunction with the word *murder* was still shocking.

Chief Dallas looked up from the picture and pinned Tori with a stare. "What reason did she have to come after you like this, Miss Sinclair?"

She'd balled her fists at her side, but released her tension at the feel of Margaret Louise's hand on her back. "I don't know, Chief. Perhaps anger? Jealousy? Revenge? I don't know, that's your job to figure out, isn't it?"

"Revenge?" he echoed.

Margaret Louise stepped forward, positioning her body between them and placing her hands on her round hips. "Were you ever a teenage girl? Or even a grown woman, Robert?"

Fred snorted.

The chief widened his stance, his hands still locked in an *X* at his upper arms. "I suspect you don't really need me to answer that, do you, Ms. Davis?"

"Well then let me give you a crash course in what you missed. Teenage girls are always lookin' 'round tryin' to see who they're competin' with. And when they find it, they either tuck their tail between their legs and give up, or they come out fightin'. And that fightin' is rarely fair."

"Competing for what?" Chief Dallas asked with a hint of boredom in his voice.

"A boy."

The chief peered around Margaret Louise. "Were you involved with the victim again, Miss Sinclair?"

"No." It was a simple answer but it was all she owed the man.

His gaze lingered on Tori's face for a full beat before meeting Margaret Louise's once again. "Then why would this woman be angry enough to set fire to Miss Sinclair's office?"

"Because girls never take their anger out on the boy. Oh no, they see the tomcat as the innocent party and sink their claws and their teeth into the competition instead."

Fred leaned against the counter. "Happened with my best friend's sister in college. Some girl was angry because her old boyfriend had decided to pursue my friend's sister. Locked her in a dorm room closet for darn near twenty-four hours before they found her."

Margaret Louise's hand shot out. "Do you see?"

For a moment Chief Dallas said nothing, a silence that only served to further elevate the tension in the room. When he finally spoke, Tori found herself wishing for his silence. "So let me get this straight. The victim—Miss Sinclair's ex-fiancé—came to town for his aunt's funeral and fell for Miss Sinclair once again?"

"That 'bout sums it up." Margaret Louise shifted her weight then pointed at the photograph. "Miss Kelly, here, didn't take too kindly to that. Turned her claws on the competition based on what Lulu is sayin'."

Fred released a sigh. "Makes you wonder if maybe this one broke the mold, doesn't it?"

All heads turned to stare at Fred. "Mold? What mold?" Chief Dallas asked.

"Well, it sure looks as if she went after Victoria. Lulu's story and what we found in the outlet pointing to that fact with the kind of clarity that's pretty tough to ignore, yes?"

The police chief nodded.

"So we've got her for the fire. But you gotta admit it's hard not to wonder if she went after the"—Fred looked at Margaret Louise for word clarification—"tomcat, too."

Chief Dallas puffed out his chest. "I'm already thinking that, son."

Tori felt the grip of tension ease from her body.

"But it's also making me wonder."

"About what?" Lulu asked sweetly.

Ignoring the little girl, Chief Dallas forged ahead. "I can't imagine this competition stuff is gender specific."

Fred pushed off the counter and came to stand beside Tori. "Girls are famous for it, but I'm sure there have been many men who have committed crimes of jealousy, too. It's the dark side of human relationships, I guess."

A spine-tingling glint flashed across the chief's face as he nodded at Fred yet kept his focus squarely on Tori.

She swallowed once, twice.

"Is there any chance someone *else* knew about the victim's intentions where you were concerned, Miss Sinclair?"

Margaret Louise hoisted her hands on her hips once again. "What are you gettin' at, Robert?"

"Only an observation, really."

"What kind of observation?" Fred asked.

Chief Dallas pursed his lips and shrugged. "About shapes. Squares, in particular."

Lulu grinned. "Those have four equal sides."

"Exactly. Which is rather unlike triangles which only have three sides, isn't that right, Miss Sinclair?"

Chapter 25

One by one they filed through her front door, sewing boxes, tote bags, and foil-covered plates in hand. Only this time, instead of feeling the burst of excitement she usually felt when it was her turn to host a circle meeting, she was aware of a very different emotion.

Dread.

It wasn't that she'd suddenly grown a distaste toward her nearly lifelong passion for sewing, because she hadn't. Sewing was as much a part of her life as reading and breathing. In fact, in addition to being a link to her late great grandmother, sewing had also become a tried-and-true form of therapy whenever life threw a curveball.

Unless, of course, the curveball had her worried to the point of being unable to sit still.

Leona leaned over Tori's table and plunked her powder blue bakery box smack-dab in the middle of the sea of covered plates. "Everything looks so . . . so *homemade* this evening."

Rose lowered herself onto the wicker rocker Tori had dragged into the room from the front porch and winced, a flash of pain in her eyes making the reason crystal clear. But before anyone could comment, she volleyed a barb across the room at Leona. "And this is different from any other Monday night because why?"

Leona fairly sashayed across the room to the plaid armchair she'd claimed as her own nearly two years earlier. "It's not, really. But that doesn't mean I'm not continually astonished by the effort everyone goes to for these meetings when Debbie's Bakery is on the way to virtually everyone's home."

"*This* from the woman who calls herself Southern Woman of the Year," mumbled Rose.

"*That* from a woman whom I've appointed as guardian to an offspring of my precious Paris." Leona lowered her chin long enough to peer over the top of her glasses at Rose. "Unless, of course, you're too infirm to care for Patches now."

Tori sucked in her breath. "Leona! That's enough."

Rose's laugh morphed into a quiet gasp, summoning Tori, Beatrice, and Georgina to her side.

"Rose? Are you okay?" Beatrice asked shyly.

Shooing all concerned sewing sisters back toward their seats, Rose said, "Nothing a few pain pills and a good nap can't address. Now scram, all of you. I don't need to be hovered over as if I've got one foot in the grave."

"Before you do, may I suggest Prada or Jimmy

Choo?" Leona reached into her bag, extracted a magazine, and flipped it open on her lap. "They would be so much more stylish than"—she peered across the room at Rose's feet—*"those."*

Debbie clapped her hands. "So, how are everyone's pillows coming along?"

"Dandy," Georgina announced, raising two pillow covers into the air. "They're really quite simple to make."

"I found this fabric at the sewing shop in Landover on the way home from the cabin yesterday morning." Beatrice's gaze skirted nervously from face to face before making a dive into her lap. "I thought it might be cheerful for the pillows."

Rose nodded. "Looks fine to me."

Relief chased uncertainty from the nanny's face, culminating in a quiet smile. "Thank you, Rose."

Leona turned her attention on Tori. "You're mighty quiet today, dear. Is everything okay?"

"It's fine." She settled onto the couch beside Margaret Louise and opened her wooden sewing box. "I'm just a wee bit tired, I guess."

"Who wouldn't be after that interrogation this afternoon. All that was missin' was the windowless room and the swingin' light." Margaret Louise shook her head then pulled one of the portable sewing machine's rolling carts to a stop between her knees and the coffee table.

Georgina looked up from her latest pillowcase, a threaded needle poised between her lips. "What interrogation?"

Tori opened her mouth to steer the conversation in another direction but she was too late. Margaret Louise, seizing the opportunity afforded by Georgina's question, rushed to answer, her loud, booming voice putting her front and center. "Chief Dallas was questionin' Victoria as if she was some kind of psychic."

"A psychic? On what?" Debbie inquired as she bent over her own pillow cover, stitching the edges by hand.

"The mind-set of her ex-fiancé's killer."

Georgina pulled the needle from her mouth. "I'm sure Robert is just being thorough, you know, not leaving any stones unturned."

"Perhaps he could work on turnin' more than throwin'." Margaret Louise slid her pillowcase up to the machine and flipped the power switch, the answering whir audible for mere seconds before it was turned off. "Would you believe he had the nerve to—"

"I don't think we need to discuss this now, Margaret Louise." Tori looked at her watch and then gestured toward the kitchen. "Should we get started on dessert?"

"We just got here," Melissa protested. "Besides, we need to get as many pillows done as possible, isn't that right, Rose?"

Rose pinned Tori with a knowing stare. "I don't think Victoria is trying to shortchange the pillows. I think she's just trying to get Margaret Louise to put a sock in it."

Reality dawned on Margaret Louise's face and she turned to Tori, wide-eyed. "I'm sorry, was I not supposed to say anything about Chief Dallas and his insinuations regardin' Milo?"

Beatrice's head snapped up. "Milo?" she whispered.

"What on earth?" Debbie chimed in.

Melissa's mouth dropped open. "He can't be serious."

Tori closed her eyes and rested her head against the back of the couch, the dread of earlier rapidly reappearing.

"He started spoutin' 'bout triangles and squares right there in front of Lulu!" Margaret Louise turned the machine on then flipped it off once again. "As if Milo Wentworth is even capable of murderous *thoughts*."

Tori pushed off the couch. "Would anyone like a drink? I made a fresh batch of sweet tea not more than thirty minutes ago."

Beatrice set her pillowcase off to the side and rose to her feet. "I'll help, Victoria."

Grateful for the opportunity to escape further discussion regarding Milo and Jeff's murder, she gladly accepted the nanny's offer, tasking her with counting hands as she disappeared into the

303

kitchen. When Beatrice followed suit with the official count, Tori forced her lips into a smile. "Thanks for helping, Beatrice."

The girl looked at the floor, her voice barely more than a whisper. "I'm sorry you're going through this sort of thing again."

She flung open the cabinet to the right of the refrigerator and counted out six glasses. "Who doesn't want a glass?"

"Rose and Dixie," Beatrice said. "They said they'll have hot tea when it's time for dessert."

Stepping to the left, she yanked open the refrigerator and extracted the pitcher of sweet tea. "Hot tea, check."

"You're not worried, are you?"

She cast a sidelong glance in Beatrice's direction. "No, hot tea will only take a moment."

Beatrice shook her head. "I meant about Milo."

Her hand shook as she tipped the pitcher to the first glass. "That Milo had anything to do with Jeff's death? Of course not."

Tea dribbled down the side of the second glass as her hand shook more. Without saying a word, Beatrice took the pitcher from Tori's hand and completed the task with efficiency and ease. When she was done, she held a glass out for Tori. "Just because someone says something doesn't mean they're inclined to do it."

Tori wrapped her hands around the glass yet said nothing.

"Think about how many of us expressed thoughts of doing away with that awful woman last spring."

She knew Beatrice was right, yet she couldn't shake the nagging reality that put Milo in town at the time Jeff died. For a visit he was still hiding from her today.

Toss in the threatening statement he'd made toward Jeff the night before the murder and, well, it was enough to give her pause.

The fact that Chief Dallas was sniffing around the same bandwagon turned the pause into genuine concern and fear.

"I just want to know *how* Jeff died," Tori whispered, the statement surprising even her.

"They do. Georgina said it was a drug-induced heart attack."

She stared at Beatrice. "Drug-induced? Are you sure?"

Beatrice blushed. "I know I wasn't supposed to be listening but it was hard not to when Georgina was talking into that phone of hers at the top of her voice in the car just now."

"Do you know who she was talking to?"

"I don't know but she has the strangest rings on her phone," Beatrice whispered, peeking around the corner into the living room as she did.

"Do you remember what song it was?" she asked as she crossed the fingers of her free hand.

"When I asked afterward, she said it was the theme song from something called Quincy."

She sucked in her breath. Quincy had featured a medical examiner and had been a show her great grandmother used to enjoy. "Did you hear anything else?"

"Only that it was a drug he hadn't been prescribed by his doctor."

"Prescribed?" she echoed as her mind worked to dissect the information. "So it wasn't a recreational drug?"

Beatrice averted her gaze to the floor. "Oh, Victoria, I shouldn't be telling you this. I was eavesdropping."

Setting her glass on the counter, she pulled the young woman in for a hug. "Would it help ease the guilt if I told you I'm less worried now?"

Red circles appeared in the nanny's cheeks as she stepped back and met Tori's eyes. "Really?"

She grinned. "Don't you see? If it was a prescription drug that killed Jeff, all of these silly questions about Milo are moot. He's the picture of good health. The only pill bottles in his house are vitamins. And last I checked those are *good* for your heart."

A quick smile lit Beatrice's eyes with an endearing sparkle. "So you feel better then?"

She reached out, squeezed the nanny's shoulder. "I feel much, much, *much* better."

"You won't tell Georgina I was listening, will you?"

"It'll be our little secret." Scooping up four of the six glasses she gestured toward the living room with her chin. "When and if Georgina decides to share the information with us, I'll act as surprised as anyone else."

Beatrice ducked her head forward then grabbed hold of the two remaining glasses. "I'm glad you feel better. It makes me sad to see you so upset. You've been through so much since you moved here and it doesn't seem fair."

"But moving here gave me the greatest friends I could have ever asked for." She bobbed her head left then right until she caught and held Beatrice's eye. "And I count you among them. I hope you know that."

The flush from earlier only deepened in Beatrice's face. "Thank you."

They fell into step together as they crossed the threshold into the living room, the familiar chatter that was synonymous with circle meetings suddenly music to her ears once again.

Beatrice stopped in her tracks. "Victoria? Do you think Georgina has a ring for me?"

She laughed. "I think she has one for all of us."

"Do you know what they are?" Beatrice asked softly.

"Not yet, but I intend to find out."

Chapter 26

The Sweet Briar Public Library was officially the place to be Tuesday morning as resident after resident stopped in to say hello, some there purely out of curiosity about the fire, others because it was as much a second home for them as it was for Tori.

Higher traffic, of course, meant extra re-shelving, but, considering the alternative had the fire not been contained, it was a pleasure.

"Isn't it wonderful to see so many people here?" Dixie asked, her voice nearly breathless. "And it's just as many adults as children."

Tori looked up from the information desk computer and scanned the room, the accuracy of Dixie's demographic observation catching her by surprise. "Wow, you're right. And what's more, the adults seem to be looking at books as much as they are visiting."

Dixie nodded in agreement.

"But I have to say, I do feel bad telling the kids we need another day or so on the children's room. They all look so crushed when I say that."

"I can stay after work today and help with some more of the cleaning in there," Dixie offered. "Maybe doing that would help ease any leftover guilt once and for all."

She reached out, touched the woman's arm. "Dixie, none of what happened here was your fault. If it hadn't been the coffeemaker that night, it would have happened the next time I plugged in something else."

"I want to believe that."

"And you should, because it's the truth."

Dixie leaned forward and brushed an unexpected kiss on the top of Tori's head. "Thank you, Victoria."

Before she could respond, Dixie wandered out from behind the counter, a stack of books to be shelved in her hands. She watched the woman for a moment, a barrage of Dixie-related memories flashing before her eyes in movie reel fashion . . .

Dixie glowering at her during circle meetings.

Dixie heckling her during her first board meeting as head librarian.

Dixie continually pointing to Tori as the reason she'd been retired from a job she'd held for more decades than Tori had been alive.

But as the reel continued, she couldn't help but notice the subtle way the images changed . . .

Dixie offering to help clean the children's room.

Dixie complimenting Tori on her job as librarian.

Dixie giving her a kiss.

"Good afternoon, Victoria, beautiful day, isn't it?"

The familiar voice broke through her woolgathering, prompting the smile that had been virtually ever-present all day to grow even wider as she took in the elderly man standing beside the information desk.

"Mr. Downing, how are you today?" she asked, soaking up every nuance of the man who was as much a staple of the library as the books that drew him in twice a week.

He tipped the lip of his ball cap forward. "I'm quite well, thank you." He circled his hand around the room. "Things look better in here than I'd hoped."

"We were certainly very fortunate. The only room that will be unusable for quite some time is my office."

"How's that young man of yours? Is he home yet?"

She felt her heart flutter. "Tomorrow night."

"I'm not surprised. I can see a light in your eyes that's been missing the past few weeks. Figured he had something to do with it."

Her face warmed at the accuracy of his words. Despite everything that had fallen on her shoulders over the past few weeks, not having Milo to talk to, Milo to go out with, or Milo to hold and be held by, had affected her more than she could have ever imagined.

"That's what happens when part of you is missing. Happened to me whenever my Evelyn wasn't around."

She met Mr. Downing's eyes, saw the brief flash of sadness that flitted across his eyes at the mention of his beloved late wife. But just as quickly as the sadness came, it was replaced by the positive outlook the man extended to everyone he met. "It's one of those rare blessings in life that make you a very lucky woman."

She knew he was right, knew she'd hit the jackpot the day she met Milo Wentworth.

It was time.

Time to give him the rest of her heart.

She sucked in her lower lip as she imagined giving him the answer he'd been patiently waiting for for months, confident the smile on her lips at that moment would be every bit as bright as the one on Milo's face.

A cough over by the computer bank snapped her back to the present and the fact that Mr. Downing was eyeing her curiously.

"I'm sorry. I guess I got lost in what you said." She pointed at the slip of paper in his hand. "Looking for something specific today?"

He handed her the paper. "I'm thinking about soliciting the paper to see if they might be interested in hiring me on as a freelance photographer."

She clapped her hands softly. "Oh, Mr.

Downing, that would be wonderful. Your photographs are always so engaging. They'd be lucky to showcase your efforts."

He grinned. "I don't know how lucky they'd be but I sure would enjoy it. It'd give me something to do with my free time instead of coming in here bothering you all the time."

"Everyone in this library treasures your visits. We always will."

"That's mighty kind of you, Victoria."

She glanced down at the title he'd written on the scrap of paper. "*Encyclopedia of Flowers*?"

Nodding, he reached inside his back pocket, extracted a folded piece of newsprint, and handed it to Tori. "I need to build a portfolio to show them what I can do. I'd like it to include shots of people—candid and posed—as well as things like buildings and plants. But I also need to show them I can caption them, which is a much easier thing to do when there are people as opposed to something stationary."

It made sense. "So you'd like to see how others have done it with something like flowers?" she asked.

"That about sums it up."

She considered his request, setting the title to the side of her computer and opening the catalogue screen. "I'll certainly see if we have this particular book but I'm going to see if there might be one that will suit your needs more."

He leaned against the counter. "How so?"

Her fingers moved across the keyboard as she explained the reason for her alternate search. "An encyclopedia of this nature is going to give very basic captions to any of their photographs. You know, its name, location, and other details— something of interest to a gardener. Whereas for your purposes, it seems a book that focuses more on their beauty rather than their facts might have more creative captions."

"This is why folks around here adore you, Victoria." He waited patiently as she found a few options, jotting down their shelf location in list format.

"Okay, let's take a look, shall we?" She climbed down off the stool and met Mr. Downing on the other side of the counter, pointing toward the shelves devoted to gardening as she did.

He trailed behind her as she rounded the first shelf, her fingers finding and locating the first book on the list with ease. The second book was found just as easily, while the third required a bit of a hunt.

"I can check the tables if you'd like. It's possible someone was looking at it today and it just hasn't made its way back onto the shelf."

Mr. Downing took the books from her hands. "These will be fine for now. If I need to see more, I can take a walk around the room myself."

She gently squeezed his forearm. "Enjoy. If you need anything else, let me know, okay?"

"Will do. And Victoria?"

"Yes?"

"That young man of yours is just as lucky. Maybe even more so."

"Thank you, Mr. Downing." She headed back toward the information desk, stopping every few feet to greet a patron and ask if they needed assistance.

When she finally reclaimed her spot at the computer, she found she couldn't concentrate on the ordering she'd intended to do. Instead, her thoughts ran the gamut from Milo and his impending homecoming to the knowledge that Kelly was being located and most likely arrested at that very moment. The charges though, were anyone's guess.

Sure, Jeff's girlfriend would be accused of arson; that was a no-brainer. But whether a charge of murder would await the woman as well remained to be seen. For now, all Tori could do was guess.

And guess she did ever since Beatrice had divulged the results of her eavesdropping the night before.

Hushed whispers off to her right made her look up, a smile spreading its way across her face for the umpteenth time that day.

"Hi, Miss Sinclair."

She waved at Lulu and her little sister Sally before greeting their grandmother. "Isn't this a nice surprise."

Margaret Louise hoisted her tote bag onto the counter, reached inside, and extracted a large scented candle from its depth. "I know you're probably a bit skittish about the notion of lightin' a match in here 'bout now but if you set it here on the counter and only burn it while you're sittin' there, it'll be fine."

"It smells like sugar cookies," Sally chimed in as she hopped from foot to foot. "Mee-Maw wanted lilac but Lulu and I knew you'd like sugar cookies better."

She laughed. "You two girls are so smart."

"Miss Sinclair?" Lulu cocked her head ever so slightly to the left, peering at Tori around the computer. "Can we go into the children's room?"

"I'm afraid you can't. We have a little more cleaning to do in there before we can open it again." She couldn't help but notice the way Sally's shoulders slumped at the news. "But don't worry, everything will be back to normal before the end of the week."

"Do you promise?" Sally asked.

"Sally, hush. Miss Sinclair can't promise somethin' like that."

"I can promise to do my best, will that work?"

Sally nodded then looked around, her

shoulders slumping once again. "Are there *any* books for us to read?"

"Miss Dixie can get something for you from the children's room if you'd like . . ."

"Can we skip around the trees instead, just this once, Mee-Maw?" Lulu asked. "That way Miss Dixie can help that man she's helping and not have to worry about us."

Tori followed the path made by Lulu's finger, stopping at the sight of her temporary assistant and Mr. Downing, their heads bent toward one another as they pored over the pictures in the man's book.

"Will you keep an eye on Sally?" Margaret Louise asked.

Lulu nodded.

"You won't take your eyes off her for one second?"

This time, Lulu shook her head.

"Then you may, but stay close to the front walkway."

"Yes, Mee-Maw." Turning to Sally, Lulu extended her hand to her little sister. "C'mon, Sally, let's go skip under the trees."

When the pair was gone, Margaret Louise leaned her plump body across the counter and lowered her voice to the closest thing to a whisper the woman could get. "Did you hear the news?"

"What news?"

"That ex of yours had Digi-something or other in his system."

She stared at her friend. "Digi-something or other? What's that?"

"Okay, so I'm not always good with names. But what I do recall is that it's some sort of heart medication. Powerful stuff that didn't take too kindly to his decision to go joggin' from what I hear."

So it was official. The news Beatrice had shared was making its way around Sweet Briar.

"I heard that."

"His doctor in Chicago said his heart was okay, and that he wasn't on any heart medication. That anyone who knew of his exercise regimen and family history wouldn't have prescribed it for him, either."

"How else would he have it in his system then?" she asked even as her mind was barely registering the more detailed information she was hearing than she'd heard the night before.

"I imagine someone found a way to slip it into his system without his knowing."

She closed her eyes as an unexpected pang of pain shot through her heart. It wasn't pain over never seeing Jeff again, but, rather, pain at the senselessness of it all.

"How would a girl, obviously skilled as an electrician, come upon a medication like that and know the effects it would have on a runner like Jeff? Is she just some sort of genius?"

"I suppose. Or maybe it wasn't her at all. Maybe it was someone who knew about medication the same way Kelly knew about electrical things."

"Maybe," she mumbled. "Maybe he dated a doctor at some point."

"Or a pharmacist," Margaret Louise suggested.

"A pharmacist," she repeated even as her thoughts began shaping a reality that not only worked but made perfect sense, too. "Margaret Louise, *you* are a genius."

Chapter 27

Dumping all library responsibilities on Dixie without so much as a moment's notice probably wasn't one of her better moves but she didn't really have any other alternative.

Except, perhaps, to wait until they closed for the day.

But when she saw how happy Dixie was to be given the responsibility again after the trauma of Friday's fire, Tori couldn't help but free herself of any guilt. Besides, had she stayed and waited until close, she would have been completely useless, her mind as far from books and patrons and post-fire related tasks as humanly possible.

No, following her gut was smart.

Unfortunately, following her gut at that very moment meant denying Margaret Louise of her second favorite thing to do—playing backup investigator to Tori.

Having Lulu and Sally for the day, though, made the timing less than ideal. And considering the fact that the woman's grandchildren claimed the top spot on her list of favorite pastimes, it made sense to visit Lynn alone.

Yet as she drove along the very same winding

roads she'd driven less than forty-eight hours earlier, Tori couldn't help but feel her excitement waning. If she was right about the identity of Jeff's killer, an innocent party was about to get hurt—an innocent party who'd been through enough trials over the last year or so to last a lifetime.

If she was right, and she said nothing in a misguided effort to help Lynn, a man would get away with murder. If she was right and told Chief Dallas, the killer would ultimately meet the justice he deserved but also set a cruel injustice in motion for a blameless bystander.

She felt her foot let up on the gas, the car slow in response.

What on earth was she doing? Was it really her place to stick her nose in business that, truly, had nothing to do with her any longer? Figuring out who killed Jeff wasn't her job, it was the police chief's. Her job was to excite people about reading and connect them with the books they sought.

It was as her great grandmother had always said, everyone had their place in life.

Pulling onto the shoulder, she slowed her car still further in preparation for the U-turn that would bring her back to Sweet Briar. Everything she was thinking was pure speculation. And, given time, Chief Dallas was perfectly capable of speculating in the same direction.

Wasn't he?

The rhetorical question played through her thoughts, followed by random images that had her wondering whether he could.

Sure, Chief Dallas was a smart man. One only had to walk into the police department and see all his certificates and awards on the wall to know that. But he wasn't always quick to look beyond his initial suspicions, narrowing in on his first guess while missing various possibilities that lurked in the periphery.

It was why she'd been propelled to snoop around when Tiffany Ann Gilbert was murdered. It was why she hadn't settled for the obvious when Debbie's husband disappeared. It was why she poked around in the death of Rose's next-door neighbor and later a fellow kindergarten parent of Debbie's and Melissa's.

Some may say her need to probe came from a lack of trust in Sweet Briar law enforcement and they weren't too far off base. But, beyond that, she was simply a curious person. Always had been. It's why she read everything she could get her hands on growing up; fiction, nonfiction, anything with a cover on it.

She simply had to know.

How a tale ended . . .

How a particular animal survived . . .

Whether a relationship lasted or fell apart . . .

I have to know.

Tightening her grip on the steering wheel, Tori thwarted her U-turn and pulled back onto the road, curiosity winning out once again.

If her suspicions were right, she'd simply have to find a way to help Lynn. Where there was a will, there was a way, right?

She zipped along the road until she came to the turnoff to Lee Station, the Calders' street coming up shortly thereafter. Slowly, she counted out the houses she passed on the left, the daytime version of Lynn's street different than the nighttime version.

As she approached the fifth house, she pulled in tight to the curb and came to a stop. If she'd been thinking, she'd have run into Debbie's Bakery before making the drive from Sweet Briar. But, as often was the case when she was following a hunch, good manners slipped from her mind.

Releasing a frustrated sigh, she pushed open her door and walked around the car, her feet following the same path they had less than two days earlier. A path that led them to Lynn's front door.

She knocked on the trim that surrounded the screen door. "Lynn? Are you home?"

Footsteps followed, then the sight of Lynn's surprised face beneath her bare head. "Victoria, what a nice surprise. Come—come in." The woman reached out, pushed open the screen door, and stepped aside to let Tori pass. "Is everything okay?"

She half shrugged. "I wanted to thank you for letting us hang on to that picture of—oh, wait. I think I have the other one I didn't intend to take." Tori separated the shoulder straps of her purse and peered inside. Rummaging around with her free hand, she came up empty. "Darn. I'm sorry. I must have forgotten it at work."

Lynn led the way into the same parlor they'd inhabited the first time, her hand gesturing to the same couch as well. "What other picture?"

She perched on the edge of the sofa and looked up at Lynn. "It was one of the shots you took of your garden. I guess it got stuck to the one of Kelly because we didn't notice it until yesterday."

Lynn waved away Tori's concern. "I have plenty of pictures like that. No worries." The woman reached up, touched her head. "I wasn't expecting company today. Didn't feel like wearing my bandana."

"You look beautiful just the way you are, Lynn." Tori patted the cushion to her left. "Do you have a moment to sit? I'd like to talk if that's okay."

"Of course."

Lynn lowered herself onto the couch, her brows furrowing as she did. "Did you show the picture to the fire chief?"

She nodded.

"And?"

Linking her hands inside one another, she set them in her lap. "And I imagine they're tracking Kelly down as we speak."

A soft clucking noise emerged from Lynn's lips. "Such a shame. One more woman is ruined because of a cheating man."

She considered the woman's words, recognized them as something she, herself, might have spoken before moving to Sweet Briar and meeting Milo. "She could have walked away, washed her hands of Jeff once and for all."

Lynn closed her eyes and leaned her head against the back of the couch. "That's not always easy. Especially when you're head over heels for the person who ripped your heart in two. You, of all people, should understand that."

She searched for the right way to articulate the place she was in, the hurt and the self-doubt she'd worked through in order to gain wisdom and happiness.

"I was hurt by Jeff, there's no doubt about that. I, too, was head over heels for him, or, rather, what I imagined was head over heels. I put his needs first, his interests first, his everything first, allowing myself to disappear in the process."

Lynn opened her eyes and fixed them on Tori. "You did that because that's what we were taught to do as women."

She shrugged. "Maybe. Maybe not. I may have thought that, but I don't think that was entirely true. At least not in my case, anyway. My great grandparents had a wonderful marriage, the kind of marriage that not only lasted but worked, too. Sure, my great grandmother made dinner every night and set aside her dreams to support my great grandfather and raise their children. But she still kept herself. She sewed, she visited friends, she even dabbled with a little writing. The difference, though, was the fact that she had a mate who encouraged her to do those things. Encouraged her to be her own person."

"Jeff wasn't like that?"

She laughed. "No. And I'm embarrassed to say I was too dumb to see that. In fact, I didn't even see that until after I moved here and was able to look back without the raw pain that blinded me after the breakup."

"What made you see it then?" Lynn asked.

"I guess I saw the move as a chance to make a life for *me*. A life with friends, and hobbies, and a job that fulfills me in so many ways."

"Then the move was your lucky break or your silver lining, yes?"

She shook her head. "No. My lucky break was Jeff showing his true colors before I got sucked into that life full-time. The silver lining is my life now."

For a moment, Lynn said nothing as her gaze

strayed to the mantel and its assortment of framed photographs. "You think Kelly would have come to that realization, too?"

"If she'd given herself time to grieve, yes. But she didn't. She opted to act out at me before taking the time to realize I wasn't interested in Jeff and that she deserved better than the respect he so clearly didn't show her."

"See, and I've had the time. Plenty of time."

"Time?" Tori asked. "Time for what?"

"To realize I'm better off without Garrett. Any man who could carry on with another woman the way he does isn't fit to be a husband. To anyone."

Pity welled up in her heart for the woman. "I concur wholeheartedly."

"But, for some of us, time isn't the issue." Lynn grabbed hold of a loose thread along the side seam of her jeans and twisted it around her finger. "Well, not in that sense, anyway. Time in the traditional sense of the word is very much an issue for me."

Tori reached across the couch, closed her hand over the top of Lynn's. "I'm so sorry for everything you're going through. I truly am."

"It's life." Lynn squeezed Tori's hand in response, then extracted her own and pushed off the couch. "Would you like something to drink?"

"No. I'm fine."

Lynn wandered over to the window and pushed

aside the sheer white panel that broke the intensity of the afternoon sun. "So what brings you by, exactly?"

She swallowed once, twice, willed herself to find the courage to ask the questions that needed to be asked.

"Was Garrett angry when he heard the terms of Vera's last will and testament?"

Lynn snorted. "Was Garrett angry? What do you think?"

"I don't know."

Slowly, Lynn turned from the window and retraced her steps back to the couch, bypassing her former spot in favor of a nearby armchair with matching ottoman. She propped her feet up. "The bulk of Vera's money came to her by way of Garrett's father. He was a very wealthy man. In his will, he left everything—the house, the cars, his money—to Vera. The only stipulation regarding his son at all was a request to allow Garrett and I to continue living in the house."

Tori nodded yet said nothing as Lynn's voice took on a fatigued quality. "Garrett wasn't thrilled at that time but he let it go, assuming that it would eventually come his way once Vera died. But that didn't happen. She left all of her money to Jeff, and this house to me."

"Wow. He must have been furious."

Lynn made a face. "That's one word for it, I suppose. Another might be near violent."

She stared at the woman. "He didn't hurt you, did he?"

"No. But he broke nearly everything that remained in Vera's room. Every lamp, every picture, every glass knickknack he could get his hands on." Lynn gestured toward the mantel. "The only reason he didn't do the same out here is because I made the mistake of pointing out the caveat in the will. Once I did that, his mind and his efforts went elsewhere."

"What caveat was that?" she inquired.

"The part that left the money to Garrett should anything happen to Jeff before the money was turned over."

Tori froze in her spot, Lynn's words essentially sewing up any conceivable hole she might have entertained in her suspicion regarding Garrett.

"H-had Jeff gotten the money yet?"

Lynn shook her head. "As of that morning, no."

"Are you sure?"

"He came and stayed here after the wake. Garrett wasn't thrilled but he agreed, something he regretted after he heard the terms of Vera's will. Anyway, Jeff checked the mailbox 'bout twenty minutes before his run that last day. Came in all long-faced because it hadn't come yet. So there I was with Garrett stewing over his lunch and Jeff pouting while I made him a protein drink. Eventually they both left—Garrett to work, or, rather, to see his mistress, and Jeff to take what turned out to be his last run."

"So Garrett now gets that money?"

"Yes he does. In fact, the check that was being written in Jeff's name was deposited in our account not more than forty-eight hours after his death."

"Garrett killed him!" The second the words were out, Tori clapped a hand over her mouth. "Oh, Lynn, I'm sorry. I shouldn't have said that but—"

"What makes you think Garrett killed Jeff? I thought you were convinced it was Kelly."

"Jeff died because of a medication that was in his system, a medication that wasn't intended for a man with his active lifestyle and family history of heart problems."

Lynn's left eyebrow rose upward. "Medication?"

"It could have been stuck in his drink or mixed in his food. But whatever it was, it messed up his heart," Tori explained, then watched as the connection she'd made at the library dawned on Lynn's face as well.

Once again, Lynn rose from her chair, this time stopping beside a shelf stocked with various books. Standing on tiptoe, Lynn pulled a large blue volume off the shelf and carried it back to the couch. Flipping it open, she thumbed through the first few letters of the alphabet before coming to a stop and holding the book out for Tori to see.

"Is that the drug that was in his system?"

Tori read the highlighted listing above Lynn's finger, the word starting exactly the way Margaret Louise had said. "That's it! Oh my gosh, that's it!"

Lynn shifted the book onto Tori's lap and leaned her head against the back of the sofa. "I don't know why I should be surprised. Garrett gets what Garrett wants. He always has."

She looked from the book to Lynn and back again then slammed the book closed. "I'm sorry, Lynn. I truly am. I know how much you've been through with Garrett and the cancer and losing Vera."

"It's life."

"That doesn't make it any less unfair." Inhaling every ounce of determination she could muster, she met and held Lynn's gaze with her own. "I know the hardship his being in prison is going to cause you, but I want you to know that I'm going to do whatever I can to help. One way or another, we'll find a way to make everything work out okay. I promise."

The faintest hint of a smile momentarily pushed exhaustion from Lynn's face. "I suppose I can look at the silver lining in all of this."

Tori held her breath, grateful for the woman's attempt to stay positive. "What silver lining is that?"

"I'm finally rid of Garrett once and for all."

Chapter 28

By the time she got back to the library, it was closed, the absence of patrons and related duties affording her time to work on getting the children's room up to snuff once again.

"Dixie?" she called, locking the front door in her wake. "Are you still here?"

A chorus of muted voices grew silent followed by the sound of a familiar voice down the hall. "We're in here."

Smiling, she made her way down the hallway, her gait slowing as she passed the taped off doorway that led to her office. The fire had been a tragedy, there was no doubt about that, but like she and Lynn had both discovered, a silver lining could almost always be found.

In the case of the fire, it was the simple fact that her office was the least important room in the building. The only one affected by its current state was Tori. And Nina when Nina finally came back.

She followed the hall a few more steps then turned left, the sight of her sewing circle sisters dispatched around the children's room further underscoring the notion of silver linings and lucky breaks.

Her mouth gaped open as she took in their collective efforts—the dusted shelves, the freshly washed and pressed stage curtain, the neatly folded dress-up clothes being transferred back to their trunk.

"You ladies are amazing. Absolutely, utterly, completely amazing." She walked into the center of the room and slowly spun around, the magical aura of the room as unmistakable as ever. "But you didn't have to do this."

"You're right, we didn't," Georgina said, peeking through a row of books one shelf over. "But we wanted to."

She nodded in gratitude at every woman in the room—Georgina, Leona, Margaret Louise, Dixie, Debbie, Melissa, and Beatrice. "Thank you. So much."

Dixie clapped her hands. "We'll be able to get the children back in here tomorrow, won't we?"

Slowly but surely she made her way around the room, taking in every shelf, every little chair, every article of clothes, every picture on the wall. Dixie was right. They were ready.

"I don't see why not," she finally said, the excitement she felt lifting her spirits tenfold.

"Not bad for a few hours work," Leona boasted from her spot beside the stage.

Margaret Louise snorted a laugh. "That would be the case if Tori hadn't already gotten a head start yesterday . . . and you actually *helped,* Twin."

Leona's chin jutted outward in indignation. "I helped."

"Oh really?" Rose accused, her wrinkled hands working alongside Beatrice to refill the dress-up trunk. "Seems to me you haven't moved from that spot since we got here."

Leona stifled a yawn with dramatic flair. "Delegation is difficult work, Rose. It's exhausting trying to make sure everyone is doing what needs to be done."

Debbie nibbled back a smirk as Melissa laughed out loud. "Aunt Leona, I don't know what we'd do without you."

"I don't either, dear." To Tori, Leona said, "My sister said you went off on a mission?"

She met Margaret Louise's curious gaze although her words stayed focused on Leona. "I guess you could call it that."

"Were you getting something naughty for Milo's return tomorrow evening?" Leona asked.

"No."

Leona made a face. "Why on earth not?"

"Because I had something more important to do."

A mumbled tsk from Leona was quickly drowned out by Debbie, who crossed to the doorway and pointed to a large plastic container stuffed to the top with pillows. "We've got thirty-three comfort pillows so far, Victoria, isn't that wonderful?"

She pulled her gaze from Margaret Louise and fixed it, instead, on the fruits of the sewing circle's labor. Blinking back an unexpected tear, she crossed the room and plucked a pillow from the bin. "I was excited about this project when Rose told us what she wanted to do and why, but now I'm even more excited."

"Why?" Melissa asked, pausing the damp cloth over the top of the mural depicting Laura Ingalls's first log cabin. "What's changed?"

"I guess it's the reality that breast cancer patients face. Instead of being something I simply read about in newspapers and magazines, now it's something real, something that affects someone I've gotten to know. I see the physical toll it's taken on her body, I see the way it's changed her perception of herself, and I see the way it's dictated some of her choices in life."

Rose closed the gap between them. "These pillows are such a little thing, really. They can't undo the physical toll, or make someone feel better about themselves, or do much of anything besides alleviating a little of the post-op discomfort. But I guess, when I came up with the idea, I was hoping it might let some of these women know we care," the elderly woman said, her voice growing more shaky with each passing word. "Like I know whenever I have to go in for an infusion."

"They give you pillows, too?" Dixie asked.

"No. But I have friends by my side, holding my hand. Not all of those ladies have that. And now that her mother-in-law is gone, I imagine Lynn won't have much of that, either."

Tori hugged the pillow to her chest. "I'm hoping that maybe she will."

Margaret Louise stepped forward, a knowing smile on her face. "I'll take a shift whenever I can."

Rose grinned. "I will, too."

"Count me in as well, Victoria," Georgina added.

She swallowed back the lump that threatened to make it difficult to speak. "I was hoping you'd say that."

Dixie waved her hand in the air. "Doesn't this woman have a husband?"

Rose rolled her eyes in disgust.

Leona snorted.

The two nodded at one another in agreement.

"Don't tell me you two are still gettin' along," Margaret Louise bellowed. "You're startin' to make me wonder if I've dropped into some parallel universe from one of them adventure novels Jake Junior keeps readin'. You know, where things that can't really be happenin' start happenin'."

The first few notes of the *Hawaii Five-O* theme song filled the room and all eyes turned toward Georgina, a hint of crimson making its way across the mayor's cheeks.

"That's your cell phone ring?" Leona questioned.

Georgina shrugged and flipped open her phone as Beatrice closed the costume trunk. "That's her cell phone ring when Chief Dallas calls. It's the theme song from"—she looked to Tori for confirmation—"*Quincy* when it's the medical examiner."

Five mouths hung open as five sets of eyes trained on Georgina.

"Does she have a different ring for everyone who calls?" Melissa asked.

"She does," Tori confirmed.

Dixie narrowed her eyes on Tori. "Does she have a different one for each of us?"

"I believe she does, yes."

Leona shot her hands in the air. "I know mine. It's got to be 'Belle of the Ball' or, possibly, 'That Lady.'"

"Or, perhaps, something along the lines of 'Devil in a Blue Dress,'" Melissa teased, earning herself an evil eye in the process.

"I hope mine is something by Kenny Rogers. Maybe 'Lady'?" Beatrice mused. "Or 'Islands in the Stream'?"

Tori tried to focus on the jokes making their

way around the room as each member of the sewing circle hypothesized about the various songs Georgina may have selected for them, but it was hard. Especially when she knew the reason for the chief's call.

Chief Dallas had been surprisingly open-minded when she'd stopped by the police station on the way back to the library. In fact, from the moment she mentioned Garrett's profession, she'd had his undivided attention, his interest peaking at the details of Vera Calder's will. By the time she'd finished and he'd made a number of phone calls, the chief was all but ready to issue a warrant for Garrett Calder's arrest.

His call to Georgina was simply the cherry on top.

Which meant Lynn's world was about to turn upside-down once again.

"How did Lynn take the news?" Margaret Louise asked as she moved in beside Tori. "Is she okay?"

"She's trying to look at the bright side. The side that gets that creep out of her house once and for all."

Margaret Louise squeezed her arm. "She'll be okay, Victoria. We'll all help see to that."

She leaned against the wall, the weight of the reality she'd been so far ignoring, suddenly zapping her energy. "I know we can help with things like dinners and companionship and hugs, but this woman is *sick*. She needs insurance, something I imagine she'll lose when Garrett is locked away."

"One way or the other, things will work out. They always do." Margaret Louise reached out, pushed an errant strand of hair from Tori's face. "And now, you can finally put all this stuff to the side. Concentrate on Milo comin' home and you finally givin' that boy the answer he's been waitin' for."

Margaret Louise was right and she knew it. The person behind the fire had been identified. The person behind Jeff's murder was virtually certain. And the person who made her life even brighter was due home in a little over twenty-four hours.

It was time to look forward. To trust that the rest would fall into place the way it was meant to, her part in bringing the truth to life complete.

"Thank you, Margaret Louise." She planted a kiss on the side of the woman's cheek just as Georgina snapped her phone closed.

"Don't think I didn't hear all of you guessing about your ringtones. And you can speculate all you want. You just won't be getting any confirmation from me," Georgina explained before focusing on Tori. "Chief Dallas told me about your meeting. Said he wished we had money in our budget to hire you on as a detective."

She couldn't help but laugh. "I wouldn't take the job even if you did."

"Couldn't handle working with Robert?" Debbie mused.

"Couldn't imagine spending my days anywhere but right here at the library."

"And neither could we," Dixie said earning a few startled looks in the process.

Tori blinked away the tears that threatened to spill down her face, Dixie's words meaning more to her than she could ever articulate aloud. Instead, she gestured into the hallway. "I'm going to give the main room a once-over and then maybe we can adjourn to the bakery for something sinful."

Leona shot a look of surprise in Debbie's direction. "Did you hire a well-built security guard? Or a handsome pastry chef?"

She couldn't help but laugh as she wandered into the hallway and toward the main room, her feet traveling a path they'd traveled nearly every day since arriving in Sweet Briar. When she reached the main room, she flipped on a few lights, her gaze sweeping across the various tables and chairs strewn about the room.

"I tried to tidy up as much as I could before everyone showed up to help with the children's room," Dixie explained as she stopped alongside Tori. "The only thing I didn't get to was Mr. Downing's books."

She waved aside Dixie's concern. "You did a

fine job, thank you. Why don't you start herding everyone toward the bakery and I'll be along as soon as I shelve his books."

"Are you sure?" Dixie asked.

"I'm sure." She watched as Dixie turned down the same hallway from which they'd both come, the woman's help and support the past few weeks a godsend she hadn't properly acknowledged. "Dixie?"

The woman turned. "Yes?"

"Thank you for everything these past few weeks. You've made operating without Nina a whole lot easier."

Dixie blushed with pleasure. "You're welcome, Victoria."

When the woman disappeared into the children's room, Tori crossed to the table and the lone stack of books waiting to be shelved. Glancing down, she leaned toward the familiar picture, the shot no better than the one she'd tucked on a shelf behind the information desk.

" 'Foxglove,' " she read aloud. " 'The common foxglove contains some powerful constituents, which are used in the medicinal world; the most active and important constituents of the common foxglove include digitoxin, digitalin, digitalein, and digitonin. Of these constituents, digitoxin is the most powerful and also an extremely poisonous drug. In addition, the constituent digitonin is a cardiac depressant.' "

Confused by what she was reading, she continued on, her finger leading her eyes down the page with rapidly increasing speed.

Foxglove poisoning can also occur by ingesting or sucking foxglove flowers, leaves, or any other part of the plant.

As she read, a frightening picture began to form in her mind—a picture so twisted it made her sick to her stomach.

"Oh no. Please, please, no."

"What's wrong, Victoria?"

She jumped at the sound of Margaret Louise's voice, the sudden movement knocking the book to the floor.

"I'll get that." Margaret Louise bent down, retrieved the still-open book, and handed it to Tori, the sinister beauty of the purple flowers staring back at her from its prominent place on the page.

"Oh Margaret Louise, I think I made a terrible, *terrible* mistake."

The woman's hand settled on her shoulder and gave it a gentle pat. "Victoria, I can't imagine what kind of mistake you could make that would get you this worked up."

"I can," she whispered. "And it's a doozy."

Chapter 29

For the second time that day, Tori found herself heading out of Sweet Briar, the trees along the rural two-lane road whipping by her window faster than she intended. Once again, Margaret Louise had wanted to come, to lend her support at a time Tori's head was reeling, but she'd declined the offer, opting to make the trek alone.

The hurt on her friend's face when she refused to divulge her concerns in favor of running out the door had stung, but it was for the best. She was the one who'd been so sure she had all the answers, not Margaret Louise.

Besides, she needed time to think. The first trip to Lee Station had been about asking questions; this one was about confirmation of what was virtually certain.

Her phone chirped indicating a call. Reaching into her purse, she extracted her cell and checked the caller ID screen.

Milo.

Inhaling deeply, she flipped the phone open and held it to her ear. "Hi, Milo."

"Twenty-four hours!"

She willed herself to find even half of the

enthusiasm she heard in his voice, but it was no use. Her mind was on other things. "That's great."

Silence hung between them as she rounded one corner and then another, her thoughts ricocheting between the flowers and Garrett.

"Is everything okay, Tori?" he finally asked. "You sound . . . funny."

She shook her head ever so slightly in an effort to dislodge her focal point just long enough to placate Milo. "I rushed to judgment about Jeff's murderer and I was wrong."

"What are you talking about?"

She breathed in, counted to ten, and then released the air from her lungs as slowly as possible. "I thought I knew who did it. The facts lined up perfectly."

"Why are you involved in this in the first place?"

Why indeed.

She searched for an answer, one that would sum up her reasons as succinctly as possible. "I wasn't. Not really. But as pieces of information began to surface about his death, an image began to form. So I checked it out."

A second, longer batch of silence was followed by a long sigh. "And?"

"And it all fit. So much so that I stopped by the police station and handed everything I knew to the chief."

"Okay . . ."

"But I was wrong." Tori let up on the gas as her turn approached. "Not about the motive, I think that's still the same, although from a different perspective than I'd originally thought. But the *who* behind it all was completely wrong."

"Then tell Chief Dallas. He'll take care of it."

She knew it was the smart thing to do, she really did. She just wasn't sure it was the right thing to do.

"I can't."

More silence was followed by yet another sigh, this one more of resignation than frustration.

"Is there anything I can do?"

She pulled to a stop in front of the Calder home once again, the warmth of Milo's voice and the unyielding support in his words bringing her up short.

She was lucky. Truly, truly lucky.

Sure, there were good guys out there. Debbie had one in Colby, Melissa in Jake. They were out there, somewhere. Yet not everyone fared so well . . .

Not Leona.

Not Georgina.

Not Kelly.

Not Lynn.

Those women had been hurt beyond belief simply because they'd handed their heart to someone else. In turn, the person they'd given it

344

to had tossed their love aside as if it meant nothing, making them doubt their self-worth and their judgment.

She knew because she'd been there.

She *got* it.

The difference, though, came down to choices.

Leona took control of her life, refusing to engage her heart in a relationship ever again, opting, instead, to keep all encounters with the opposite sex light and fleeting. But the pain was still there, affecting her choices in life even decades later.

Georgina employed her infamous take-charge attitude, wiping her hands of the public disgrace that had been her second husband. But the pain was still there, dulling what had once been a natural sparkle.

Kelly had seen the writing on the wall where Jeff was concerned, but rather than lash out at him, she'd opted to pin it on Tori, a choice that would have untold ripple effects throughout the rest of her life.

And then there was Lynn. A woman who had choices restricted by options . . .

"Tori? You still there?"

She shifted her car into park and turned off the engine, her focus moving to the house on her right.

Lynn never had options.

Not the kind most people would want, anyway.

"Milo? What do you think it would be like to be trapped in a cage with no real way to get out?"

"I think it would be hell."

"I do, too," she whispered as much to herself as the voice in her ear. "Milo? I need to go. But I can't wait to see you tomorrow night. I've missed you so much."

His smile was audible in her ear. "You have no idea how badly I needed to hear that."

When they hung up, she stepped from the car, the lone picture held tightly in her hand as she made the now familiar walk to Lynn Calder's front door. She knocked on the door trim.

A smiling Lynn appeared inside the foyer, a powder blue bandana wrapped smartly around her head. "Victoria! I didn't expect you back so soon." The woman pushed the door open. "Come in, come in!"

Tori stopped just inside the entryway and looked around, a homey scent instantly lifting her nose into the air. "Are you baking?"

Lynn grinned still wider. "I'm in the middle of baking chocolate chip cookies. Would you like some?"

She gave a half nod before holding out the photograph. "I—I figured I should bring you your picture."

Plucking the picture from Tori's hand, Lynn made a face. "You drove all the way out here, *again,* just to bring me this?"

Not sure what to say, she simply shrugged.

Lynn set the picture on the hall table and pointed into the living room. "Why don't you settle yourself in there and I'll get this last batch of cookies on the trays and into the oven lickety-split."

She wandered into the living room and over to the mantel, her gaze lingering on the picture of Jeff.

"I'm thinking about entering my garden in a local contest. All I need to do is send in a few pictures for the judges to see," Lynn called from the kitchen.

She sucked in a breath of determination. "I'm surprised those flowers are allowed around here."

The sound of a pan being pulled from a cabinet was quickly followed by its thud on top of a counter. "What are you talking about?"

"From what I read this evening, foxglove is highly poisonous. If any part of the plant is ingested, it can cause hallucinations, blurred vision, vomiting, even an irregular heartbeat, which could be fatal to someone with certain heart conditions."

Her own heart thumped in her chest as she waited for a response, but there was nothing. Only silence.

"I'm sorry," Lynn finally called. "I didn't quite catch what you said. Let me pop these in the oven and I'll be right there."

Seconds turned to minutes before Lynn reappeared with a dish towel in her hands. "Okay, that's better. Now what were you saying?"

Tori turned and faced Lynn, the courage she'd had when they were rooms apart suddenly fading into the background. "Um, so where's Garrett? Is he here?"

"Not anymore."

Something about Lynn's tone gave her pause. "Is he at work?"

"Nope." Lynn glanced down at her wristwatch and then back up at Tori. "With any luck he's being fingerprinted and tossed in jail as we speak."

She stared at Lynn. "You mean they came and got him?"

A smile spread across the woman's face. "About two hours after you left. He'd stopped in to get a change of clothes and the police were sitting in here waiting for him."

She swallowed. "Wow. I didn't think they'd move *that* fast."

"I imagine that little tramp of his is bawling her eyes out right about now." The smile moved into Lynn's eyes as she continued. "The second they took him out of here it was as if I could breathe for the first time in years."

Tori searched for something to say but came up empty.

"I remember that moment when I'd packed my bags and was headed out the door, my anger at Garrett over having a mistress giving me the shove I needed to get as far from this town and that man as humanly possible."

"What stopped you?" Tori asked.

"A phone call from my doctor. The one that told me I had cancer. My whole world changed at that moment."

Overcome by conflicting emotions, she wrapped her arms around herself. "I can only imagine how awful that call must have been."

"Realizing I had to stay and endure the ongoing humiliation of Garrett and his mistress has been just as bad." Lynn's voice took on a wooden quality as her gaze fixed on a spot somewhere over Tori's head. "I had two choices. Leave and die physically, or stay and die emotionally. Vera convinced me to stay."

"Why?"

Lynn pinned her with a stare. "Because she was a strong believer in what goes around, comes around. Only it never seemed to come around . . . until today."

"Today?" she echoed.

"When you figured it out the way I hoped you would." Pivoting on her feet, Lynn waved Tori to follow. "The cookies should be just about done."

The way she hoped I would . . .

The swinging door flapped shut behind Tori as

she trailed Lynn into the kitchen, the enticing smell of chocolate chip cookies hovering in the room. Grabbing an oven mitt, Lynn opened the door and lifted the hot tray onto the counter. "I'd like you to try one, they're from a special recipe."

Tori glanced toward the batch cooling on a nearby plate. "Sure, okay, I'll take one." She reached her hand toward the plate only to have it thwarted midway.

"No, you need one fresh from the oven. They're extra delicious that way." With careful fingers, Lynn pried a cookie from the pan and held it out to Tori. "Here. Try."

Taking the cookie, Tori held it to her lips and took a bite, her gaze dropping to the counter and the sprig of foxglove lying beside the now-empty mixing bowl. Warning bells sounded in her head and she spit the cookie onto the floor.

Lynn's face fell. "I would have thought that you, of all people, would have understood."

She grabbed a glass from the dishwasher and held it under the faucet. Quickly she took a sip, gargled it around her mouth, then spit it into the sink. "Understood? Sure, I understood. I understood your pain and your heartache. I empathized with what you faced every day. But this? No. I don't understand."

"I couldn't leave Garrett because there was no money to split. I stayed because Vera kept a roof over my head and made sure there was food on the table. But once she was gone, I knew I couldn't handle living here with Garrett any longer. The pain and humiliation was too great.

"But when Vera's will was read, and Garrett was listed as the secondary beneficiary behind Jeff, I realized there was a way."

"A way to what?" she challenged.

"A way to have the money I needed and be rid of Garrett once and for all." Lynn slumped against the kitchen counter. "If I made Jeff's death look as if Garrett was at fault, he'd be locked up. With him in jail, I could remain his wife and have access to his money without having to watch him with *her* anymore. And Vera's money was enough to get private insurance."

Tori rubbed her hand across her face, absorbing Lynn's words. The thinking was sound, genius, even. But still . . .

Pulling her phone from her pocket, she dialed the Sweet Briar Police Department. When the dispatcher answered, she asked to speak with the chief, underscoring the importance of her call even as Lynn sank to the floor in tears.

"Good evening, Miss Sinclair. You'll be pleased to know I have our man."

Summoning every ounce of courage she could find, Tori spoke into the phone. "You have the wrong person."

"What are you talking about? Garrett Calder is sitting in the cell down the hallway right now."

"He didn't kill Jeff. His wife did."

"His wife?" the chief repeated, shock evident in his voice. "But the will . . . the drug . . . the—"

"All twisted to point in Garrett's direction. By his wife, Lynn."

"Where are you right now?" he barked.

"Standing in the Calders' kitchen."

"Is she there?"

She eyed the woman on the other side of the kitchen, the powder blue bandana shielding her view of Lynn's face. "Yes."

"I'm on my way."

Nodding, she snapped the phone closed. "I'm sorry, Lynn. I truly am. But two wrongs never make a right."

Chapter 30

By the time she got home from work on Wednesday, every backyard fence in all of Sweet Briar had played host to the biggest news in town since spring. Those who didn't hear it across the fence heard it while sipping coffee at Debbie's Bakery or lunching at Johnson's Diner or shopping at Leeson's Market or while strolling around the square.

The only certainty was the fact that everyone knew.

And that everyone had an opinion.

Those who lived a life of black and white felt Lynn's arrest was simply justice being served. Those who'd been wronged by love in the past weren't so certain. To them, Lynn had been backed into a corner from which the only way out was to fight and the direction she lashed out in didn't really deserve any better.

It was the same argument Tori had played out in her thoughts throughout the day. When she'd shelved, she'd thought of Mr. Downing's flower book and the insidiousness of what Lynn had done when she set out to frame her philandering pharmacist husband. When she'd been reading fairy tales to a group of preschoolers in the newly reopened children's room, she couldn't help but feel as if Lynn had been cheated of her chance to meet the Prince Charming she surely deserved.

Either way, the situation as it played out had left her feeling blue and in dire need of a little solitude before her own Prince Charming finally returned.

Tossing her keys onto the table beside the front door, Tori wandered into her living room and plopped into the plaid armchair she'd purchased shortly after arriving in Sweet Briar. In the nearly two years since her arrival, the chair had become her place to think, to read, and to sew—all activities that afforded an opportunity to take a breath and start fresh.

Something Lynn Calder will never be able to do again.

Shaking her head free of the thought, she looked around for something, anything, that could take her mind off everything that had happened. Her To Be Read pile teetered on the corner of the end table to her left, a potpourri of mysteries, romances, and women's fiction novels just waiting to be devoured. But to read, she needed to focus. A tall order when every little thing brought her back to the image of Lynn Calder being led away in handcuffs.

She pushed off her chair and wandered into the

sewing alcove she'd created in a far corner, the depth and width of the area leaving little room for anything besides her sewing machine and a gooseneck lamp. The wooden sewing box Leona had given her after the Tiffany Ann Gilbert fiasco sat exactly where she'd left it when she got home from bringing the initial packet of pictures to Lynn in the wake of Monday night's sewing circle meeting. Beside the box was her latest contribution to the circle's current group project.

"So much for making comfort pillows," she mumbled under her breath as she grabbed hold of the soft pink covered pillow and tossed it onto the couch. "Our intended recipient has shown a preference for stripes."

A knock at her front door was followed by the sound of Margaret Louise's voice in the foyer. "Victoria? Are you home?"

"Perhaps you should have waited to see if she came to the door," Leona reprimanded. "If she's home, she'll answer. If she's not, she won't."

"Leona is right. Maybe we should just wait and—"

"Oh, move out of my way, Beatrice." Rose's voice, shaky yet firm, preceded her frail body into the living room. "When loved ones are worried, they get a special pass. And I'm worried."

And, just like that, the distraction she needed to get back on track stepped into her line of vision.

"There's no need to worry, Rose, I'm right here." She lifted her hand and waved as, one by one, her friends filed into the room.

Rose.

Leona.

Margaret Louise.

Beatrice.

Melissa.

Dixie.

And Georgina, carrying a large plastic bin.

Tori looked around at the crew as they distributed themselves around her living room in record fashion. "I'm sorry, but is there a sewing circle meeting I wasn't aware of?"

Dixie gestured around the room. "Where's the rocking chairs?"

"I'll get 'em." Margaret Louise disappeared down the hallway, the door opening and shutting in her wake. Seconds later, the sound repeated and she strode into the room carrying both rockers from the front porch. She set one down behind Dixie and the other behind Rose. "There you go, you're all set."

Leona sat down primly on the edge of the plaid armchair and crossed her legs. "So what's this I hear about Lynn executing a nearly flawless attack on that buffoon she was married to?"

Georgina set the container beside Dixie's rocker then made her way over to the couch. "Lynn Calder killed Victoria's ex and then tried to frame her husband for the murder. Her plan was to have him locked up and then use all of Vera Calder's inheritance money to survive while he was in prison."

Leona's eyebrows arched. "It's a shame she got caught."

Beatrice gasped. "She killed someone, Leona."

"Technically, yes, but think of all the innocent women out there she saved from heartache at Jeff's hands."

"Aunt Leona, stop," Melissa chided.

"And the one she lined up to take the fall for it? He was just as bad, worse, even." Leona bent her fingers at the knuckles and studied her fingernails closely. "Frankly, I think that woman should have gotten a prize for her efforts, not jail."

Tori met Margaret Louise's eye across the room, tried her best to gauge the extent of everyone's knowledge, but it was no use.

"I turned her in," she finally admitted.

Leona peered at Tori over the top of her glasses. "Why on God's green earth would you have done such a thing?"

"Because it was the right thing to do." Margaret Louise closed the gap between the rocking chairs and the sewing alcove in several quick steps.

"Was Jeff right when he broke Victoria's heart?" Leona asked.

"Of course not," Debbie answered. "He was awful for doing that."

"Was Garrett right when he took up with that little hussy in plain sight of his wife?"

"No," Dixie chimed in. "Of course not."

"Then from what I can see, Lynn Calder took care of business, that's all."

Georgina sat forward on the couch. "Do you want to know something, Leona?"

Leona flicked a bored hand in the air.

"I spoke with Mrs. Calder this morning."

Tori took two steps toward the couch and then sat on the floor, waiting.

"Do you know what she told me?" Georgina prompted.

Heads shook around the room as all eyes focused on the town's mayor.

"She told me she was wrong. That just because something awful was done to her didn't mean she was justified in doing something awful in return." Georgina turned and smiled at Tori. "She said you taught her that."

She blinked against the sudden stinging sensation in her eyes. "She did?" she whispered.

Georgina nodded.

Suddenly, the weight she'd carried around all day dissipated, leaving her as close to content as possible at that very moment. "That helps. Thank you, Georgina."

The first few notes of a popular emergency room

drama sprang from Georgina's pocket, earning the mayor more than her fair share of curious looks. "Excuse me, that's the hospital." Jumping to her feet, Georgina escaped into the kitchen.

"I know what song she has for you, Beatrice," Margaret Louise teased. "I was eatin' dinner with her today when you called."

The nanny sat forward in her chair, anticipation etched across her every facial feature. "Is it 'Lady'?"

Margaret Louise shook her head.

"'Islands in the Stream'?" Beatrice asked, breathless.

"Nope, not that, either."

"Oooh, what? What?"

"'Spoonful of Sugar.'"

Beatrice made a face. "'Spoonful of Sugar'?"

Dixie laughed. "That's perfect!"

"Perfect?" Beatrice echoed.

"You're a nanny, aren't you, dear?" Leona mused in a voice dripping with boredom. "It's a perfectly logical choice."

Georgina swept back into the room bringing all further discussion on the matter to a crashing halt. "That was the hospital. I have an appointment for us to drop off the comfort pillows on Saturday morning."

"But Lynn is in jail." Tori rocked back on her feet, hugging her knees to her chest. "What good are they going to do now?"

"We made forty, Victoria, remember? We may have undertaken the project *because* of Lynn but the pillows we made were for women *like* her. Women who battle the effects of breast cancer day in and day out."

Because of Lynn.

A plan formed in her head. "Do you think we could donate them in honor of Lynn? As a tribute to the strong woman she was before . . . well, you know."

Georgina smiled. "I think that's a fine idea, Victoria."

"So do I," Rose agreed.

She exhaled a burst of air through her lips, grateful that the drama of the past few weeks was finally behind them all. "Can I tell all of you something?"

"Of course," Melissa answered, as all but Leona nodded. "You can tell us anything. Always."

Tori studied Leona, the familiar tug of curiosity distracting her momentarily as she tried to figure out what the woman was doing hunched over in the chair. But, in the end, she simply pulled her left hand from around her legs and stared down at her empty ring finger. "I'm going to say yes."

"Hallelujah," whooped Margaret Louise as hands clapped around the room. "It's 'bout time, ain't it, ladies?"

"Oh, Victoria, that's wonderful news. Colby and the kids are going to be so—"

A muffled, yet familiar jingle emerged from Georgina's pocket, cutting Debbie off mid-sentence.

"Here comes Peter Cottontail, hopping down the bunny trail, hippity, hoppity . . ."

Georgina's face drained of all color as she scrambled to retrieve her phone from the depths of her trouser pocket. Without so much as a glance at the screen, she pointed an accusing finger in the direction of the white-knuckled woman holding court in the plaid armchair. "Leee-ona!"

Sewing Tips

- A razor blade, box cutter, or craft knife can double as a seam ripper. They cut through thread quickly, but care must be taken to avoid slicing into the fabric or fingers.

- Try clipping seam allowances with a craft knife instead of scissors. Place your item on a cutting mat. Use your craft knife to cut from the seam to the raw edge of the seam allowance. Cutting from your seam instead of toward it will lessen the chances of cutting through your stitching.

- When cleaning your sewing machine, repurposing a few household items can help get the job done. A small sable paintbrush or disposable mascara wand can help brush away lint and dust, while an empty squeeze bottle can blow away any bits that remain.

- When changing your sewing machine needle, place a piece of paper or cloth over the needle plate to prevent the needle from falling through the small hole and down into the machine, which could require a trip to the repair shop to get it removed.

- When laying out and cutting slippery fabric, place a flannel-backed vinyl tablecloth (flannel side up) over the cutting table to help keep the fabric in place and prevent it from sliding around while you work.

- Keep freshly pressed fabrics from getting wrinkled by allowing them to cool down for a few minutes before moving them from the ironing board.

- Keep the hem on a knit garment from curling to the outside with a strip of fusible lightweight knit interfacing. Cut a strip of interfacing the width of the hem on the cross-grain so it stretches with the fabric. Apply the interfacing, then turn up the hem and stitch into place.

- When basting by hand or machine, choose thread in a color that contrasts with your fabric. That way, it will be easier to see and remove later.

- Instead of basting or pinning, try holding patch pockets in place with cellophane tape.

Stitch right through the tape, and then pull off the tape after you are finished sewing.

• Small hair scrunchies are superb for putting around spools of thread and keeping the thread from coming unraveled. In addition, they are just the right size for slipping around partially used packages of rickrack, bias tape, etc., to keep them from coming undone also.

Have a sewing tip you'd like to share?
Stop by my website,
www.elizabethlynncasey.com,
and let me know!

Sewing Patterns

Comfort Pillow

Pillowcase Directions:
Cut two pieces of washable material 9″ x 13″ or fold a piece of material to form a 9″ x 13″ pattern.

With the right sides placed facing each other, sew the three sides.

Sew, lace, or hem the open end.

Turn right side out and place over the pillow.

Pillow Directions:
Cut two pieces of washable material 8″ x 12″ (something strong and soft, like cotton).

With the right sides placed facing each other, sew the three sides and part of the fourth.

Turn the pillow right side out.

Stuff the pillow to the point of being firm, without overstuffing.

Turn the remaining open end in and topstitch it closed.

Center Point Publishing
600 Brooks Road ● PO Box 1
Thorndike ME 04986-0001 USA

(207) 568-3717

US & Canada:
1 800 929-9108
www.centerpointlargeprint.com